Beautiful Criminals

a novel

STORY BY ERIC TIPTON
AND MATTHEW STRAVITZ

WRITTEN BY ERIC TIPTON
AND SUSANNA ROSENBLUM

EMILY BESTLER BOOKS
—
ATRIA
NEW YORK   LONDON   TORONTO   SYDNEY   NEW DELHI

EMILY
BESTLER
BOOKS

ATRIA

An Imprint of Simon & Schuster, Inc.
1230 Avenue of the Americas
New York, NY 10020

First Emily Bestler Books/Atria Paperback edition August 2017

EMILY BESTLER BOOKS / ATRIA PAPERBACK and colophon are trademarks of Simon & Schuster, Inc.

For information about special discounts for bulk purchases, please contact Simon & Schuster Special Sales at 1-866-506-1949 or business@simonandschuster.com.

The Simon & Schuster Speakers Bureau can bring authors to your live event. For more information or to book an event, contact the Simon & Schuster Speakers Bureau at 1-866-248-3049 or visit our website at www.simonspeakers.com.

Interior design by Laura Levatino

Manufactured in the United States of America

10 9 8 7 6 5 4 3 2 1

Library of Congress Cataloging-in-Publication Data is available.

ISBN 978-1-5011-3651-1
ISBN 978-1-5011-3653-5 (ebook)

FOR ELIZABETH AND JOSIE

1

Amanda stepped into the parking lot as Tiny (that's what they called her on the inside, anyway) locked the gate behind her with an awful vibrating clang. Amanda prayed that Tiny would send her off with some words of encouragement and not some disparaging, crass, sexual innuendo. She wanted to start her new life with confidence in the sisterhood and womankind. But it was fifty-fifty with Tiny. You never knew what you were going to get.

"Hey, Candy Girl." Candy Girl was Amanda's nickname in prison. Perhaps because Candy rhymed with Mandy. Or because her cellmate, Jocelyn, started singing that New Edition song in falsetto whenever Amanda walked by. Amanda was apparently Jocelyn's "world." (And there were other implications that Amanda shuddered to think about.)

Sometimes they also called her "White Collar" because of her whiteness, obviously, but also the nature of her crimes. They eventually abbreviated this to just "Collah."

"Candy Girl," Tiny said again as Amanda turned to look at her. Tiny's entire body fit between two rails of the steel gate. She held up a miniature thumb and said, "You got this, Collah."

"Thanks, Tiny. Good luck. Happy Thanksgiving."

Amanda stood for a second, remembering to breathe. In for four, hold for seven, out for eight. It was Thanksgiving in So Cal, but it didn't feel like it. No crisp air, skeletal trees, or carpets of dry, brown leaves covering a quiet, snow-dappled forest floor.

Only the sun. That ubiquitous sun, staining everything, even today's uninspired turkey dinners cooked mostly in the microwave, with a yellowy, piss-colored cheer. Amanda disliked LA.

She squinted against the glare and tried to locate the glint of her mother's silvery blue minivan, but as usual, her mother was late. Amanda had calculated that she'd probably spent a quarter of her life waiting for her mother. This had actually benefited her in prison. At forty-two, she'd already had a long education in waiting things out.

What she wasn't prepared for was the paucity of prison supplies. Washing her hair with soap. Wearing enormous cotton underpants. And using maxi pads for God's sake. There were no tampons in the big house. Luckily, her periods were different now. They came on slowly, torturing her with a week of bloating, headaches, and rage as they crept up on her, and then they happened all at once in a projectile burst, like her uterus was sick of all this crap (who could blame it?). The period part only lasted one day. She got to trade the rest of her maxi pads for cigarettes or cream rinse.

Right now, she'd trade a gallon of cream rinse for a pair of cheap sunglasses. It was relentless, the sun. She'd been locked away from it for way too long.

She sat on the curb and pulled out her notebook. She had vowed during the last two years that the waiting was going to stop. As soon as she could, she would write her own destiny. Take charge of her own life. Put herself in the driver's seat and all that crap. She'd taken poetry classes on the inside. Gotten her associate's degree. Had begun to write in a journal. Had a job at the commissary, where she'd begun to learn how to keep track of things and stay organized. She'd developed habits, actual habits that she hoped to carry on in the real world. Writing, exercise, tidying up, three meals a day. And even though she had never been drunk in her life (someone needed to be in control of their faculties in her family), she went to every prison AA meeting. At first to get out of kitchen duty, but once she surrendered to it, she actually found all that one-day-at-a-time bullshit pretty transcendental. She might even want to be an addiction counselor one day. If she could keep up the routines, get a job, work her way up. If. She might have a normal life. Maybe. Finally.

She heard the scraping in the distance and reluctantly looked up from her notebook. She had just written a cool if useless line for a poem, "Lashing, licking tongues on fire tangled in her dress," when she saw the minivan trailing sparks from whatever it was dragging behind it. The muffler? Probably. But as it took a careening left into the parking lot she could see the tin cans on a rope, and instead of "Just Married," someone had used a bar of Ivory soap to write "Welcome home, Amanda!" on the rear window. In the distance some sort of raptor circled and eerily screeched an echoing screech into the desert. Amanda tried not to take it as an omen.

"Get in," Joyce said after Amanda yanked the cans off the bumper and let them bask, coiled in the sun like a futuristic reptilian desert animal. Green beans, corn, peas, cranberry sauce. At least Taylor was getting vegetables. Albeit in a *can*. She used her finger to cross out her name on the rear window like you're supposed to do for good luck on your birthday cake.

"You've lost weight," her mother said, when she climbed into the passenger seat. Joyce stared straight ahead, barely able to look at her daughter. What was it with that generation and *communication* or *introspection* or *love*? Amanda could have used a hug. No matter. She couldn't reinvent the wheel. *God grant me the serenity to accept the things I cannot change.*

It looked as if her mother had had some work done around her beautiful Barbie-blue eyes. The skin covering her cheekbones was waxy and a bit too taut. But the woman was still beautiful. Beautywise, she cast a long shadow. Amanda looked like her, blond and wiry and taut, but her features were softer. A bit more diluted. Her nose a bit more knobby, a bit less Roman. She was the jab to her mother's uppercut. Together they were a proverbial one-two punch.

"What's with the car?"

"It's a celebratory occasion, isn't it?" said Joyce sarcastically. Her mother was still semi-furious with her. Not for committing a crime. For getting caught.

"Yes, I'm so proud," Amanda said. "Where's Taylor?"

Her mother's face slackened a little as she peered straight ahead and hit the gas. "That's going to take a while, Bird."

Amanda had a theory that when they cut the umbilical cord, some invisible, frayed end of it floated up through the mother's body and tethered itself to her heart. Whenever she thought of her daughter she felt an aching in a line that extended from her womb to her throat. The love you have for your child is so indistinguishable from fear that she couldn't understand how some people seemed so relaxed and cavalier about having children. How could a woman possibly bear more than one of them?

Her insides contracted. Taylor was fourteen when she left. At the crux of needing her mother the most. It's possible that Amanda had lost her forever. Breathe, she reminded herself. In for four, hold for seven, out for eight. She'd taken some parenting classes in prison, and she was excited to practice some of what she'd learned. There were only two years of high school left, but she was going to go to PTA meetings. Bake some shit for the bake sales. Help with the college applications. Anything it took, she was going to do. From now on.

She had spent the last two years living with people who hadn't been parented, and bad things happen when you parent yourself. The prisoners were infantile, most of them. Throwing tantrum after tantrum about stupid shit, like someone stealing a comb or taking an extra peanut butter packet. Who even uses combs anymore? The cheap fine-tooth plastic ones that they handed out before school pictures. No one. Amanda was able to stay out of most of it. But in the meantime, she'd learned the importance of parenting with a capital P.

And she was grateful for whatever small amount of it she had received. No matter how messed up Joyce was, she always sensed that Joyce cared. She looked at her mother staring hawkeyed out the front.

She did the best she could, Amanda knew. But she wondered if that was just a cop out. Parents proclaiming they did the best they could. Just do better, right? She would do better if it wasn't too late.

"What are you craving?" Joyce asked.

"I saw something on TV about froyo. Is frozen yogurt back?"

"Yup. It's serve yourself now. All the little piglets line up to suckle at the sugar hose," she said, adjusting her lipstick in the rearview mirror on the straightaway.

"Mom. Don't judge."

"What do you mean, don't judge? Just because it has the word *yogurt* in it doesn't mean it's a health food. People are getting obese on the stuff," she said, narrowing her eyes in that defeated look of disappointment that could still make Amanda feel like she swallowed her own heart. "I was afraid this would happen."

"What?"

"They took away your edge. That's all you have in this life, Amanda. Your edge. Lose that and you're sunk."

Amanda gazed at her mother's profile silhouetted by the blazing edge of the noontime sun. She practically glowed with the burn of last-life. She would not be around forever. "I love you, Mom," Amanda replied, daring to touch her mother's age-spotted hand on the steering wheel.

"Ah, Jesus H. Christ," Joyce barked.

———

In 1968 when Joyce got off the bus in Vegas she was a fresh-faced Jersey-born ingénue with dreams of stardom who quickly became a Rat Pack "mascot" (read into that word what you will) during the very last days of the Rat Pack.

Her conquests (and to Joyce "conquests" could mean anything from serving them a drink to spending the night) were among the steeliest of the steely blue-eyed Hollywood gods of the era. Steve

McQueen, Clint Eastwood, Paul Newman, Peter Fonda, all guests of
Sinatra at the Sands. Even Ol' Blue Eyes himself was rumored to have
asked her to sit on his lap and tell him a joke.

Of course everyone would ask her, "Which joke did you tell
him?" and she'd say, wryly, "The one about the (fill in the blank)." She
changed it every time.

Her whole life, Amanda had heard Joyce's tall tales of waking up
next to Sammy Davis's eye submerged in a glass of whiskey on the
nightstand or using smelling salts to wake Dean Martin in order to
get him out of her room before dawn. These were the glory days of
her career. Frank had promised her a role in the "anti-Western" he was
filming that year, and she got fitted for her dress in the saloon scene.
Even got to walk on set, fanning her face with a fan, but then the di-
rector hated the color of her dress and waved her away into oblivion.
"Oblivion" because it was then that she met Amanda's father, John. A
bar manager at the Golden Nugget with big dreams of owning a casino.

Casino owning necessitated a bevy of skills he would never ac-
quire, though. Like making nice with the mob, number one. And
being able to stay sober for twenty-four hours at a time and not gambling away one's entire salary. Joyce had fallen for him in spite of that,
because, as that wise duo Emily Dickinson and Selena Gomez will
remind us, "the heart wants what it wants."

He practically pimped Joyce out to the Rat Pack trying to get her
to work her connections and get him a loan to start their big project.
But luck was not on their side. And in Vegas (and everywhere) luck is
a big part of everything. Especially impossible dreams.

She got pregnant with Amanda, which cut into Joyce's cocktail
waitress career, and John started getting abusive. Hit some low lows.
Stopped coming home.

Her mom fled in his old maroon '74 Mustang in the middle of the
night during one of his drunken rages, taking with her only six-year-
old Amanda, thankfully, some clean underwear, and an eight-track of
Helen Reddy songs.

"It's you and me against the world, kiddo," Amanda remembered her mother quoting as she wrapped Amanda in a blanket in the backseat and wiped away the only tear Amanda ever saw her shed.

The concept of paternity was a little more fluid at the time. People were not testing DNA or fighting for custody, also a burgeoning concept. Custody almost always went to the mother. So Amanda never knew her father. Sometimes she looked in the mirror at her green eyes, so different from her mother's, and wondered if she were the Dean Martin, bastard-child equivalent to Mia Farrow's hot Sinatra son. But then she put it out of her mind. If that were true, she was sure her mother would have worked that angle to death. Plastering Amanda's photo all over the *National Enquirer* until the Martin estate paid her off to keep quiet. No. Amanda had to be the daughter of plain old John Cooper. A name she never got used to, which made it easy to surrender when she had to become someone else.

—

"We're here," her mom said. "Home sweet home."

The minivan had pulled into a garage built directly underneath a stucco apartment in a building that may have, in a past life, been some painted pink motor lodge, catering to rubes from New Jersey checking out Hollywood for the first time. Its square, thin-paned sliding window looked out at the driveway below with a fragile stare.

"What's this?" Amanda asked.

"Home. I had to downsize because, not naming any names, some of our wage earners landed themselves in prison."

"It's beautiful. The epitome of soulessness."

"Yeah, yeah. That can be the title of your new book, Steinbeck." Amanda didn't know why she'd told Joyce she'd taken up writing. "Your room's down the hall."

Her mom had sold everything, down to her Precious Moments tchotchkes and their special glass case. Nothing in the carpeted apartment with the popcorn ceilings and Formica countertops was vaguely familiar.

Amanda was too worried at the moment about seeing Taylor to wonder whether her mother had gotten hold of her own possessions and liquidated those, too. Her stomach clenched into a fist. In for four, hold for seven, out for eight, she breathed. "Taylor," Amanda ventured, "I'm home." *The courage to change the things I can.*

While it didn't look like home, it certainly smelled like it. Someone's home, anyway. A cheap oak oval dining room table in the area between the living room and kitchen was set for two. The window was fogged with steam from recently boiled things and you could almost taste the crackling drippings from a recently roasted fowl.

"What's all this?" Joyce squawked.

"I made dinner," Taylor said, emerging from a bedroom in the middle of the dank, dark hallway. Amanda almost didn't recognize her. Her once wavy hair was very long, ironed straight and dyed an ombré blue. She wore a black T-shirt just short enough to reveal a strip of her tanned belly adorned with a requisite diamond belly button ring. "It's Thanksgiving, right?"

"It's those cooking shows. I worry about her," Joyce complained. "She has a crush on that Iron Chef woman."

"It's not a crush!" Taylor protested.

"You know, the sad, serious-looking one with the ponytail and the man's name?"

"Alex Guarnaschelli? I love her," Amanda gushed. The women in prison used to love watching her, too. "Taylor, thank you, I'm so proud of you," she said and held out her arms for a hug.

Taylor looked to the floor, grounded there in her palpable sadness. "I'm going to have to think about what that means to me," she said, without looking up. " . . . if anything."

"Taylor, come on," said Joyce.

"It's okay, Mom," Amanda said. Her social worker had warned her it would not be an easy road back to motherhood. The fist of her stomach clenched tighter, though, and she almost doubled over from disappointment. *Easy does it*, she thought. *This too shall pass.*

Taylor made her way toward the door and donned a cute leather moto jacket. "I'll see you later," she said.

"You're not going to eat with us?" Amanda asked.

"Baby steps," Taylor replied.

"If you're going out, don't forget Grammy's juice," Joyce said. "Here's a twenty."

Oh god. "Grammy's juice" was Amanda's first professional scam during the days they were on the run and living out of their car. Amanda was only six. Her mom would pull up to some kind of convenience store and give Amanda a ten-dollar bill. "This is our last one, darling, so you know what to do," she'd say, straightening out her little pinafore dress and spit-cleaning a little dirt off her cheek. "Come back with change. Don't forget Mommy's juice. And get something nice for yourself."

Amanda would walk through the aisles collecting the white bread and peanut butter and milk. Then she'd slip a couple of lollipops in her pocket before heading to the liquor section. She'd toss a pint of vodka into the basket and when she was paying make a big stink about not getting enough change. "But I gave you a twenty," Amanda would cry. She was a good little actress and exercised just enough restraint to make it seem real. She'd squeeze out only one tear and say, "My mommy said to bring back change. I gave you a twenty. She's going to kill me."

The clerk usually protested at first, at which point Amanda would step up the volume, making sure all the customers would hear her building tantrum.

"All right, all right," the clerk would concede. "I got it. You're right. You gave me a twenty." And Amanda would walk out with more than she came in with.

"That's my girl," Joyce would say, when she slid into the slippery front bench seat of the Mustang. And in spite of herself Amanda would bask in the glow of her mother's approval. They would drive off then, Joyce taking a swig, Amanda sucking on her lollipop, and they'd sing "Delta Dawn" at the top of their lungs as they drove into the desert sunset.

They were poor, but things were simple then. Amanda looked over at her mother, who was sampling the mashed potatoes and nodding her head. Things are so complicated now. How can the most primal relationship of our lives become fraught with such tension? Communicating with her mother was like trying to smash through a brick wall with a toothpick. All she could do was scratch the surface.

God, if there is a God, must get such a kick out of this. "Watch this," she could hear God saying. "I'm going to make them need their mothers so much it hurts, and then I'm going to simultaneously make it the most enmeshed, gut-wrenching, impossible relationship of their lives. Lol."

Good one, God.

Speaking of guts, Amanda's clenched again, in anger this time. It was getting harder to breathe, especially in the heavy steam of the after-cooking.

"Grammy's juice?" she yelled at Joyce. "Please tell me you're not embroiling her in your bullshit."

"My 'bullshit' is what pays for this dump, my prison princess. You haven't exactly been around to help out."

"Oh, and whose fault is that?" Amanda began but then remembered her AA. Step ten: *Continue to take a personal inventory and when we're wrong promptly admit it.* She was the one who passed the checks. She signed every one with a name that wasn't her own. *Mercedes Douplas, Irene Stanford, Melissa Morgan, Jamie Torricelli . . .* She'd written long letters of apology to each of them when she was working steps eight and nine: *Made a list of all persons we had harmed, and became willing to make amends to them all. Make direct amends to such people wherever possible, except when to do so would injure them or others.*

"Come on," said Joyce. "We may as well eat it while it's hot." Joyce hardly ever ate, so Amanda was surprised by her mother's sudden appetite. Joyce plopped a huge spoon of stuffing on a plate, drizzled some gravy over a slice of turkey, and handed it to Amanda. "Here. You haven't had real food for two years. Eat."

"I thought I'd never hear you say that." Her mother had restricted her diet, too, giving her the evil eye if she ever reached for seconds—or firsts, for that matter. Their self-worth, income, and entire existence depended on maintaining what men thought was an ideal figure in the eighties. Starvation was their normal state of being.

Amanda sat down and picked at her plate. Her mother had taken one small piece of dry white meat and a couple of string beans. "Eat. Don't tell me they turned you into a tree-hugging vegetarian in there. I'll die if you say you won't eat anything with a face."

"Just not really hungry," Amanda said.

"She looks good, though, doesn't she? Did you see the bazooms on her? I put her on the pill as soon as the acne started. Cleared up her face and gave her giant boobies. Win-win. Not to mention, the peace of mind, if you know what I mean."

"You did that without telling me?"

"I wasn't going to be left in charge of a pregnant teen."

"Do you think she's . . . ?"

"Probably not. She's quiet, that one. Studious. But hard to know exactly what she's up to. A little sneaky. She'd be an asset to the corporation."

Amanda hated it when her mother called her shenanigans "the corporation," as if it were a legit enterprise. "Don't you dare," Amanda warned.

"It might be a little too late," Joyce replied with a sheepish grin. "Only small stuff. She's a cool cucumber, Mandy. Like her hero, Alex Guarnaschelli. Cool under pressure."

"Excuse me, please," Amanda said, pushing herself away from the table.

"What, Amanda? What's so bad about bringing her into the life? Has yours been so terrible?"

"I'm not talking to you right now."

"Amanda . . ."

"Mom. You ask me that question on the same day you pick me up from women's prison? There's obviously no talking to you."

"The best of us go to prison. Martha Stewart went to prison. Martin Luther King. Socrates. All prisoners."

"Mom."

"It's not such a miserable life."

"I want more for her, Mom, which I guess I have to explain to you since you never wanted more for me."

"What's that supposed to mean? I was there, wasn't I? With you. Always."

You wanted me with you because misery loves company. You couldn't bear to see me succeed when you didn't. You were envious of my potential so you squashed it, Amanda thought. "I'm breaking the chain. She goes to college, Mom. She gets legit. She has a real life. She goes to prison over my dead body."

"Good luck with that."

"What is that supposed to mean?"

"You'll see," Joyce said as she sat down and lit a Pall Mall, exhaling, and then ashing into her tiny dollop of mashed potatoes.

"Where are my things? I do still have things, don't I?"

"Second door on the left."

Amanda rushed to the carpeted cookie-cutter bedroom laid out in a perfect square with a twin bed in the middle. She slid open the cheap mirrored door to the closet and exhaled. Her three Rolie Bags were still there, piled on top of one another. Amanda pulled the zipper of the black one and lifted the top to reveal the hundred-dollar bills packed wall to wall in perfect hundred-dollar-bill-sized blocks.

She unzipped a secret compartment and said a little prayer before fishing around and extracting an enormous three-carat diamond engagement ring.

She held it up to the light and let it diffract the sun into tiny, dancing spots on the ceiling. She tried to think of an appropriate AA prayer for this moment. *Attitude of Gratitude?* She was so grateful that her mother didn't sell off her nest egg, but at the same time she knew her newfound "sober" conscience would not approve. *You're only as sick as your secrets*, she reminded herself. But she needed this last secret. It was a means to an end. Her life's work. She had to capitalize on this last secret to create a new life for herself and Taylor.

As if it were a crystal ball, she looked into the diamond—emerald cut and as big as a skating rink for a flea circus—and saw her future: She and Taylor in a house, a *stand-alone* house, making dinner with their daily bounty carried home from the farmers' market in their reusable canvas bags and talking about their day. Hers at the counseling center where she was helping her fellow humans grapple with recovery, and Taylor's at college where her mind was being sufficiently blown. They would be the kind of people who went to the farmers' market and even had an herb garden of their own on the patio. They would snip away at it every night before dinner with their special herb garden scissors. They would read books and talk about them. They would listen to NPR and drink hot chocolate beneath a homemade quilt. That's how things were going to be.

First things first, Amanda thought, snapping herself out of her reverie. Tomorrow she would land a job. A regular job. The first one she'd ever had.

2

She'd tried to keep her expectations as low as Markdown's prices. But she was excited. Sure, it was the bottom of the proverbial barrel, but she had to start somewhere. She tore through her suitcases looking for an appropriate outfit to wear to an interview at Markdown. She'd actually never been inside one.

Most of what she owned were tight, expensive cocktail dresses and shiny, lacquered Jimmy Choo pumps. She wore seductive attire because that's what she did. Seduced. An interview was a sort of seduction and she had the skills to sell herself. But even she knew you didn't wear Jimmy Choos into the "Mark."

"Taylor," she called. It was 10 AM and Taylor was still in bed. She got home late last night because she was hanging out with a bunch of her smart friends who were home from college for Thanksgiving. At least that's the story Amanda told herself. She really had no idea where Taylor was, and she hadn't yet earned back the right to know. At least Taylor hadn't kicked her out when she found Amanda curled in a blanket sleeping on the floor next to T's bed. She'd slept there for a couple of reasons. One: it had been two years since she'd slept in a room by herself, and two: the Kangaroo Principle. People don't tell you this when you have a child, but, even when they are almost grown, you will still, occasionally, have the impulse to stick them in your pouch and carry them with you wherever you go. If T wasn't going to talk to her, at least Amanda could fight back with proximity. And so she slept on her floor and listened to her daughter breathe and thrash around under the covers all night.

"Tay?"

Taylor, eyes smudged like a panda bear's with last night's makeup and hair askew, appeared half-asleep at the entrance to Amanda's room. She slumped against the doorjamb wordlessly.

"I have an interview at Markdown."

One eyebrow raised in a combination of disgust, amusement, and pity.

"Can I wear this?" Amanda lifted the plainest dress she could find from a heap on her bed. A halter-style green number.

Taylor just shook her head and looked at the pile incredulously. Then she disappeared and silently came back with a pair of tan slacks, a neatly pressed white blouse, and some cute beaded moccasin flats.

"Why do you have these?" she asked. But actually, Amanda did not want to know. It was either some costume Joyce concocted to make Taylor look older for one of her scams or it was Joyce's own outfit. Either was horrifying, but Amanda had to wear it. She had nothing else.

"Taylor," she said now, "I'm not going to force you to talk to me, but I'll be here when you're ready, okay? I know this has thrust you into some adult stuff you were not ready for. I know you're pissed. It sucks. I'm sorry. But I'm trying to turn it around, okay?"

Taylor said nothing, but looked down at her phone and *beep, beep, bopped* on it for a second and then held it up to show Amanda a picture of Yoda. *Do or Do Not. There is No Try*, the caption read.

"Fine. I'm doing."

Taylor just shrugged and went back to bed.

Amanda tried breathing again. In for four, hold for seven, out for eight. She got dressed and then stole the keys to Joyce's minivan. She climbed into it, a used beast from 1999, and tried not to think of the microbes from spilled sippy cups that had been baking and growing for years in the brushed velvet blue seat that currently enveloped her tan-slacked ass. She adjusted the mirrors and backed slowly into the macadam driveway behind her. She looked both ways seven times, paralyzed by the possibility of hitting one of the little kids who'd left their scooters, helmets, and bouncy balls strewn about. Her hands sweat and shook. She suddenly didn't know if she could do this. Drive. The risks were so high. She'd never felt this before. The dread, this feeling of imminent danger. This fear of getting caught. The big house changed her.

Do or Do Not, she reminded herself, and got her shit together.

The boulevard, lined on either side with tufted palm trees from another, more glamorous era, was bumper to bumper, and the sun, glinting and glaring and searing into the back of her brain, was giving her a headache. Did Ken, her parole officer, realize he'd set her up for an interview at Markdown on Black Friday?

She'd developed a very close relationship with Ken. She couldn't help it. She was bred for bribery. She hated herself for using her wiles and, honestly, her white privilege with him when she knew her fellow prisoners could not. But she connived herself into prison, so she could certainly connive her way out.

Ken was a family man in midlife just beginning to realize that the bald spot growing on the back of his head for the past decade was actually evidence that he was going bald. Slow on the uptake, men are, and loath to think anything aside from the fact that they are unbelievably handsome. So different from women. It has to do with how we mother them. Women idolize their sons and resent their daughters. Fear for their daughters, really. And so they knock them down a peg. Keep them in check and all that. Make sure they are obsessed with their beauty so they will survive in this messed-up world. Ah, the world.

She was stopped at a red light and so she called Ken, whom she had on speed dial. *Everyone has their parole officer on speed dial, right?* Amanda joked with herself. Oy. She could not believe this was her life. Ken had told her to call him whenever she wanted. Of course he did. He was dying to see how far he could get with her on the outside—away from surveillance cameras and the threat of being fired.

His wife, whom he used to find adorable, was just starting to show signs of aging. She cut her hair short and began losing interest in sex. She was either withering up or becoming a lesbian, or both, he told Amanda.

"I live with a withered old lesbian," he complained. He showed her a picture, though, and Amanda found his wife's pixie to be darling and feminine and youthful. Ken was just going through the standard boring midlife crisis. Too easy a target not to take advantage of. So, in their parole hearing, Amanda only had to mention how great he looked and how he must be working out, things his wife may have thought but was just too harried to communicate, and it got her six months off her sentence.

"Ken," she said, when he picked up. "Did you know you got me an interview at Markdown on Black Friday?"

"Amanda, baby, is this you?"

"Easy with the baby, darling. We have an issue. Black Friday. Seriously? Are you sure my interview is today? How am I even going to get in the door?"

"You're the one who wanted out by Thanksgiving."

"And what a fabulous Thanksgiving it was . . ."

"Taylor not cooperating?"

"She'll come around."

"My kids are brats, too. They're all just kids, you know. Little gluttonous monsters. You can't expect too much, I guess. It's all about the low expectations."

"Nice pep talk," she said. "I'm inspired. So. You sure about this interview?" Amanda slowed down for another red light and reapplied her bland, interview-colored lipstick.

"Yeah. Russ is . . . you'll see. A little manic I guess. Undiagnosed ADHD or whatever. He thrives on chaos. Black Friday is perfect. He might even put you out on the floor today. Trial by fire and all that. Call me and let me know how it goes."

"Okay." Amanda was suddenly leery about having to stay in close contact with her parole officer. Six months was a long time to string him along and fend him off at the same time.

"And Amanda . . ." he continued.

"Yes?"

"It was nice to hear your voice."

Ah jeez. "Yeah. You, too."

She pulled into the Markdown parking lot with ten minutes to spare, and it was mobbed. She tried to get a spot by following people around the lot in hopes that they were leaving but that didn't work. Shoppers were loading their cars and heading back into the store for more schlock. She was going to be late. Her old self would have jumped a curb and created her own parking spot on the grass. Her old self followed only the rules that made sense to her. But her new self was wiser. Rules are in place for a reason, even if the reason isn't exactly clear to you. *When all else fails, follow directions*, she remembered from the Big Book. And parolees must demonstrate that they can follow rules. All the rules. But she now had only two minutes until her interview and parolees were also not supposed to be late.

She would just *bend* the rules. She reached into the glove compartment where she knew her mother would be hiding a stolen handicap tag, hung it on the rearview, and peeled into one of the spots right in front of the entrance.

It was so mobbish and hot that she had to slide skin to skin against people to get through the door and to the registers. Inside she realized exactly why Ken set her up for a Black Friday interview. Ken was not a stupid man. This was a test. Could Amanda walk through the mess of carelessly abandoned pocketbooks and bent-over bottoms with wallets hanging out of their back pockets and, instead of stealing them and heading straight to the store for this week's groceries, interview for a forty-hour-a-week piece-of-shit job that would not even cover a quarter of her mother's rent, not to mention any of the groceries? Could she eschew the easy way out on day two of her parole when the easy way out was bending over and shoving itself in her face?"

Indeed she could. "Excuse me," she said to the gentleman's bent-over ass in aisle one as she stepped around it, even daring to finger the corner of his wallet as she walked by, just for practice.

What Ken didn't know was that she could never steal from someone who deigned to shop at Markdown. She and her mother (and now Taylor, she feared) made it a rule to steal from the rich. How could they live with themselves otherwise? Her mother envisioned herself as a veritable Robin Hood. This was LA. Wealth needed some redistributing, she would say. What they did was always *just* in her mother's eyes. It was either grifting or food stamps, and these days, welfare was viewed as an even worse kind of crime. So she may as well get what she needed with some secret dignity intact. And Joyce gave to the poor, too. At first it was part of her little old lady act. A way to get the fuzz off her trail. But Joyce had become genuinely passionate about making it to her church circle every week where they made dresses for orphans in Haiti or knit hats for preemies or donated money to women's homeless shelters. She wasn't all bad, the old bat.

—

In this hostile, well-lit sea of humans, jostling and elbowing for position, trying to grab the last of the knock-off Uggs and hoverboards, Amanda looked up and found one tranquil face glowing in a ray of fluorescent light behind the steady ship of the customer service desk. According to her name tag she was called Lupita. Lupita took a millisecond to smile at Amanda and Amanda waded her way toward her.

"You look like you could use some assistance," Lupita said to her.

"Yes. I have an interview with Russ. Ken Johnson sent me."

"I thought so," Lupita said. She had beautiful mahogany eyes done up in expert cat-eye makeup.

"How could you tell? Did I wear the wrong thing? My daughter picked it out."

"Relax, *mami*. Only I can tell. It takes one to know one, you know? You just look so 109.10 right now, that's all."

That was the prison code for prisoner out of place. "Yeah. This is not my scene."

"Just another type of prison. You show up for the count, do your bid, three squares and lights out. Do it all over again tomorrow."

"At least they pay you for it though, right?"

"Um. Yeah," said Lupita. "You'll probably still need food stamps, though. Did you fill that out?"

"No. I don't—"

"Got kids, right?"

"One."

"You'll need the food stamps. Come on."

Lupita led her past the women's section, where Amanda eyed a black sequined dress that also looked seriously 109.10 in this dump. She wondered who would come to Markdown to buy such a beautiful dress. She glanced at the price; $79.99 was more than most would normally spend here. And then she looked around. She noticed a few people—well-toned gym bodies with smooth super tans and the perfectly highlighted haircuts of movie stars—sprinkled in with the normal sloppy-jeaned, fast-food eaters and realized, *This is how rich people get rich. By finding ways to cut corners.* "To get rich, you've got to be tight as a clam's ass," she remembered Bruce, her mother's boyfriend, saying.

There was no hope for her then. She'd rather be poor than cheap. She'd been raised on luxury and generosity, albeit ill-begotten luxuries, and she was used to a certain level of comfort. Pinching pennies did not come naturally.

No matter. She didn't need to be rich. Making a living didn't have to mean making a killing. It just had to mean having enough of a little luxury. Perhaps Ken was right. She would keep her expectations low.

But when she turned the corner down the dank hallway at the back of the store to Russ's office she realized she didn't go low enough.

Lupita knocked on the door and opened it. A mustachioed Russ sat behind the desk and granted them entrance.

The first thing Amanda thought was: *Masturbation happens here.* She couldn't help it. If she and Lupita were simply a different kind of prisoner at Markdown, then Russ was just another kind of lonely prison guard. Sitting back on his cheap rolling-office-chair cushion full of farts, salivating and abusing the power of his surveillance cameras.

"Whoa, we have a live one," he said, getting up and holding his hand out to Amanda, which she was loath to take. "Ken didn't mention your staggering beauty."

"Thanks, I guess?" Amanda said. "Amanda Cooper." She bravely took his hand, which was bloated, slightly purple, and knotted tightly at the knuckles like a twisted balloon animal.

"Russell Crowe. Ha. No. Russell Pulaski. Russ. The pleasure is all mine. So when can you start? It's the busy season obvs." His hair was rusty brown but discolored in some parts and Amanda couldn't tell if it was badly dyed, a hairpiece, or perhaps a hack job by Hair Club for Men. Sad, really. She pitied him already. And yet he had all the power.

Amanda looked around his office at the half-open boxes of merchandise foaming at the mouth with Styrofoam peanuts, the spreadsheets scattered around his desk, the old-timey phone with those lit-up cubes urging him to pick up, and the *Game of Thrones* poster on the wall.

"Sunday?" Amanda ventured tentatively.

"Great. Here's a shirt. Size small, I take it," he said, eyeing her. "And remember the company motto," he said, pointing to an eight-by-eleven laser-printed poster taped sloppily to the wall with Scotch tape: *In these times, you're lucky to have a job at all.* "Basically, check your complaints at the door because I don't want to hear them." Then he looked her up and down again, practically drooling. Amanda shivered. "I'm trying to decide if you're a Cersei or a Daenerys. Time will tell, I guess. Either way, I'll need to keep you in check. Welcome aboard, milady."

"What did that mean?" she asked Lupita as they made their way back to the front of the store.

"*Game of Thrones* reference. Basically means you're a white princess who can do whatever she wants and get promoted months before I do."

"Won't let that happen."

"We'll see," Lupita said and brought her to the register. "I'm going to do you a favor and train you on the register. You're welcome."

"Don't people usually get trained?"

"Ha."

The next hour was spent learning code after code, rule after rule, procedure after procedure. It's true that most of cashiering is simply sliding tags over a laser, but when things went wrong, as they often did, then you had to quickly become a scratch problem solver. Lupita was good at it. "Can I buy you a drink?" Amanda asked when they were clocking out.

"Nah."

"You a friend of Bill's?" Amanda asked, referring to her alcoholic status and whether or not she went to meetings.

"AA's a white people thing." Lupita laughed. "I just don't like to drink. And I have to get home to my babies."

"Right," Amanda said as she headed back out to the parking lot. It was only 3 PM but it felt like she'd been in that box for days. That fluorescent light was even worse than the LA sun. What could she possibly wear on her face to look good in that light? Then she wondered why it mattered to her.

———

Driving again was nerve-racking. Amanda felt like the minivan had become some *Star Wars*–y rocket ship with lasery tasery things darting at her from every direction. She'd have to get used to the overstimulation of it all.

She pulled into the driveway, hands still shaking, and almost ran right over a man stooping to pick up a newspaper in a plastic bag. The brakes squealed as she stopped for him just in time.

He stood up calmly and walked to her window. A sort of lumber-sexual kind of dude, complete with five o'clock shadow, plaid shirt, jeans faded with the dust of drywall, and work boots. Why did she suddenly think work boots were the sexiest thing she'd ever seen? And then she remembered. Prison. Two years. No sex. Forced abstinence.

"Hello," she said when he got to her window. "I'm so sorry," she said. "I haven't been . . ." She was about to say she hadn't been driving for two years, but then realized she shouldn't overshare. No one, especially strangers, had to know where she'd been the past two years. It was okay not to share everything. Sharing was fine for AA but not for the day-to-day. Ken actually taught her that in preparation for her release. "Wait, you actually still get a paper, paper?" she said. "Who does that?"

"So this is my fault for getting a paper," he joked, but his smile was kind, gentle, intelligent. Not sharp and wolfish like her usual real estate developer targets dressed to the nines in three-piece suits and shiny Italian shoes, flashing snarky grins full of impossibly white teeth bleached one too many times. This, she admitted to herself, was a real man. Just stooping in front of her minivan to pick up his newspaper. *There are no coincidences in AA*, she thought. *Expect miracles*. Then she got hold of herself. Even though there were multitudes in this man's deep brown eyes (his stare and maybe his hair—dark, thick, and scruffy—were kind of biblical), it didn't mean he was put here in the driveway for her by her higher power. "I'm Ben," he said.

"Amanda," she said. "So sorry about that. I'll be more careful in the future."

"Not a problem. Nice to meet you, neighbor," he said, and then simply walked away.

3

"Oh, I'm glad you're back," Joyce said when Amanda got in the door. "I have an appointment at four. I need you to drive me."

Amanda threw her new Markdown shirt over the back of the dining room chair. "I'm hired!"

"What is that? The Mark? Oh honey. You cannot do that."

"You mean because it will embarrass you?" Amanda asked. "I don't care. I'm doing the next best thing. Just got to keep *doing the next best thing*, according to AA. This is the opportunity that presented itself and I'm going to take advantage of it. And it is a special condition of my parole."

"No, I mean *can't* as in you are *unable* to do that. You'll last an hour in that joint."

"You want to make a bet?" After all this time, mothers still haven't realized that telling a child they can't do something is like laying down the gauntlet. Tell a kid they *can't* and watch them kill themselves trying to prove you wrong.

"I'd love to make a bet. A thousand, which is what you'd make with me in two days rather than a month full-time at the Mark. Do you realize how much it costs just to keep Taylor shod? Do you know how much it costs to buy her groceries and not convenience-store crap from the food desert, like you instructed me to do? Those were your last words. 'No crap from the food desert.' Well, grass-fed beef costs ten bucks a pound."

"I can use my employee discount. And working *with you*, if you haven't noticed, lands people in prison."

"Ach. God. Employee. The word gives me the shivers. You are better than that, Amanda. I did not raise you to be an *employee*. I give you one week in that place, you'll see."

"What are you wearing?" Amanda changed the subject.

"I told you. I have a doctor's appointment."

Her mother was clad in bright yellow stretch pants with pantyhose peeking out above the waistband in the back, a short-sleeved acrylic sweater with a yellow stripe that matched the pants exactly, and orthopedic taupe-colored sneakers. Her hair had been curled with rollers and teased and set, rather than how she usually styled it in a piece-y shaggy cut that framed her face à la Jane Fonda.

"You can't wear your rag and bone jeans to the doctor?"

"Not this time, honey. Come on," she said, springing up off the couch and almost sprinting to the door. "Grab the walker." She pointed to the space between the fridge and the counter where Amanda saw a folded-up walker with tennis balls on the bottom.

"No. Mom. I got out of prison *yesterday*."

"I just need a ride. It's part of the act. I can't have them thinking I can drive myself around. But you don't have to say a peep. Pinky swear. If you won't do it, I'll call Tay . . ."

"Oh god! Fine, get in the car."

—

On the ride over her mother put on some very chalky, matte, coral-colored lipstick and doused herself in Jean Naté.

"Where do you even *find* that stuff," Amanda asked, opening a window to air out the van.

"Rite-Aid. Keeps me in character."

Her mother, it must be said, was actually a fine actor. Not fine as in "just okay" kind of fine. Fine as in "fine art." If luck had gone her way, she really could have been somebody. Like Judi Dench or her nemesis Shirley MacLaine. When she could afford it—or could swindle it—she continued to take a secret master class taught by Bill Esper in the back of a Chinese restaurant in the Palisades. Every once in a while she'd audition and easily get a part in a show at the Santa Monica community theater, but she needed to be careful to keep a low profile, so she only indulged every other year or so. Amanda had to admit Joyce was brilliant as the evil stepmother in the company's performance of *Cinderella* a few years back. Joyce considered her acting skills transferable and used them in the meantime to take care of herself. You had to find some way, when you were cursed with it, to compensate for bad luck. So. This was her way.

Joyce kept her eyes closed, doing deep breathing exercises and clenching her face muscles as she calmly sighed out directions to Amanda. "Left on Sepulveda . . ." When she started in with the vocal scales, Amanda asked, "What are you doing?"

"Proper Preparation Prevents Poor Performance," she barked, exaggerating all her *p*s.

Amanda shook her head. At least her mother had stopped trying to force her into show business. When they got to LA in the eighties, Joyce ran into the mother of Eve Plumb. *The* Eve Plumb, who played Jan on *The Brady Bunch*. She was Van Nuys's most famous resident. Joyce hounded Mrs. Plumb for tips on how to get Amanda started. "Mrs. Plumb says you need this haircut," she would say. "Mrs. Plumb says freckles are in right now." "Mrs. Plumb told me about an audition on Sunset." She dragged poor eight-year-old Amanda to auditions for commercials and TV shows and the new *Mickey Mouse Club*, but the only gigs she ever acquired were a modeling contract for a flimsy newspaper insert for Sears kids' clothing and a radio commercial where she said, "Have it your way," and someone else said, "At Burger King." That was it. She was chubby with anemic-looking hair and just wasn't what anyone was "looking for."

"You still have a couple of years left, if you would just audition," her mom had said to her before the prison thing happened. But forty-two was way over the hill for her now. No one would ever hire a haggard old ex-con with crow's-feet and slightly flabby triceps. American actresses do not have crow's-feet, her mother knew, and so she'd finally gotten off her back about it.

"Take a right," her mom said as she directed her into the parking lot of a two-story strip mall with a cupcake store, a pet emporium, a dollar store, and an MD's office on the first floor. Joyce took out the handicap tag as Amanda pulled into the spot. A gold plaque next to the door read MICHAEL MORRISON, MD.

"Showtime," said Joyce, and Amanda knew her mother loved her job. Job security, zero. Job satisfaction, ten. "Get the walker, dear," she said in the frail voice of a "Mrs. Alfrieda Johannsen."

Amanda unfolded the walker and held it sturdily in front of her mother. She'd done this before, so she knew her mother would stay put until Amanda physically helped her swing both feet out the passenger side and then, using the crook of her elbow under her mother's armpit, hoisted her ass out of the seat as her mom held shakily onto the walker and practiced Alfrieda's arthritic hunch. Amanda held on to her mom's arm as Joyce slowly pushed the walker in front of her a foot at a time and then shuffled her feet behind it à la Tim Conway on *The Carol Burnett Show* until she got to the curb and paused to take an imaginary rest. It would be hilarious if it weren't so pathetic.

They got in the door and Amanda whispered, "Take it down a notch," to Joyce, who acceded and straightened up a tiny bit and took slightly bigger steps so she actually looked decrepit and not like a ridiculous parody of decrepitude.

Joyce had promised Amanda she wouldn't have to speak and jeopardize her parole, but this was already aiding and abetting. And Amanda, when faced with the choice between looking like a horrible daughter to a bunch of office workers she would never see again or further violating her parole, chose the latter. She couldn't just leave the poor woman in the waiting room. Joyce was so "affecting."

She waited in one of the germy vinyl chairs and helped Joyce up when Alfrieda's name was called and assisted her down the hallway to the examination room. But that was where it stopped. Joyce would have to manage the rest on her own. She went back to the waiting room to play *Words with Friends*. She tried to connect with Taylor like they used to do before the big house but "snazzygem6" would not accept her request.

Twenty minutes later a dark-haired, swarthy doc in a white lab coat and hiking boots—the total California type, ready to rip off his office attire and jump on a mountain bike or a surfboard the second the quitting bell rang—escorted her hobbling mother down the hallway.

"Here she is, Doctor," Joyce said in her humble, respectful, and shaky Alfrieda voice. "My beautiful single daughter," she winked, playing the adorable old lady matchmaker role to the room, but really indicating to Amanda that she should jump on this ticket and use Michael Morrison, MD, as her next target.

"Nice to meet you," Amanda said, holding out her hand to the doctor, but shooting her mother the evil eye. "Thanks for squeezing my mother in today. She's been pretty uncomfortable." Agh. She was now complicit in the whole thing. Why couldn't she keep her mouth shut?

"Well, we gave her something for the pain, but she should call me for more tests in a couple of weeks."

"Will do," Amanda said and caught Dr. Michael checking out her ass as she turned to escort her mom out the door.

They had to keep up the charade until the car door was closed and then Joyce opened her sturdy purse and threw Amanda a prescription for OxyContin. "Ah god. What a moron. Fill this for me, will you, Amanda?" She winced as she slid off the clunky, apparently painful, clip-on old lady earrings, wiped the nasty lipstick off with a tissue, and ruffled the set curls out of her hair so that it flew back into its mod, piece-y look.

Amanda was about to protest (she wanted to start a career as an addiction counselor after all, not leak more oxy onto the street) when she noticed a Lincoln SUV idling behind her in the parking lot. It was a conspicuous step up from the rusted Kias and Hyundais in the parking lot.

"That's just Uber," Joyce said, following her gaze. "Fuckers are everywhere."

"What's Uber?"

"Something you missed in the big house. The uber-obnoxious rise of Uber. They're just glorified taxis."

"Really?"

"Yeah," Joyce said, taking a peek in the side view. "Here's the number for the unsuspecting Doctor Morrison, for when you're ready to let go of your Markdown dreams."

With a shake of her head, Amanda drove her mother back to the apartment and then continued on to a remote pharmacy in Westwood where a photocopy of her mother's face wouldn't be taped up behind the drop-off counter and, in spite of herself, filled the prescription with Alfrieda Johannsen's forged Medicare card. *Just this once*, she told herself, and realized at that moment that her mother's bullshit was her addiction. If she was going to get healthy, she had to learn to say no. One day at a time. She had to start *acting*, as a matter of fact. She had to act as if she didn't need her mother's methods to survive. In AA they say, *Act as if. Fake it 'til you make it*. And she forgave herself as she threw the pills onto the passenger seat. She'd try again tomorrow to resist her mother.

She felt calmer and resolved, but when she turned to back out of the lot, she saw it again. The shiny Lincoln SUV, and she could swear the same dark-haired man in dark sunglasses was driving it. *Prison paranoia*, she thought, and continued home where she threw the pill bottle onto her mother's bed and said, "Never. Again." in four declarative syllables of resistance.

Her mother just smirked and raised an incredulous eyebrow above her reading glasses as she continued to mark up the racing papers from her reclined perch on the flowery comforter of her bed.

4

Saturday was a new day! All Amanda had to do was resist her mother for one day. Today. So she got up before anyone else and walked to the Coffee Bean. She listened to the mesmerizing whir of the industrial coffee grinder and sipped her coffee with the smart little trust-fund brats scribbling their "breakout" screenplays. Everyone here was trying to break out. Or break in.

Amanda just wanted to be. To grasp at and hold on to contentment for just one moment. She was never any good at drawing, but she couldn't really explain what she wanted in words, so she took out her journal and drew a hand reaching for a radiant lotus flower and then a picture of herself sitting cross-legged with the flower glowing inside her belly. As if she had swallowed it, whatever that meant. It would make an awesome bumper sticker, though. Or the name of a blog. Swallow the Lotus dot com.

At ten she made her way to Radford Hall on Victory for an AA meeting on the eleventh step, which is: *Sought through prayer and meditation to improve our conscious contact with God* as we understood Him, *praying only for knowledge of His will for us and the power to carry that out.*

It was her first meeting on the outside, so she didn't know what to expect, but she loved it. Compared to a prison meeting, it was so civilized. No one was rudely interrupting the speaker or using the time to sneakily hold hands and play footsie with their prison girlfriend.

It was a bunch of quasi-professional people with regular stories about having some hard times.

At the refreshments table, Amanda ran into a short woman in her sixties wearing sunglasses and a poncho. She sampled the day-old cannoli donated from the Italian bakery down the street, taking a small bite of each flavor and then throwing the rest in the trash.

"How do you understand 'Him'?" the woman asked Amanda, who was loitering around the coffee samovar, delaying her inevitable trip back to her mother's house.

"You mean God? That's kind of a personal question, isn't it?" Amanda asked. The woman looked familiar, somehow, but she couldn't place her.

"It's kind of a riot that they think they're tolerant enough to let you describe your own god, but then they go ahead and call it a *him*. Seriously?" The woman threw away a second half-eaten cannoli wrapped in a napkin.

"How do you understand your higher power?" Amanda asked her.

"I don't pretend to understand it at all. I mean, isn't that the human condition? The fact that we will never understand what it all means? Why we're here and all that gobbledygook? Once we understand that, we'll be superhuman. I'm human. I have no idea what the fuck God is or what the hell *he* wants from us."

"Whom do you pray to then?"

"*Whom*. Oh. I love a gal who knows her objects of the preposition. My dog. I pray to my dog."

"I guess it is *god* spelled backward."

"Ha, right. I never thought of that," the woman said, brushing some powdered sugar off her hands and looking Amanda squarely in the eye through her very dark Ray-Bans.

Is she wearing a wig?

"I'm Amanda," Amanda said as she held out her hand, hoping to perhaps make a friend or get a sponsor or something.

"Right," the woman said, refusing her hand. "Well, my dog's will for me is to come home and take him for a walk, so I gotta run. May the Force be with you," she said and then walked slowly to the glass door exit and disappeared into the parking lot.

———

"You guys!" Amanda said breathlessly as she entered the stucco apartment. "The weirdest thing happened." She had decided to do some shopping after AA to grab some cheap khakis and polo shirts (God help her) for Markdown, had lost track of time, and was now starving. It was already time for dinner. The cheap, hollow front door was lighter than she thought, so she almost swung it off its hinges. She was about to admit that she may have been visited by the ghost of Carrie Fisher at AA. What other explanation could there be? She'd gone over it again and again. The woman felt so real. So close. And yet also ethereal. Drifting, perhaps between here and there. Wherever *there* was. Maybe because no one on the planet (heck, universe) wanted to believe Carrie Fisher was gone, the collective grief of the entire populace was keeping her wandering spirit trapped in LA. That's the wacko theory Amanda concocted to explain it away and excuse herself from any hint of psychosis. "You are not going to believe this," she continued, struggling to disentangle herself from the handles of her plastic bags, when she was interrupted by a yell of "Surprise!"

"Come get a hug from your father figure," Bruce joked. He was wearing his pilled clumpy brown fleece robe tied loosely around his potbelly. "I'll never get used to this goddamn desert climate," he often complained in his Brooklyn accent. "I'm always cold in this town. The weather is like the people around here. Sunny on the outside and frigid at the core."

"Hi, Bruce," Amanda said and let herself melt into an Old Spice–scented hug.

"Hiya, Mandy," he said with genuine love in his voice. "I came over to make you a steak."

"Bloody to feed my blood?" she asked.

"Bloody to feed your blood," he said. It was their favorite line from *Moonstruck*.

"Be careful, I don't know if she eats innocent cows anymore. They turned her into a wuss in prison," Joyce said.

Bruce ignored her. "We're celebrating your homecoming, right Taylor?" he said, glancing at Tay, who was in the corner of the dining room sulkily setting the table against her will. Or pretending it was against her will. Deep down, Amanda knew she wanted to be there or she wouldn't be. Eventually they would break the ice. "I heard you got a job, too. Right off the bat."

"I start tomorrow," Amanda said, not realizing until this second how much she'd missed him. Always the voice of reason. Maybe Bruce was her higher power. He was kind of mystical, like "The Dude" in *The Big Lebowski*. He had the same bathrobe and nonchalance but he was a little saltier with East Coast grit. He had a habit of every other Thursday buying a Filet-O-Fish at the McDonald's on Ventura.

Bruce met Joyce soon after she and Amanda landed in LA. Joyce found him at a shady back-alley poker game and impressed him by running the table full of tough ex-cons, Vietnam vets, mafia dropouts, and media moguls down on their luck. He had to protect her on the way out because the men were furious to have lost everything to a woman, and when he escorted her to her car, he saw six-year-old Amanda asleep in the back and realized they were living out of it.

Her mom never again wanted to be dependent on a man, however, so she wouldn't let him take them in or give them anything she couldn't repay in a week. Bruce ended up being Amanda's satellite stepdad, always orbiting around them but never cohabitating. He was their entire family really. They were all lucky to have him. He was pretty successful and entrepreneurial, too. He had started and successfully sold a few businesses since Amanda had known him. Convenience store, a lube-job franchise, and now a storage facility. He was a legit businessman except for maybe seeking out a few tax loopholes. He knew not to ask Joyce questions about her own enterprise, which kept the relationship intact.

"Oh yes, the job," Joyce moaned, drying her hair with a towel as she walked into the living room.

"Don't start, Joycey," Bruce said. "I'm proud of her, if this is what she wants."

"She doesn't understand the world."

"Um, I was just in prison," Amanda said. " 'I have been in Sorrow's kitchen and licked out all the pots,' so to speak."

"Zora Neale Hurston," mumbled Taylor from the corner.

"Good, Taylor! Did you read that in AP English?" Amanda asked, trying to get a school discussion going. Amanda would love to hear about what Taylor was doing in school. She had probably been reading the same things herself while getting her associate's in prison.

"I don't care what you licked in prison, they did not teach you about the world," Joyce cut in. "They brainwashed you into thinking you could change. Take charge of your own life by playing by their rules and all that. But you can't, Amanda. Don't you get that the entire game is rigged?"

"What's that supposed to mean?"

"It means, dear daughter, that the world does not operate under a system of merit. Of course you merit a wonderful life. You are beautiful and kind and better than everyone on the planet. But you don't have power." With this, she squinted her eyes at Amanda and pointed a slightly arthritic bent-at-the-tip finger at her. The fingernail was cracked and yellowing, too. *A lot can change in two years*, Amanda thought. Her mother was getting old.

"And you can't get power unless a powerful person gives it to you. Powerful people can 'make' you. *If* they choose you. If they don't, which they haven't in your case, then you're fucked. If you're not lucky enough to be chosen, to be made, then you need to honey badger your way through life. You've seen the video on YouTube. A honey badger does what, Taylor?" she asked, pointing to Taylor in the corner without taking her eyes off Amanda.

"Takeswhatitwants," Taylor mumbled.

"I can't hear you," said Joyce.

"It takes what it wants," Taylor said, louder this time.

"Exactly. It takes what it wants."

Amanda stared at Bruce for a second, who was pretending to be engrossed in mixing spices for his rub. "Why are you so quiet?" she asked him. "Do you agree with all this?"

Usually Bruce would take her side. Defend her from the acidic burn of her mother's rage and fear. That's what fathers were for, after all. To balance out the crazy. Stabilize the ship. Good fathers were psychosocial gyroscopes, taking the roll out of the ocean, so families didn't sink.

"Um," he said now, choosing his words very carefully and trying to stay as neutral as possible on the subject, "I feel like, sometimes, you need to take the bull by the horns, I guess . . . Take what you want . . . But it's always an issue of timing."

"What timing?" Joyce squawked. "You see what you want, you take it, right Taylor? You need to get back on board," she finished, pointing drunkenly at Amanda.

"Here's a news flash, Mom," Amanda started. It was becoming clearer and clearer just how much living with her grandmother had influenced Taylor. "Because I think you need to hear this: I am not you. My life is different from yours. I can be patient. I can do the next best thing, one day at a time, to earn my way back into society. I am not you."

"This has nothing to do with me, sweetheart. Or whether you're better than me. Six months is a long time to work at Markdown when you're old enough to count the months you have left in your life with simple math, dear daughter. What is it that they say at school, Taylor?"

"YOLO?" Taylor tried.

"Ha. Yes. YOLO. YOLO, Amanda. *YOLO* means you can't waste precious time working at Markdown."

"It's a perfectly fine job. And it's a condition of my parole. Bruce, you tell her. You're a legitimate business owner. You had a vision and you played by the rules and look at you now."

"Ha! Yes, you tell her, Bruce," Joyce said, retreating to the bathroom, locking the door, and turning on the blow-dryer full steam.

"What's that supposed to mean?" Amanda asked.

"Nothing, sweetheart. Let's have our steaks," he said, and he winced as he hobbled a little to the balcony to take the meat off the grill. He had a bad leg from Vietnam that had been getting worse and worse.

"When you going to get that checked out?" Amanda asked.

—

Joyce, sufficiently coiffed and greased up with wrinkle cream, sat at the table and picked at her steak, then whipped out her racing papers, which were scribbled with a complicated labyrinth of marks from a blue ballpoint pen. "So who wants to come to Santa Anita with me tomorrow? Speaking of rigged. I know everything. Win. Place. Show. Etcetera. Every race."

"What do you mean, you know?" Amanda asked. "How can you know?"

"You think powerful people just leave these things to chance? It's all rigged, Amanda. There's no such thing as luck."

"I'll go," Taylor chimed in before Amanda could craft her rebuttal.

"Oh no," Amanda said. "You are not going out gambling with your granny."

"Why?" Taylor dared to look at Amanda for the first time, albeit from the side of her eye. *Good ole Cap'n Side-eye.* That's okay. Her daughter hated her in this moment, which for a sixteen-year-old was in the range of normal. She would take any emotion at all from her daughter that was in the range of normal and proved that Taylor hadn't entirely given up on caring about her entirely.

"Why?" Amanda repeated incredulously. "It's gambling, Taylor. And you're sixteen."

"It's a lot more wholesome an activity than most people my age will be engaging in tomorrow night," Taylor mumbled. "Would you rather I got high on oxy and slept with some scumbag movie producer trolling the high school pool parties for wannabes?"

"These are not your choices, Taylor. You can choose other things. And I don't want you choosing her road . . ." Amanda said, pointing at her mother and then immediately regretting it. The ship was about to roll again.

"Her road has kept me safe and sound for two years. Where were you when my best friend threatened to commit suicide while she was on the phone with me? Where were you when I almost failed Geometry? You need geometry for college, Mom. Where were you when I was bullied because I had to wear the same jeans every day because you weren't here to get me to the mall? Where were you?"

Amanda put her head down.

"Right. Whatever. You don't get to tell me what to do. Ever. Again."

"Taylor. Apologize," Bruce said, steady-as-she-goes, yet menacingly pushing his belly away from the table and threatening to stand up. "This is your mother and she will always get to tell you what to do."

"Why?" Taylor crossed her arms over her chest.

"That's your favorite question tonight, isn't it? Because it's in the fucking Bible, Taylor. The most important fucking thing in the Bible. Honor your mother. Now straighten up and apologize right now," he said, putting his sandaled foot down. "Amanda, honey, why don't you take her shopping tomorrow," he suggested.

"Because I have to work at Markdown," Amanda sighed.

"Ah, Jeezus H. Christ," Joyce piped in from the peanut gallery.

5

"Do you have any more of these in the back?" asked a bespectacled, haggard-looking mother. Her dirty-faced child, who had fluorescent-green slime hanging out of his nose, whined again about wanting Spiderman slippers.

Amanda was extremely polite, even though the mother ignored her child when he screamed again and started a tantrum right there in the shopping cart, purposefully slamming his head against the side. *Maybe he'd be more comfortable if he were wearing a shirt*, thought Amanda, but she kept her judgments to herself and calmly said, "Everything we have is out on the floor right now, ma'am. Were you looking for a particular size?"

"Are you sure? Can't you go look in the back?" she said, ignoring the fact that her kid had now climbed out of the cart and was kicking and screaming bare-backed on the dirty Markdown floor.

"Um, I think maybe he needs a nap," Amanda offered. "Maybe you can come back later?" Amanda *obviously* was not the perfect mother, but she never let her kid have a tantrum in public, always stuck to a strict napping schedule, and *never* woke her sleeping baby. Those rules, especially the ones about sleep, were responsible for Taylor becoming so smart and beautiful in spite of everything else going on.

"Excuse me? Did you just tell me how to parent my kid? Did I ask you for parenting advice? I asked you to go and get me one of these from the back," she said, holding up a red and black plaid shirt, bedazzled with some silvery rhinestones on the collar. "And while you're there, get your manager so I can speak to him about this," she said as her kid came over and kicked Amanda in the shin.

"Get me Spiderman slippers," he said and then threw himself face-down on the floor in another fit of screaming tears.

Amanda was about to say that there was no "back." Where did this lady think she was, at some boutique on Montana? Markdown has a front and that's it. Things come off the truck and onto the sales floor. They don't hold stock in some elusive back area just to frustrate people. But then she remembered *Act as if*. She would act as if there were a back.

"Yes, ma'am," she said. "I apologize. I'll check in the back." As Amanda walked away, holding her ears against the primal screams of the three-year-old, the intercom blared, "Customer assistance to Personal Care," and since she was the only one on the floor thanks to the six people who had called out sick, Amanda made her way to Personal Care and forgot all about the woman and the plaid shirt.

In aisle seventeen, she found a lanky, pimply kid in shredded skinny jeans holding his skateboard and looking down at the floor. He was standing in front of the condoms, which were high on the top shelf, encased in plastic and under lock and key.

"Can I help you?" Amanda asked.

The boy, who must have been seventeen or eighteen, just kind of looked up at the Trojans and then back down at his feet.

"Do you need those?" Amanda asked. "Which ones?"

The boy pointed to a black box and Amanda used the special key Russ gave her to unlock the specialty items. She thought the key would be reserved for diamond jewelry or high-priced electronics, not condoms. Then, she went ahead and unlocked all the plastic cases in that entire aisle, the ones for the condoms and the pregnancy tests, and ripped the cases off.

"Ridiculous," she said. "God, you can just go to Sporting Goods to buy a gun, but you need me to unlock the condoms? Tell your friends,

I've set them free," she said, and then the intercom squawked, "Customer assistance to Housewares," so she left the boy and hurried to aisle five.

Amanda endured several hours of this, running from aisle to aisle, trying to assist with demands: "I want this dishtowel but it's packaged with two others. Can I just rip it out and pay for one?" "Do you have *Lego Marvel Super Heroes* for Xbox? No, not *Lego Batman*! *Lego Marvel Super Heroes.*" "Can you put this on so I can see how it would look on my wife?" She told one woman that her daughter would get much more use out of a hula hoop than *Disney Infinity*, which she would play exactly three times before becoming bored with it. The woman seemed grateful. Amanda was helping people. Doing a good job, she thought.

It was after that, though, when she heard from the squawk box, "Amanda Cooper to the management office, please. Amanda Cooper."

She was relieved, because she hadn't had a break and would have loved to get some coffee and maybe switch to cashiering for a bit. She confidently knocked on the door to Russ's office and was shocked to see his red, angry face.

"What the hell do you think you're doing out there?" he asked.

"Serving customers?"

"Sit down, Daenerys," he said, standing up. "I've just been going over your tapes and have seen seven violations in as many minutes."

"Tapes?"

"Sit down," he said, indicating a coffee- (or something) stained chair that Amanda was loath to sit in, but she complied.

"What violations?"

"See for yourself," Russ said as he pushed Play on his remote and aimed it at a tiny TV that played back surveillance-camera footage. A black-and-white Amanda, her blond hair tied back in a neat ponytail, looking pretty professional, Amanda thought, climbed up the shelves in aisle seventeen. Strangely, the camera was zeroed in on her butt as she set the condoms free.

"What is that about? You just go ahead and make your own store policy?" Russ said, leaning over her and using textbook intimidation body language techniques.

Amanda tried to stay strong. "I thought it was a mistake that all the condoms were locked away."

"I'm sure you've heard this before, but we don't pay you to think. Locking up the birth control is not a mistake. Markdown doesn't make mistakes. We need the poor people to make more and more poor babies so that they will come in and buy the cheap diapers. It's a strategy."

"I'm sorry," Amanda said.

"And what about this?" he said, holding up a customer complaint form. "You insult a mother's parenting style at Markdown? And then you dissuade a woman from buying a hundred-dollar video game in favor of a $4.99 hula hoop?"

"Well, it's my first . . . Wow, you really keep close . . ." Amanda began, but Russ kicked his wastebasket across the room, and then smoothed down his hair plugs with both hands.

"This is obviously not working out," Russ started.

"I will do better tomorrow, though. I just wasn't sure . . ."

"Look," Russ said, calming down. "Maybe the floor is not for you. But I do have another job on the loading dock, where you won't have to interact with customers."

In spite of herself, Amanda's heart sank a little bit. She'd thought she was doing a pretty good job with the customers. She was using every ounce of patience she could muster and giving them good advice.

"Come with me." Russ had her follow him to the rolling garage door where a couple of kids were unloading a truck full of televisions and other premium electronics. Russ handed her a spreadsheet. "See these highlighted packing slip numbers? I need you to find the matching boxes and put them on that pallet over there," he said, indicating a six-by-six square wooden plank structure that stood six inches off the ground. "Then when you've finished, label the stack 'Damaged. For Russ.'"

"Do you need me to open the boxes to verify the damage?" Amanda asked. In her job training in prison they encouraged new hires to try to go the extra mile. Ask how you can be of further assistance.

"What was it that I told you inside?" Russ said. "We don't pay you to think. Grab the boxes. Pile them over there. Label them 'For Russ.' One, two, three. You can count to three, right?"

"I can . . ."

"Then get to work. Last chance. If you can't do this, you lose your job. Lose your job and you go back to the parole board, although I'm sure you've already blown Ken to get yourself this gig, so perhaps you can 'persuade' him to get you another," he said, moving closer, staring down at her and fingering the name tag pin above her breast. "Pretty name, Amanda. Don't screw this up. I'd love to keep you around, just for eye candy."

Amanda shuddered. But this wasn't the worst abuse she'd endured in the recent past. She just got out of prison after all, where such talk was run of the mill. She shook it off and got to work.

—

Just as Amanda suspected, none of the boxes on her list was actually damaged. She went through about half of them, her anger building. How dare Russ bully her into his scheme because he thought she had no choice? How dare he? She understood right away that Russ would just take advantage of the natural retail shrinkage numbers, claim the merchandise lost, and then sell it on the black market. It wasn't difficult to connect the dots.

The cement loading dock was freezing and her back started to hurt from the damp cold and the lifting of televisions. She hated Russ and pictured herself making a potbellied, fake-haired loser of a Russ voodoo doll and poking it in the head with a large needle. *Take that*, she thought, hoping he would feel the crippling pain of it just by her thinking it into being.

"Hey," she heard. It was Lupita, carrying a Styrofoam cup of nasty breakroom coffee and a glazed donut that had been sitting out since 7 AM.

"Hey," Amanda said. "Is that for me?"

"Yeah. I had a feeling he would trounce you pretty hard today."

"Why is he doing this?"

"Because he can, *mamacita*. Because he can. Don't worry. He'll have you do this for a couple of months and then he'll transition you when he gets in his next victim."

"Transition me to what?" Amanda asked.

"The next step is moving the merchandise," said Lupita, taking a bite of her own donut. She was a thin woman. A "vata" in Ayurveda. The kind of person who could care less about real food, eat only sugar when they do eat, and never gain an ounce. She herself, she'd read in *Glamour* while she waited for Joyce at the doctor's office, was a "kapha." Doe-eyed and content, with a super-slow metabolism. She had to be careful about what she ate, so she threw the stale donut in the garbage can.

"On the street?" Amanda asked.

"*Si*. On the street . . . *La playa* . . . Venice mostly."

"God, why doesn't Ken shake him down?"

"Ay, *mami*, Ken's in on it, too," she said, staring out the square loading dock door and taking a sip of her coffee.

"Lupita . . ."

"What?" Amanda could tell from the numbness on her face that she was resigned to it. Willing to put in even more time on top of her time.

"Why don't you leave?" Amanda asked.

"Where am I to go? My babies. I can't go back to prison. I have two months of this left and then I will help my sister-in-law make gowns for weddings and quinceañeras. She's doing it out of her house now but we will open a shop."

"What were you in for?"

"Immigration. Unlawful reentry. I went to visit my dying mother and they caught me on the way back in, strip-searched me. Worse . . . The American dream. You are the lucky one, *gringa*."

"There is no luck." Amanda suddenly realized that her mother was right. *Goddammit, why are mothers always right?* Was there really no way to get ahead by playing fair and square? She didn't want to believe it was true. But maybe it was. Times had changed. There was no mobility anymore unless you were the one making the rules.

She considered her options. Submit to Russ's bullshit and continue to do her time, but she'd *still* be risking getting caught and violating her parole. If anyone found out about this fucking Toastergate, she'd be the first one thrown under the bus. They would blame it all on her. She was an ex-con, after all. Well, fuck it. If she was going to be forced to break the law, it may as well be on her terms, right? It may as well benefit her and her family. If she was going to have to play dirty, she may as well profit from it.

She imagined Russ's smug, idiotic face, a bright, angry, ripe pimple on the side of his nose, tight, shiny, and ready to burst. It flashed through her brain as she relived the way he fingered her name tag as if she were his property.

She couldn't be a pawn in other people's two-bit games when she was perfectly qualified to run a game herself. On her own terms. "This is bullshit, Lupita," she said as she squashed her coffee cup and threw it out the opening into the parking lot. Then she stood and stormed into Russ's office. "I quit!" she yelled, tearing off the red vest and throwing it at him. "I'll be damned if I have to do your dirty work, you insignificant pimple on the ass of humanity."

Russ stepped around his desk, leaning back against it, and stared her in the eye. "Oh, so now it comes out. Your royal princess side. I knew you weren't a team player at heart, Cersei."

"I tried to be a team player, asshole. This is not a team; it's a racket," she said. "Guess what? I can run my own racket. My racket could eat yours for breakfast. I'm out."

While she ranted, Russ must have hit some button under his desk, because a three-hundred-pound security guard snuck in behind Amanda and grabbed the back of her arms.

"Let me go, Hank," she said, and Hank did, because he liked her.

She ran down the hall and pushed through the swinging door out onto the sales floor.

"Where are you going?" Lupita said, but her voice got farther away as the anger welled up behind Amanda's ears and her face turned red. She whirled up to the front of Women's and snagged the 109.10 dress off the hanger, the hot black one with the tasteful sequins for $79.99, then she stormed out the front door.

"A honey badger takes what it wants," she hissed as the dress triggered the alarm. She could hear the alarm pounding at the back of her head long after she'd already driven home and hung the black dress in her cheap mirrored closet.

"You're home early," her mother said, eyebrow raised.

"Here," Amanda said, slamming ten hundreds from her house down-payment savings onto the table in front of her. "You were right."

"Ah, a mother's favorite words. But keep it," she said, holding the money up. "At least you've come to your senses. Come give your mama a hug. We'll do it right this time, baby. You won't go back to prison," she said as she embraced Amanda lightly for ten seconds and then gave her three light taps on the back, which signaled the end of it and meant *This was nice but I'm done with the mush for now.*

It's not easy to love a honey badger.

6

Effing hipsters and their effing "outdoor rooms," Amanda thought. The trend was just beginning when she went to prison, but now it seemed you couldn't go anywhere in LA and sit indoors at a proper *bar*. You had to go outside and sit around some designer fire pit and pretend you weren't freezing your ass off as you watched the sunset burn off the last of the smog over the Hollywood Hills. The decor was always the same, too. Inchworm-green and brown faux bamboo couches arranged in pits and surrounded by white orchids, which they shouldn't be watering in this drought. Even her old standby, the Four Seasons, had moved everything to the outdoor room. When she pulled up wearing the beautiful (she had to admit) stolen Markdown dress this evening, she not only had to suffer the humiliation of valet parking the dented silver minivan, but she also had to endure the prospect of the "outdoor room." How the hell was she going to work that? She needed some intimacy and gel lighting to disguise her crow's-feet.

"Ms. Vanessa!" the concierge yelled at her from across the lobby at his marble desk in the corner. Amanda almost forgot she was "Vanessa" two years ago. How did this guy remember? And what was his name?

She walked over to him, and, thank god, he was wearing a name tag. "Roderigo, how have you been?"

"*Where* have you been? That is the question," he said. "I've seen

Mr. Evan now and then, but always alone. Have you been breaking hearts?" he asked, wagging his finger back and forth.

Crap, Amanda thought, *Evan*. She knew she shouldn't have come back to the Seasons. Number one rule: You don't shit where you eat. Or, in this case, eat where you shit. Or whatever. Her life was one big shit-eating fiasco.

"Roderigo, dear," she said, ignoring his question. "Please tell me you still have a proper bar. Inside the hotel."

"Oh yes, Ms. Vanessa. It's small, but there's still a bar in the Italian restaurant upstairs. Will you be needing Lakers tickets on the floor for tomorrow's game? Do you need reservations at Maude? I have a guy . . ."

"No thanks, hon," she said. "Just here for a drink tonight, but hey," she paused, thinking, "can you do me a favor? If you do see uh . . . Mr. Evan," she said, lowering her voice, "please don't tell him you saw me." She handed him a hundred. It was stupid of her to be so careless with her paltry savings, but she had to keep up appearances if she was going to step back into the life. And now that the rusty gears were getting lubricated, she was feeling excited to get back in the driver's seat.

"Sure, Ms. Vanessa," he said. "Yes. No problem."

———

The bar, thankfully, was dark and dignified. And, thankfully, was manned by a new hot young actor wannabe, not one Amanda remembered from the old days. She took a look around and sat strategically in the far corner, facing the entrance. From here she could see who was already drinking and who was walking in. She could dangle her crossed and toned calf out and use it as a lure for the perfect target.

Of course, she could be missing an opportunity by not heading out to the fire pit. There was a lot of very young hipster wealth in this city that, because of their youth and casual attire, could be underestimated at first sight. But Amanda preferred hitting up douchebags instead of hipsters: over-tan, fossil-fuel-wasting, Hummer-driving, flipped-up-collar-wearing, possible Segway-owning, sexist, narcissist assholes who deserved what was coming to them.

And speak of the devil. Twelve o'clock. Two pastel Izod shirts with both collars popped, aviators, hair product, expensive jeans, loafers, no tassels. Amanda flipped her hair, made eye contact and then looked away pretending to be very involved in her iPhone. Men liked women who had their own stuff going on. That's usually all it took. She expected her next move to be accepting a drink from him, but when she looked up, he had slid onto a stool next to a younger woman, twenty-seven at most, and she was working him hard. Laughing at his tired jokes, touching her neck, gazing into his eyes. The young, wrinkleless girl stopped these shenanigans for a moment to catch Amanda's stare and then gave her a nasty wink to punctuate Amanda's pathetic obsolescence.

Was Amanda that old? Had she already peaked? Maybe she *would* have to head back to Markdown. *For there is only one thing in the world worse than being talked about, and that is not being talked about,* Amanda thought to herself with a sigh, remembering her Oscar Wilde. *The Picture of Dorian Gray* was one of the first books she picked from the prison library. It was an old green hardcover with yellowing pages that fit in the palm of her hand and smelled like musty rotten glue. If she ever got rich she would donate to the prison library system. She was about to pack up when a white-haired man sat down next to her and slid a glistening glass of Pinot Grigio in front of her. It caught the overhead track lighting and threw a golden yellow ball of light onto the wood.

"I can tell you're a woman of sophisticated tastes," the man said. Little did he know that she drove here in a minivan and that her dress was from Markdown. "This is a 2002 Reserve from the Alsace region. But you probably already know that because of the nose."

Amanda played along, swirling the glass beneath her own nose and pretending to pick up the peachiness of it with exotic hints of allspice and ginger.

"Exactly," he said. "I knew you were a winner."

"Is that what I am?" Amanda asked, tilting her head. "I wasn't sure."

"Thank god there are some real women left in the world," the man continued. "I'm sure you wouldn't step foot on that patio."

"No, that's barbaric," Amanda said, grinning. "I'm Amity," she said and held out her hand.

She had done some preliminary identity thieving before she left the house, first finding a name for herself that was exotic but affable and not at all wife-y. (Typical wife names like Michelle or Jennifer or Elizabeth or Karen, God forbid, were strictly off-limits.) She chose a name that could encompass both sides of the virgin/whore binary that men found so attractive if you knew which one to play when, and if you never showed them anything in between. Then she easily hacked into Amity Michaels's Amazon account, which led her to the credit card info, which got her to a checking account, a social security number, and eventually to the DMV. She was prepared after tonight to get an Amity Michaels California driver's license.

"I'm Charles," the gentleman announced, taking her hand and placing a light kiss on top. "Charmed." He wasn't bad looking. His hair, while white, was thick and perfectly barbered. His features were masculine and not boyish, and his teeth were straight enough and white enough without being perfectly aligned like dentures. He had slight traces of acne scars but they were disguised now by the gruff cut of his distinguishing wrinkles. He clearly exercised, his biceps pushing at the seams of his navy blue sport coat. Not bad.

"I also don't do brunch," Amanda continued, looking him in the eye just for a second before turning her gaze back to the wine she was only going to pretend to drink and tracing her coaster with her seductive index finger. "Or Matcha coffee, or gourmet donuts, or artisanal cheese, or red velvet cupcakes, or food trucks, or, God forbid, selfies."

"I think I love you already," Charles said, shifting on his seat. "I bet you even still have some of your pubic hair," he whispered.

Wow, not wasting any time. "Of course. God gave us that for a reason."

"Oh good. I don't like going to bed with someone who looks like a ten-year-old down there. Makes me feel dirty."

"What makes you think we're going to bed, though?" Amanda asked, sneaking her hand beneath the bar and finding the sharp seam of his polyester wool blend pants. She traced it to his knee, where she lingered for a moment before letting her finger travel back up the inseam.

"We're not getting any younger. Thought we shouldn't beat around the bush, so to speak."

"Hilarious," Amanda said with a wink. She had decided ahead of time that "Amity" was a big winker. The wink was irresistible. It signaled to Charles that she would never take things too seriously or utter the words "Can we talk?"

"No, really. We could make beautiful music together."

"Are you a musician? I wasn't reading musician. Your hands are too strong," she said, grasping his hand lightly and flipping it over onto the bar as though she was about to read his palm. "You're a chef, I think. Or by now, restaurateur." Another wink.

"Wow. That's uncanny," he said. "Seventeen restaurants nationwide."

"I have a way with that," Amanda said. She didn't really read his palm, obviously. She read the cuff links engraved with the Cross of the Holy Spirit, the symbol for the gastronomically gifted medieval knights who wore that cross on a blue ribbon and became the inspiration for Le Cordon Bleu, the world's greatest culinary institute.

"Really?" Charles said. "What about that guy over there?" he asked, pointing to her original lost target. She took in the pastel shirts and loafers again.

"Real estate," Amanda stated. "Definitely real estate. Maybe even celebrity, reality-show real estate."

Amanda glanced out to the patio then and thought she was hallucinating. She probably was hallucinating. She shook her head and looked again. But it was no mirage. Mirages don't stare back at you with your own eyes and rebelliously take a sip from their ill-gotten beer bottle. Taylor sat out there on the slimy, inchworm-green outdoor couch, face fully made up and glistening from some glitter products. She talked animatedly to a man with a full beard. Not a boy. A man.

Amanda shuddered and shook herself back into the present moment where Charles was going on and on about how small plates made him big money. He, apparently, singlehandedly popularized the entire tapas scene in America.

"Excuse me," Amanda said. "I need to go." She wasn't sure whether she or Taylor was the one who was busted. But neither of them should be there right now. It wasn't part of the farmers' market, herb garden, NPR-listening future she had planned for them.

Charles wasn't used to being interrupted, however, and he didn't like it. He grabbed Amanda's wrist, encircling it with his thumb and finger like a handcuff. "Not so fast," he said. "We were just getting to know each other, Amity." Again, Amanda thought, this is our own fault. It's how mothers mother boys, treating them like God's gift to the universe.

"Listen, Charles," Amanda said. "I'm letting you off easy. Consider yourself hashtag blessed."

"What does that mean?"

"It means I do this for a living, Charles. I meet egomaniacs like you. I bolster said egos and pretend to love every single word uttered from their mouths. God, the drivel I've endured." Amanda shook her head, remembering the bald dude with the puffy cheeks who would state the obvious as if making brilliant revelations about human nature (actually, this was all of them). The cultish ones who couldn't stop talking about their families as if evaluating whether you'd fit into the fold. The awkward ones who used sarcasm as a shield and couldn't sit for one moment with a genuine emotion. So boring and predictable, all of them.

"You men are just so much more boring than you realize," she continued. "Anyway. I toggle seamlessly from virgin to whore, since you can understand women only in the most simplistic biblical ways. I get you to wine and dine me. And then I get you to open me a bank account. I hack into your business accounts and put a tiny pinhole in each of them so you don't even notice the additional slow drip of ten thousand a month or so trickling into my pocket. I feed my kid with that money. And let her get an iPhone so she can be on a level playing field with the likes of your spoiled progeny. I think up a scheme, like needing extra money to pay the medical bills of my dying mother. Then the pièce de résistance, I get you to buy me a ring, Charles. A big ring. A ring so big, the sale of it acts as a year's salary for me while I clean up shop and plan to open another operation. And then I disappear."

His grip around her wrist instinctively tightened at the word *disappear*, as if he were a preschooler getting ready for a tug-of-war with his favorite toy. *Mine*, she could feel him thinking.

"And you. You are too devastated to pursue me, Charles. To prosecute me. Your ego can't believe that someone like you could make such a big mistake. So. This is your lucky day, Charles. I'm letting you off the hook. Now let me go," Amanda said, looking deliberately at her restrained wrist and then up at the innocent bartender, who noticed and, bless his heart, strolled confidently over to the end of the bar and said, "Can I help you, miss?"

Charles released the vise grip and muttered "bitch," or "cunt," or "witch," or whatever they like to mutter these days, and Amanda strode out to the lobby. In for four, hold for seven, out for eight, she breathed. And then she texted Taylor: *I am not going to embarrass you and drag you by the hair off that patio, but if I don't see you at home in 20 minutes, you can guarantee I will hunt you down. Home. Now.* House emoji house emoji house emoji.

She tried to make a dramatic exit, but it was hampered by the time she had to wait at the valet stand, and when the driver pulled up in the beat-up minivan, it grumbled and practically backfired just as Taylor was exiting with her much older beau. He had his arm around her proprietarily and she slumped into him. So familiar. So comfortable. So old. How was this her child? How had this become her life? Amanda climbed into the minivan.

Just three years ago she was spending weekends (and then some) in Vegas with "Mr. Evan." Mr. Evan happened to own a casino. So Mr. Evan was a big deal, born on the right side of luck. She hated him. He was her job. But the fringe benefits of gold-digging work sometimes made it worth it. Pampering. Designer clothes. Drivers. Personal chefs. Hobnobbing with celebs at the caviar bar at N9NE. Clubbing all night in the VIP section of LAX in the Luxor. Sleeping all day Sunday. Private jets from LA to Vegas. Getaways to exclusive private island resorts. She even started to learn how to golf and ski and scuba dive. A person could get used to that.

Sadly, though, she did her job too well. Evan actually fell in love with her. Or fell into his version of love with her, which meant possessing her like he possessed everything else. He was a vicious specimen, prone to jealous tantrums and sociopathic emotional abuse. But luckily, because he saw his mother brutally beaten by his father, he drew the line at that. He never, ever hit her.

Her hatred for him gave her license to slowly extort the thousands of dollars that would one day be the down payment on her and Taylor's house. It was a huge investment of time and energy for Amanda, not only because she couldn't siphon off too much at once, but because it took months for her to break through the firewall. She obviously wasn't a computer engineer and had to learn all her skills from the message boards on Hack In The Box. Eventually though, she was able to get things rolling, build up a nest egg, and then disappear.

—

She would have been scot-free and on to another target had she not been caught for passing fake checks and sent to prison.

And now where was she? She couldn't stomach going back to that life. Was Markdown really her only option?

She called Ken.

"How are the kids?" she asked him.

"Is this really a social call?"

"No. I screwed up, I think. I had it out with Russ and I need you to smooth things over."

"It's going to cost you," he said.

"Please don't say that," Amanda practically begged. "I've been doing the right things, Ken. I'm trying to do the right things," she said. Was she going to cry? *Please God, don't let me cry.*

"I can't work with a parolee that employers don't like," Ken warned. "I need to keep my channels open for other losers."

Amanda stopped her tears by biting her lip. "I know what I want now, Ken. Your program has actually reformed me. I've gotten to the age where I want to give back. I want to help others. I'm applying to counseling school in the spring. I just . . ."

"Everyone just needs just one more favor, Candy Girl," he said, sighing. "Sorry. It's been a long day. Let me call Russ and see what I can do. But this is it. Just do what he says until you can make your six months. The only other work-order jobs available are for mechanics."

"Ten-four."

"And Amanda?"

"What?"

"It was nice to hear your voice."

She swallowed. "Yours, too," she lied.

7

Amanda looked into the rearview to make sure the tears hadn't actually spilled over and destroyed her makeup. She still had Taylor to deal with at home and she had to look put together in order to elicit some respect. They have whole programs in prison called Dress for Success that tell you how to comport yourself in order to be taken seriously. Amanda realized now that it might be true for parenting as well. A put-together mom might be able to make headway and penetrate the thick skull of her teenager. What was Taylor doing with that man? He had to be twice her age. Amanda cringed.

Suddenly, peering back at her in the rearview mirror were the two bright, bearlike eyes of a black SUV. Uber again? Were they this ubiquitous? Were they known for tailgating? She tried not to seem paranoid and turned up the radio, which had surprisingly great speakers for a minivan. Must have belonged to a musical family. She let herself hum along to "Hotel California" even though she hated the Eagles so fucking much. Their music was so nostalgic, though. It evoked some good, innocent times like the first time she sat on the beach with her high school boyfriend and he tried to show her how artsy he could be by playing this song on his acoustic. That moment was perfect. His klutzy fingers squeaking against the strings as they maladroitly searched for the next chord. The cold sand between her toes. The newfound freedom.

"We are programmed to receive," she sang out loud in her ghostly "Hotel California" voice.

She took a few lazy turns trying to ignore the headlights that still seemed too close for comfort. They trailed behind her, suspiciously with no decisive direction of their own. They were obviously on the hunt. She got off at Wilshire and banged a right onto Coldwater Canyon. The lights followed her, keeping steadily on her tail. Fuck. The next light was turning yellow, so she slowed until she got under it and then sped up, passing through the intersection as the light turned red. She heard the horns from the crossing traffic blare at him as he continued to follow right behind.

Amanda could feel her heart pound through her entire body, and her palms began to sweat. She thought of the last time she was followed. Right before her arrest, how she was innocently breezing through the security pre-check at LAX about to meet Evan in Vegas when she felt anticipatory goose bumps crawl all over her flesh before the tall man next to her, undercover in jeans and an Under Armour mock turtleneck of all things, grabbed her around the bicep and read her her rights. Stone-cold busted.

There was no way she was letting that happen again. She made a U-turn in the middle of the street, tore through another red light, wound her way back down toward Hollywood, and banged a right into the parking lot of Temple Beth El. She turned off her lights and waited in the pitch dark.

"Amanda Cooper?"

In the rearview, she could see, so very close to her right earlobe, a black, shadowy figure speaking to her from *inside the van*. It was every bad suburban legend come true. He's talking from Inside the Van. Amanda's brain tried to process it. After a five-second delay, she screamed. And screamed and screamed again, and then blindly drove the minivan over two curbs into another parking lot where she crashed into a Jack in the Box speaker head. It fell off the post and lolled around on the pavement for a second, hampered by its pointy hat.

"Welcome to Jack in the Box," the headless speaker squawked. "What can I get for you?"

Amanda threw the car into park, opened the door, and tried to run.

"Freeze," the shadow said, although he was delayed for a moment by the slow opening of the automatic sliding door of the minivan. "Dammit," he muttered.

Amanda ran again. *Run*, she thought. *Just run.* And she did so without even feeling her legs. Her legs were that big cloudy, circular whorl of cartoon Road Runner legs, and she was floating on top of them, stretching out her neck, moving fast. *Meep meep.*

And then she tripped. Of course. And then he stood over her, straddling her face in black jeans, a sexy black T-shirt, and black Frye boots. "At least it's not Under Armour," she said.

"What?" he asked, out of breath.

"Never mind," she said. And in a last-ditch effort, curled her knees into her chest and tried to blast her foot into his crotch. She missed and he stepped his boot on her bicep, grounding it into the pavement. "Ow," she said. "Get. Off." She would have a bruise on her arm in the shape of his heel for weeks.

He cocked the trigger, pointed it at her forehead, stepped off her arm, and said, "Get up," kicking some dirt on her as she heaved herself upright.

"Are you a member of law enforcement?" she asked, and he flashed her some golden badge that he fished from his pocket with his left hand, keeping the gun pointed at her with his right. "Because I've done this before, and your throwing the book at me is not going by the book. Ow," Amanda said, inspecting a huge raspberry scrape on her kneecap.

"Stand up!" said the man in black.

"Okay," she said. Her hands were shaking involuntarily as she showed them to him, but she pretended to be in control. "I don't think we've been formally introduced."

"Agent Antoine Stevens. FBI."

"What. Do. You. Want?" Amanda asked, still trying to catch her breath.

"I can think of a lot of things right now," he said, eyeing her from head to toe.

"Right," Amanda breathed. "Nothing gets you folks riled up like a little game of cat and mouse. Especially when there's a weapon thrown into the mix. Let me help you focus. My name's Amanda. And you are chasing me with a gun. Why? That's what I meant by what do you want." She bent over and gasped for air again.

He looked around suspiciously then motioned with the revolver toward the car. "I want you back in the car."

"That really doesn't seem like a safe choice for me." She got chatty when she was nervous. "I don't want to be found dead in the trunk like in those suburban mall parking lot legends. Let's clear this up out in the open, shall we? Have you radioed for backup? Because that's what they did the last time. It was all official, with police cars and Miranda rights and nosy people in their socks staring at me as they removed their belts and placed their laptops in the gray bins and rolled them along the conveyor belt. *There must be some mistake*," Amanda said. "That's what I kept saying over and over. There must be some mistake. And then I couldn't stop crying."

"Shut up and get back in the car."

"You are a man of few words. How long is this going to take? I have some parenting to do. And again, there must be some mistake. I haven't done anything wrong."

She was stalling, wondering whether she was busted for the Markdown scam already or the pharmacy thing where she got the oxy for her mother. Some kind of gig was up.

A heavy pressure built behind her eyes and forced a hot tear out the corner of each of them. "What did I do?" she asked Stevens.

Amanda suddenly felt exhausted. It was getting late. It'd been a long day and she just wanted to get home. The window on a possible talk with Taylor was closing by the minute. She walked back to the car and climbed in and wiped the snot off her nose with the back of her arm.

Stevens heaved himself into the passenger seat and exhaled a long breath that seemed to release his entire long history on this planet, which was not a happy one. Agent Stevens had seen a lot of shit. You could tell. He even had a scar running from the corner of his mouth to his ear.

"Here," Stevens said, handing her a tissue for the blood that was trickling down her leg. And then another one for her face. Did he actually walk around carrying tissue travel packs? Or did he pull it from the glove box? He was handsome, Amanda couldn't help noticing. Like he wasn't just a cop, but also played one on TV. Defined pecs. Toned biceps that he was trying too hard to display in the T-shirt. Perfect amount of body hair. Not smooth and slippery like a seal, but not Sasquatch either. And praise to God he was not blond.

"Do you know this man?" he asked, holding up a picture of Bruce wearing his brown robe and slippers. He still wore his terry-cloth tennis headband to keep his comb-over in place until he could spray it down with Aqua Net.

"You know I do. Why?" she asked.

"I need to know how he runs his business."

"His storage business? Well. It's like this, Agent Stevens," Amanda said, daring to wink a bit like Amity would. "People have so much crap in this country that they have to rent tiny little houses in which to store the shit they can't fit in their giant, already oversized houses with enormous closets.

"They have so much money that they keep buying more crap, and eventually, they forget that the extra crap in the little houses still exists. They even forget that they're paying actual rent for the stuff they forgot about. They even die, just leaving all this shit in the tiny house, and it stays there until someone develops a reality show about digging through the extra shit of rich people who forgot about their shit."

"That's the business model?"

"In a nutshell, yes."

"I think I like you," he said, barely eking out a smile with the right corner of his mouth. "You seriously believe that *the* Bruce Ackerman is running a legit storage facility?"

"What do you mean 'the'?" Amanda asked, making air quotes.

"Bruce Ackerman . . ." Stevens looked at her, incredulous now. "You don't know the history of Bruce Ackerman?"

"I've known him for thirty-six years. He's just a nice guy who is great for my mother."

Agent Stevens looked at her, baffled. He opened his mouth, as if struggling with where to begin. Then he shook his head. "No matter. I just need you to find out how he's trading weapons for drugs with the Mexican cartels."

"What?" Amanda asked. "I can't. Because he's not doing that. That's absolutely ridiculous." She had known a few women in prison who were wrapped up in the cartels. Prison was a vacation for them, because those people were vicious. Cartel women were treated like animals, given all kinds of ludicrous plastic surgery to suit the whims of their cartel boyfriends and then eventually plugged with drugs in every orifice and sent away on airplanes. They were completely expendable beings, less valued than actual mules. "Bruce would not be a part of that. He votes for the Democrats," Amanda said out loud, as if that would speak to his upstanding-ness as a person. "He's no machismo scumbag. I won't spy on him."

"Well, maybe you can do something else for me, then," Stevens said, sliding the back of his hand gently down her cheek and splaying his legs wide in the passenger seat, giving his erection a little room to breathe as it pressed against the confines of his button fly.

As disgusting as it made Amanda feel about herself, she was almost tempted. Two years. Women's prison. A little Stockholm syndrome thrown into the mix. But she shook her head. "Absolutely not. God."

"Shame," Stevens said, looking her in the eye and pushing a strand of hair out of her face. "Well, then. Your choice. Life's about choices. Get me Bruce."

"You don't get to tell me what my choices are."

"It should be easy," he said, ignoring her. "We have evidence that it's happening, Amanda. We just don't know *how* he's communicating with his cartel. We've got no phone records, nothing on the computer. He's got some old-school racket going on that we can't trace, and we need you to give us some clue. I can't be hanging around him. It would be suspicious. They'd spot me in a second. We need you. You could be a highly valuable informant. Which is a paid position. Not an unpaid internship."

"I don't care how much you pay me. I'm not a snitch." If there's one thing you learn in prison, it is not to be a snitch. "And he's basically my father. Why would I snitch on my father, who, by the way, is definitely innocent?"

"So prove it to us that he's innocent."

"No."

"Okay, then, let me ask you this: Do you know this person?" Agent Stevens held up a picture of Joyce in a wig at the pickup counter of some random CVS.

"Yes, I do, actually. I was in residence once in her womb. Terrible accommodations. Swimming in whiskey, I was."

"You don't give us what we need on 'Daddy,'" Stevens said with air quotes, "then we're going after Mommy. We've been following her to get closer to Bruce, but we have so much shit on her that this little old lady will die in prison," he said, wobbling the photograph for emphasis. "Rock and a hard place, baby. Rock and a hard place."

"Why does everyone think they can call me 'baby,' lately? You go to prison and suddenly you're everyone's baby. Well, listen, *baby*, I want no part of this. Have you spoken to Ken?"

"I don't need to speak to Ken, whoever that loser is, because I'm FBI," he said, pointing to his badge for emphasis. "Listen, Amanda. I shit you not, we will go after Joyce."

"I hate people who say 'shit you not.' So classless and vulgar."

"Well, I do."

"What?"

"I shit you not."

"Well, thanks for not, um, shitting me. That's courteous of you. Can you please leave my vehicle?" Amanda asked as calmly as she could. Inside—to use another of her least favorite phrases—she was shitting a brick. How was she going to spy on Bruce to save Joyce, while working at Markdown and parenting Taylor and behaving herself, so she could have the farmers' market, NPR life? "Inconceivable," she said, lisping and spitting the sibilant s sound like Wallace Shawn in *The Princess Bride*.

"What?" asked Stevens.

"Never mind," she said. "What would you do if someone asked you to spy on your father?"

"You have a week," he said, disappearing as quickly and quietly as he'd shown up.

8

"Where have you been?" Taylor asked Amanda when she finally came in the door later that night. "I could have stayed out."

"No, Taylor, you couldn't have, because I asked you to get your butt home. Do you know why?"

"Not really, actually. I was just hanging out. At a nice place. With a nice guy."

"Ew. Gah. Yuk," Amanda said, trying to shake off Taylor's idea of a nice guy. "Honey. Listen. I know. We've all been there, right? It's flattering to get attention from an older man. Very flattering."

"You seemed to be enjoying it," Taylor deadpanned.

"That was something else. Anyway. You're absolutely beautiful and deserving of attention from anyone. Honey. Really, you're stunning. Every time I look at you I'm taken aback. I can't believe I made this beautiful thing," Amanda said, swirling her hand around as if to encircle Taylor. "But you have to think . . . What is wrong with a thirtysomething guy who wants to date high school kids? Because there is. Honey. There is something very wrong with a thirty-year-old who wants to date high school kids. He wants to control you hon, because the rest of his life must be completely out of control. He knows he can control you, and so he wants to and that's just creepy," Amanda continued, and then flopped onto the tan rental couch that was hopefully fumigated after its previous stint in someone else's drug den. *There are no bedbugs here. There are no bedbugs here. There are no bedbugs here*, Amanda tried to convince herself.

"Once again you completely misunderstood," Taylor said, getting off the couch and storming toward her bedroom.

"How? Hon? How did I misunderstand? Can you tell me? Taylor . . .Tay?" Amanda was exhausted. "Have you at least done your homework?"

"Ha! You're asking me that question now?" Taylor's face grew mean and narrow. "I've been in school for twelve years, and that is the first time you have *ever* asked me that, you clueless . . ." She had the self-control to stop herself before uttering something like "selfish bitch." "How dare you?" she finished.

"How dare I what? Ask about homework? Don't I have the right as your mother?"

"You haven't earned it," Taylor spat.

"I never asked because you seemed to have everything under control, Taylor."

"Right, because that's the perfect description of a teenager. Someone who has everything under control. You have no idea what it's like out there."

"I lived it, too."

"Times have changed."

"That's what they all say. Listen, Taylor. Everything I've done, I've done to support you."

"I don't want your nasty sex-con money."

"Taylor."

"I don't." Her eyes welled up in a green-gray storm of fury and abandonment. "I don't want anything from you. And look at you," she said, pointing in disgust at the dress. "Looks like you're back in action. It didn't even take a week. Are you addicted to whoring?"

Shocked, Amanda barely resisted slapping her across the face.

"I'm sorry, Taylor. This is all I know. But I want to change everything. I want to earn my way back into your life."

"Good start," Taylor said, eyeing the dress again. She shook her head and then went to her room, slamming the door.

"If you don't want to live here, then why are you here, Taylor?" Amanda screamed through the door.

"Because Grammy needs me. And believe it or not, my father is more of a douchebag than you are."

"That I believe." Her father was now a remarried corporate lawyer, defending big business against the small claims of regular people. He never had time for Taylor. Never offered much. Made her beg for shoe money while he sent his new and improved kids to private school. "Taylor. Open the door. I'm here because I want to change things. Things are going to change."

"From my experience people don't change. I don't know if they can't or they won't, but I know that they don't," Taylor said. And then Amanda heard the loud static fizz of Taylor's headphone music, and knew that she had checked out.

She leaned against Taylor's door and slid down to the carpet where she also hoped there were no bedbugs and fell asleep.

—

"Oh no." She heard Bruce *tsking* above her. "We can't have this."

Amanda's legs were tingling and itchy from having slept on the carpet all night and her neck hurt from having been propped up against Taylor's door.

"What do you mean?" she asked, wiping the drool off her mouth with the back of her hand. Bruce was backlit from the light in the kitchen and looked like a mystical, slovenly godhead, reaching out to her with open arms. She grabbed onto his calloused hand and he pulled her up, groaning with pain from his bad leg. "Bruce. You really need to get that checked out. Get some cortisone or something."

"You really need to get hold of yourself," he whispered insistently. "You want Taylor back, you can't be showing her your *desperation*."

He shook his head. "Haven't I taught you anything? Never show your cards."

"Why does this family never say things like 'honesty is the best policy' or whatever? Like normal people?"

"Because it isn't the best policy. Here," he said, handing her a cup of coffee in the small basic china mug that came with the apartment. She took it from him and he shook some powdered nondairy creamer into it.

"Fancy. Thanks," she said, and took it out to the iron railing on the balcony off the living room that was beginning to rust and seemed very precarious. The floor was made of cement, spotted here and there with yellow pebbles and seashells. She leaned over the railing and took in the view. A flat stretch of road reached endlessly toward the shadow of the purply hills beyond. The hills and the self-conscious, overly tall palm trees were the only hint of nature. The rest was a lined-up train of stagnant, dying retail boxes. Payless, 76, Hertz, Appliance Parts, oh, and a bail bond shop next to the check-cashing center. Classy. She bet there was some hipster pop-up, though—some trendy, hole-in-the-wall gourmet Korean barbeque or something—tucked in between all the kitsch. That's the kind of stuff that made LA tolerable. The hi-lo of it all.

"Hello," Amanda said.

The lumbersexual from next door had come out to retrieve his paper in his drywall jeans and construction boots. He took a side glance at the sequined cougar dress from Markdown that she was *still* wearing. On the boulevard, all the traffic lights simultaneously turned red.

"Neighbor," he said, giving her a little salute with the rolled-up paper.

"Neighbor." She smiled back, playing it cool. Speaking of hi-lo. This was the epitome of it wrapped up in one hunkalicious package. She bet he was uber-intellectual and *chose* to be a carpenter. Like Jesus.

"Calm down, cougar," she told herself. People in their first year of recovery should avoid romance for one year. *Um, but you don't drink,* the devilish part of her said. *What is all this AA bullshit for if you don't drink?* "It's helping me," she said back. "I need to recover from . . . I don't know what. I just need to recover."

"Are you talking to yourself now?" Bruce said as she stepped out and slid the glass door closed. "Here. Let's switch coffees." His, she knew, was spiked with Irish whiskey.

"I'm good," she said, and stared into Bruce's aging, yellowing eyes, trying to find a hint of the criminality Stevens was accusing him of last night. Did she know Bruce at all? Bruce was the guy who secretly paid her tuition for the one year she tried college but dropped out because she was so lonely. (She couldn't connect to other eighteen-year-olds whose "concerns" seemed so flighty.) Bruce was the guy who secretly, behind Joyce's back, sent her gift cards to Whole Foods so he knew Taylor was eating properly. The guy who wrote her letters in prison, keeping things light and simply describing how things were going on the outside. How she looked forward to those letters in his surprisingly graceful hand. Her Bruce—the only father she has ever known— was not dealing weapons for drugs with a Mexican cartel.

She looked at him yawning now in his bathrobe. Such a regular guy. If he was so good at deception that he could deceive even her, then he was borderline evil, right? Or he was, like most men, a brilliant compartmentalizer—never letting one aspect of his life bleed into another. Amanda didn't know anything anymore. She felt like she needed Gyroscope Bruce to stabilize the ship, keep things grounded so she could step off in her own direction. If he, too, was running his own scam, then there was no way, anymore, to see which way was up. She contemplated calling Taylor's father for support, but whenever she did that, she felt like she was giving him fodder for a custody battle. Not that he would want to raise Taylor necessarily. He would just love to "win" her. It wouldn't matter much now. There were only two years of child rearing left.

Speaking of custody. "Excuse me," she said coldly to Bruce, and she slipped back into the apartment and got to work making heart-shaped pancakes for Taylor, like she used to whenever she got home from a long stint in Vegas with Evan.

Until the prison sentence, Taylor didn't know exactly what her mother did, just that she traveled a lot and did something called "consulting." Everyone was just a different kind of whore, Amanda rationalized. Even consultants. She called herself a consultant, like a lot of the kids' daddies in preschool called themselves. And Taylor never asked questions. Kids had no curiosity about their parents, as long as they got what they needed from them. And until prison, Taylor had. She went to the best, albeit public, schools in the best neighborhoods in LA. Amanda wasn't a soccer coach or a dance mom or a member of the PTA, God forbid, but she signed Taylor up for all the right things. Dropped her off at the right people's houses for playdates.

"That's a wuss move," Bruce said, pointing to the elaborate pancake topped with whipped cream and strawberries and *I love you, Taylor* written around the paper plate with chocolate syrup. "Back off, baby, and she'll come around faster."

"Again with the baby! I am not your baby!" she yelled with unexpected vitriol.

"Hey, Mandy," Bruce tried. "This time of life isn't easy." He walked up behind her and gave her a fatherly squeeze across the shoulders. Amanda usually melted when Bruce showed her affection, since she was so starved from it by her mother. She was like one of those baby monkeys in that famous psychological experiment from years ago— the baby monkeys who died because they'd been given stark wire-monkey mother substitutes instead of soft plush stuffed ones capable of hugging.

This time when Bruce hugged her though, she felt a tremor of distrust quake through her body. Bruce turned to the open cabinet where he kept his cigarillos. "I'll be around when you want to talk though, okay babe? I've raised a teen or two in my day, don't forget." Amanda had a couple of "stepsiblings" scattered around the country, whom she saw occasionally when they needed money. "Worst years of my life."

Just then, Taylor walked past the kitchen, grabbed her jacket on the hook next to the door, and left without a word. "This is killing me," Amanda admitted.

"Don't worry," Bruce said, needing to have the last word. "You need to play it cool. She'll come around when she needs something. She's a Cooper, after all," he said with a sly smile and a gesture toward her mother's bedroom.

I should just ask him, Amanda thought. *Just come right out and ask . . . Are you running drugs for the Mexican cartels?* They could have a good laugh and that would be the end of it. But then she thought better of it and took Bruce's own advice. *Don't show your cards*, she thought.

"Wait. What did you say?" she asked him now, shifting gears.

"Play it cool?"

"No, after that."

"She's a Cooper, after all?"

"Yes. That," Amanda said. And it suddenly hit her. Taylor was not that upset about Amanda and her racket. Some of last night's emotion was genuine emotion. But some of it was a cover-up. A calculated, dramatic distraction to get Amanda off her back. That child was as brilliant an actress as her grandmother. That thirty-year-old wasn't playing her. She was trying to play him. She was trying to emulate her mother in the worst way possible. Taylor was not supposed to emulate her until everything was reset and her life was role-model worthy.

"Wait," she said, and she opened the door, ran down the steps, and looked for Taylor up and down the street. "Tay!" she shouted. "Taylor!" Taylor's perfectly proportioned shoulders turned toward her for a moment as she strutted down the street. She folded a piece of gum into her mouth, flicked the wrapper at her mother, and was gone, absorbed into the hustle and bustle as the city started waking up and stretching its legs. Amanda didn't care how desperate it seemed and whether Taylor saw her do it. She walked down the street. Found the gum wrapper and threw it in the trash. It's what mothers do. They clean up your garbage.

—

She found a meeting at a Unitarian Universalist church in Brentwood. Because she was *sick and tired of being sick and tired* and she knew that the program would only work if she KCBed. *Kept Coming Back.* The coffee was much better here and the snacks organic and artisanal and heirloom and whatnot. Everything here in the church basement had been either yarn-bombed or hand-quilted. Quilted wall hangings of the Serenity Prayer. Felt pillows in the shape of hearts. It was a crafty congregation and evidence of some folks with too much time on their hands.

The hominess bolstered her, though. She actually even stood up and shared at the meeting.

"Um," she started. "Hi, my name is Amanda, and I'm an alcoholic," she lied.

The entire room said, "Hi Amanda." And she balked. There was something so wrong about trying to come clean by lying to people, so she shifted gears.

"I mean, truthfully, I'm not actually an alcoholic. I just started to go to these meetings in prison to get out of kitchen duty."

Amanda scanned the room. She saw some snickers from those who believed her and some incredulous eye rolls from a couple of women who sat knitting in the corner, like, *Right. She's not an alcoholic. God do we have to start with step fucking one again. Why didn't anyone tell her that this meeting was more evolved than that?*

"Anyway," she continued, "I'm having trouble gaining back the trust of my daughter." Her voice was caught, then, by a sob that snatched her words like a Venus flytrap. She was going to cry in front of all these people. Joyce would be appalled. Her breath wouldn't even come to her. She expected someone to shoo her off the stage. Or talk over her. Or come to her rescue. But they didn't. Everyone sat in their cold steel folding chairs painted the color of clay and patiently waited. Blinking occasionally. It was as if she had taken an emotional stage dive into the mosh pit and these people knew how to catch her.

"How do I get her back?" she managed desperately.

"We're only supposed to fucking listen," said the jaded knitting lady from the back of the room. "But if you want my opinion, you need to keep a promise for once. The kid is sick of broken promises."

A skinny bearded guy with his guitar still strapped to his back chimed in with, "Yeah. Just keep one promise. One promise at a time." And then he took out a tiny Moleskine notebook and wrote that down, apparently to use as lyrics.

A man with short, neatly coiffed hair who had just come from the gym said, "Yes. Being a workaholic and an alcoholic is hard for me . . . I let my kids down a lot. But it's all to benefit them in the end, right?"

"We're not talking about you, Jason. This is not about you. God," a thin wiry man chimed in from the center of the room. "Proceed, Amanda."

"Thank you," sighed a pink-haired woman with Betty Boop tattooed on her forearm. "How does he always make this about him?"

"I'm just trying to empathize," said Jason.

"It's okay," Amanda said. "I think I get it. Keep a promise. I can do that." Amanda stepped down in a haze and found her seat while the tall ex-model facilitator in her sixties who'd resorted to long capes and obnoxious, art-piece eyeglasses to make herself look interesting said, "Jason, would you like to share next?"

Amanda blocked out the rest of Jason's rant about how people don't appreciate him, and when it was over, after they recited the Lord's Prayer, she headed up the stairs toward the sun that was blasting through the glass door of the vestibule like a hydrogen bomb. "Psst," she heard. She turned and had to blink away the sun glare before noticing the shorter woman she encountered at the last meeting, standing beneath the stairwell. Big round sunglasses. Navajo blanket–style poncho. Strawberry-blond wig. "Stop oversharing," the woman said.

"But that was my first time sharing, ever."

"Not here. I don't mean here, Einstein. I mean with the kid. Don't let her know what you're going through. Don't inflict that on her. Make your conversations only about the kid's life, right? She doesn't need to hear about yours."

"Okay," Amanda said, but the yellow sun snuck from behind her, around her body, and caught the corner of her eye, blinding her again so she had trouble seeing the woman beneath the stairs. And when she had finally focused on the spot where she heard the voice, the woman had disappeared.

"I like you," said the voice. It was above her now in the vestibule, opening the door. "You seem authentic."

"My entire life is housed in a castle of lies," said Amanda.

"Ah, but see, most people never come to that realization. Good luck," she said, and then, once again, left before Amanda could verify if she was a real person or the ghost of you-know-who.

9

Before going to work the next day and apologizing to Russ, Amanda sheepishly knocked on Taylor's door. She breathed in for a second and realized that she had always been a little afraid of her daughter. The sheer force of her daughter's will terrified her. Even when Taylor was five and would ask for a playdate they didn't have time for, or a cupcake from the shop all the way across town, or a toy they couldn't afford, and she had to say no, she was terrified of the fallout. And Taylor could read it. Like a German shepherd. Dogs can smell fear, and so could Taylor. Whenever Amanda said no, Taylor, normally so sedate and pulled together, would lash out barking, straining at the leash, showing her teeth, sometimes pitching an hour-long tantrum until Amanda would submit, just to shut her up and find herself driving an hour in traffic to buy the effing cupcake.

"Taylor," she said now.

No response.

"Taylor, open the door. Now, Tay."

Amanda waited, and breathed in and remembered the Power Pose seminar they had in prison, where some woman in really bad jeans showed them how to supposedly gain confidence before a confrontation—you could position your body in a powerful shape and immediately feel emboldened. She tried it, spreading her legs wide and holding her arms up in a Y shape. Just moving her body and taking up space did kind of make her feel strong for a second.

"Are you fucking power posing?" a voice asked her. "You know that's fake, right?"

Amanda looked at the door and saw that it had opened just enough to reveal only one of Taylor's green-gray eyes and a strip of her pale pink sweatshirt.

"What? No. I'm stretching," Amanda said with a fake yawn.

"You rang?" said the cynical eye.

"I'm picking you up at school today, Taylor. Four forty-five. After Model UN. We're going shopping." Amanda's gut clenched, girding itself for a fight. She stood her ground, powerfully pressing her foot into the carpet and steadying herself with her hand on the doorjamb. She was not backing down.

"Okay," said the eye.

"Okay?"

"Yeah. Okay."

"All right, then," Amanda said. "Good talk. I'll see you then. Four forty-five in front of school."

The eye rolled for a second then retreated again behind the closed door. Mission accomplished.

She still had an hour before work, so she went to the Coffee Bean, broke out her journal, and drew a tree, using its branches to try to compartmentalize her life. Like a dude would. Like Bruce must.

Dudes knew how to keep everything separate. They didn't become overwhelmed by the fucked-up interconnectedness of all of the things at once. They did one thing at a time, slowly and thoroughly, at a glacial pace, while ignoring all else until one thing at a time was finished. It was a brilliant method of self-preservation. She was going to learn how to do it with the tree. And she called it "the dude tree." Or "the dude tree of the mind."

She labeled one branch "Taylor." And on each of four leaves, she wrote "School," "Friends," "Boys," "Me." The last leaf was the most important right now. If she didn't open up a line of communication with Taylor, she'd never find out about the rest. Then she crafted a branch for each of the other problems in her life and tried to figure out which leaf to prioritize for each branch. She came up with the following list:

Taylor: Me
Bruce: Intel
Russ: Obey
Joyce: Ignore

The tree worked. She did feel less overwhelmed. She just had to obey Russ for a bit, while she got some intel on Bruce (she would decide what to do with it later). And she would definitely figure out how to get closer to Taylor.

Like the AA folks suggested, she would keep her promise to Taylor and take her to the mall at four forty-five.

As if from above, though, she could hear the voice of the shadowy woman she kept bumping into at AA. Amanda imagined the woman leaning over her shoulder and looking at the notebook, saying, *There's no branch for yourself. What happened to fixing yourself?*

Oh right, but there's no time for that right now, Amanda thought. And then she realized a little eerily that Carrie Fisher had become her higher power.

—

Ken must have done a good job convincing Russ to let Amanda back into the Mark because he asked few questions when she showed up for her shift at ten and he even let her out front on the register next to Lupita. She kept a low profile. Nose to the grindstone and all that. She tried to make things more interesting by figuring out the story behind people's purchases. Like the guy who bought butter, WD-40, a metal cutter, a six-pack of beer, and pork rinds. *His wife just left him*, she thought, *and he's trying to saw off his wedding ring.* The next customer had white gumballs, poster board, green paint, and a basketball net. *School project. Replica of a soccer field.* This occupied her mind until she got to hot sauce, cat food, and puff pastry. And then child-sized Bud Light slippers and a bacon-scented pillow. After that she just had to look away, and then Russ had called her to the loading dock to continue her work on the "damaged goods" project.

Since she had to do it, she took the job seriously. She wore one of those black cummerbund-style back braces and some gloves from Home and Garden, and she got to work. She figured out what Russ wanted from each shipment, and was very methodical and organized like a dude.

She noticed, however, that if he didn't want to get caught, he was going to need to cast his net a little wider and use a more open mind about what merchandise he could move on the street. Right now ninety percent of his stuff was coming from Electronics and Entertainment. That was going to send a red flag to Corporate for sure.

"Russ," she said, knocking on the door of his office, which now smelled like a combination of onions and sweaty gym shorts.

"And to what do I owe this beautiful interruption?" he asked creepily as he rushed to hide the cell phone on which he was playing some kind of geeky dungeon game.

"I was just thinking . . ."

"What did I tell you last time? Here. I put a sign up just for you." He pointed to the cinderblock wall next to the *In these times, you're lucky to have a job at all* poster, where he had taped a new one that read *I don't pay you to think.*

"But . . ."

"Amanda. Read the sign."

"I'm just saying that your initiative is a little too concentrated on the electronics side of the business. You should cast a wider net. Call less attention to yourself." *And call less attention to* me, Amanda thought. She shivered remembering the headlights two nights ago tracking her like a bloodhound. It was a stark reminder that she needed to cover her tracks. She'd realized that if she wanted to protect herself from getting busted, she had to rescue this entire bullshit Markdown operation.

"Electronics is where the most organic, shall we say, shrinkage occurs. People steal that stuff all the time."

"But you can mix it up a little," she said, pointing to some lines on her spreadsheet that were not highlighted.

"And how do you propose—"

"Well, if you pulled a report from As Seen on TV items, Small Appliances, and Wedding Registries, I think you'd find a ton of stuff you can move."

"Go on . . ." he said, leaning back in his chair. His basketball-sized belly was barely covered by his shirt—the buttons stretched to the limit and about to pop. He put the end of his pencil in his mouth, and because it had just been in his ear scratching something, Amanda gagged a little.

"Well," she said, gaining composure. "As Seen on TV. You know the stuff. Miracle cures for potbellies and arthritis pain and hair removal. 'Ove' Gloves, Pillow Pets, the thing that cuts your vegetables in the shape of spaghetti, the thing that cooks your egg in the microwave like an Egg McMuffin. Wax Vacs. And then in Kitchen, you need to grab some high-powered blenders. Everyone's drinking the green juice. And some slow cookers and anything that looks like a Le Creuset."

"What the eff is a Le . . . Creuset?"

"You wouldn't have genuine Le Creuset here," Amanda said, thinking about the merch she'd seen in aisle five. "But you have some imitations that would fool people on the street. You need to grab some. Trust me. Oh, and those god-awful one-cup coffeemakers that are destroying the environment one tiny plastic pod at a time."

"Keurigs?"

"Yes, the Keurigs."

"Little lady," Russ said, standing up out of his chair as crumbs from his breakfast spilled to the floor. A piece of egg hung in his mustache.

"What?"

"You just got yourself a desk job, and if this works, maybe a promotion."

"Only if Lupita gets one, too."

"Oh. You *are* a Daenerys, aren't you? Sexy," he said, and then he actually growled a little before Amanda closed the door and ran back to the loading dock.

Her shift was supposed to end at four, which would give her just enough time to get through traffic and meet Taylor at school and fulfill her promise of taking her to the mall. But at 3:59, when she headed to the break room, Russ was there buying a Dr Pepper from the soda machine. Lupita widened her eyes and waved her arms at Amanda, but Amanda didn't understand what she was trying to tell her. She walked over to the ancient Fred Flintstone time clock, took out her time card, and punched it with a satisfying clunk. She was ready to run out and slide down the brontosaurus tail and into her car screaming "Yabba Dabba Doo" when Russ walked over to her, standing too close, and said, "Where are you going?"

"Home. I have an appointment," she said.

"Wouldn't you like to have a Pepper, too?" he asked, swinging the can in front of her face.

"No. I'm good." Amanda noticed his mood swing and Lupita's gaunt, terrorized expression and realized Russ was definitely high on something.

"Well, you're not leaving," he said with crazy eyes, and he stiff-armed the breakroom door shut so that his arm was clotheslining Amanda's face.

"Hey, Russ," Amanda tried. "This behavior feels a little intimidating to me, so . . ." She tried to limbo beneath his arm and get to the other side of the room.

"Just like you dirtbags to promise what you can't deliver."

"What does that mean?" Amanda asked.

"I want the reports. Before you leave. I need the damaged goods reports from the departments you were talking about. And show her how to pull them," he said, indicating Lupita.

"I don't know how to pull them," Amanda answered.

"Figure it out, smarty-pants."

"It can't wait until tomorrow? I was supposed to meet—"

"No problem, Russ!" Lupita interrupted. "She will show me. No problem."

"No problemo?" Russ asked her rudely.

"That's what I said," Lupita answered, staring him down with those gorgeous tiger eyes.

"Okay. I need it before the delivery at six," he said, and then stumbled out the door.

"I can't do this!" Amanda said to Lupita. "I promised my daughter I'd meet her at four forty-five, and if I don't show up, I don't know if she'll ever talk to me again."

"Can you show me what to do? I'm a quick study. If you show me, I will do it and give them to him."

In for four, hold for seven, out for eight, Amanda breathed. "Okay," she said, and they found the computer out by the loading dock that people used to check things in. She opened the database program that she saw Russ using and tried to manipulate it. By the time they had figured out just one step in the process it was already four thirty.

They kept working, with Russ pacing behind them every now and then, until they were able to print a list of Le Creuset–like cookware, As Seen On TV items, and fast blenders. They were just printing out the wedding registries at five.

"Russ," Amanda begged at his next pass. "May I please text my daughter?" They were strictly prohibited from using phones on the sales floor or loading dock. "Please," she begged.

"No phones on the loading dock," he slurred. Amanda looked at his belt and realized he was actually carrying a pistol in a holster and he strummed his fingers against it in intimidation. *Fucking NRA*, she thought. If this were an open-carry state, it would actually be legal for him to be intimidating her like this.

"But Russ, it's important that she knows where I am. I can't break another promise." Amanda pictured Taylor waiting outside the school alone. Since she'd been home, she hadn't actually seen Taylor with anyone her age or heard her giggling on the phone or seen her smiling at all. She seemed so lonely. The thing Amanda was charged with sheltering her from. If she couldn't shelter her from loneliness, she'd failed at the most basic task of being a mother.

"Well, you made a promise to me, too, right?" Russ said. "You're letting everyone down today, Daenerys." He was coming down off of whatever he was on and getting tired and dopey. He'd be asleep in fifteen minutes, but it was already too late. The damage was done.

When he finally sauntered toward his office, she knew she could get away.

"Go," Lupita said.

Amanda hugged Lupita and then sprinted out the employee entrance to the minivan parked in the back. She called, but Taylor, naturally, did not pick up. "Dammit," Amanda said. "Dammit, dammit, dammit." But she drove to the school anyway on the off chance that Taylor had decided to wait.

She knew some back roads through the gentrified neighborhoods that she could cut through, so she barreled through gated communities of beautiful manses with Spanish-tiled roofs and walls draped with bougainvillea, hurtling the van over speed bumps installed to keep the white children safe. Not even just the children, to keep the dogs of the white people safe. She hurled over them, sending the van three feet in the air. She was practically flying, then almost died as she squealed around a hairpin turn that hugged the edge of a cliff that dropped precipitously into the Pacific.

She collected herself and continued driving, honking brainlessly at people stopped at a red light, and when it was five thirty, she started to cry.

I'm sorry, she texted Taylor, and she got the three little bubbles of hope as she awaited a reply, but then they disappeared and she got nothing. The light turned green.

When she got to the school, whose art-deco facade could be the soundstage for a school, with the requisite stately tree standing in front and a group of red-and-white-clad cheerleaders clumped together and posing for a photo, she jumped out of the car and walked around a little. "Taylor," she said. And then she screamed it. "Taylor!"

"She's gone, lady," one of the boys said.

"Fuck!" she said out loud as she walked in a little circle and then sat down on an embankment.

"Language . . ." warned two boys loaded down with big backpacks. They had the audacity to wave a shaming finger at her, and then crack up as they continued home to enjoy their joyous, carefree, masculine existence.

WWCFD? Amanda wondered. Carrie Fisher would definitely have wallowed in her shame and self-pity for a second, and then she might have apologized. So Amanda pulled out her phone and apologized. Profusely. *Taylor, I'm so, so sorry. I got stuck at work* . . . etc., etc.

No three bubbles. No reply. Nothing.

Tay? she texted, but it was too late.

10

On the way home, she kept breathing, hoping the blob of disappointment lodged in her esophagus would melt away, but no luck. Her phone jangled a few times, but it was not Taylor. It was just the Google alerts she had set up for her initial surveillance of Bruce's L'Affordable Storage.

The name of the place made Amanda even more certain that this was an honorable business. Bruce had thought about search engine optimization and made a business plan based on it. Whoever googled "LA affordable storage" would get his site first. Why would he bother doing that if the place were just a front?

And the inquiries she hacked into were seemingly legit folks from Los Angeles moving in with their boyfriends or whatever. No inquiries at all from Mexico or even close to the border. So. Take that, Agent Stevens.

She pulled in to the garage beneath the apartment, suddenly wondering what kind of fumes they were inhaling and if they were all going to get lung cancer from living on top of their garage. They needed to get out of this place, she thought as she climbed the stairs and tried not to let the tiny bubble of hope that Taylor would be home grow into a massive disappointment bomb when she found out she wasn't there.

"I'm home," she said as she dropped the keys on the kitchen table. "Is Taylor here?"

"Hi honey," Joyce said, using the saccharine voice that meant a non-family member was in the house. Amanda hoped it wasn't Agent Stevens, stopping by to terrorize the neighborhood. Joyce fluttered into the kitchen and whispered, "Taylor's not here. Why do you look like shit?" Whenever Amanda cried these days—because: aging—the thin skin under her eyes loosened and hung there like skin hammocks. Amanda remembered her tree. Ignore Joyce. And then she asked, "Who's here?"

Before she could get an answer, Gentle Ben from next door sauntered down the carpeted hallway wiping down a wrench, and said, "All set, Joyce. Faucet should work now."

"I was having trouble with the hot water," Joyce explained to Amanda.

"Story of your life," she mumbled to Joyce, and then, mortified to be caught in her Markdown uniform, she turned to Ben. "We meet again," she said.

"Yes," he said. "Y'all just needed a washer in the hall bathroom."

"Ben here helps me out when I need a hand. It's not easy being an old woman on her own, and Bruce is useless these days with the leg," Joyce said, putting on a version of her old lady act. In reality Joyce could probably change the washer with her teeth.

"Happy to help out," Ben said graciously. He had just enough of a beard to highlight his facial features without looking like a mountain man. His plaid work shirt swung unbuttoned and loose over a black T-shirt that perfectly hugged his pecs.

Amanda shook herself out of it, and said, "Hey. It's been a long day. Can I offer you a beer?"

"I don't drink."

"Me either, actually. I can offer you some filtered water from the Brita with some local Van Nuys lemons harvested from the driveway..."

"My favorite. That would be wonderful," he said, finishing wiping off his wrench and sliding it into his suede tool belt.

Ouch, thought Amanda. *Tool belt*. She had no defense against a tool belt.

"Let me just wash up," he said, and went to wash his hands in the bathroom while Joyce said, "Slow down, cougar. I've looked into it. He's broke and savvy. You'll get nowhere with his one debit card and paltry savings."

"I'm just looking for a friend, Mom. Something you'd never understa—" she cut off as Ben came back into the kitchen.

"Shall we take it on the veranda?" Amanda joked, and they went out to the tiny balcony, sat down on the cement, and hung their legs through the railing. "Cheers," Amanda said as they clinked their plastic tumblers.

"So how did someone like you end up in a place like this?" she asked.

"A confluence of events." *Confluence.* Amanda knew he was brilliant. "Was getting separated from my wife in Virginia and my mom was simultaneously going downhill, so I moved out here to help her out," he continued.

"Where does your mom live?"

"Deceased," he said, looking down into his lemon water.

"I'm so sorry."

"That's okay. I have Joyce. I've adopted her."

"Proceed with caution," Amanda said. "She is not who you think she is."

"I know all about her racket. She's a pip," he said, taking a sip and sitting for a moment in a comfortable silence.

"That's one word for it," Amanda finally said, and then had a sudden moment of panic. "So. What do you know about me?"

"Nothing that would scare me away. Why was it a long day?" he asked, generously changing the subject. "Aside from the fact that you have to be in that place?" he said, tipping his drink toward the emblem on her shirt.

"Parenting. You have kids?"

"No. That was our issue. We couldn't. She couldn't. And she couldn't move on."

"People get stuck on that."

"Yeah."

"There's still time for you, I guess," Amanda said. "What are you, forty?"

"I could never do that to her." He shrugged. "I'm okay. We gave it a go. And not for nothing, I think you're okay, too. Taylor's a good kid."

"You think so?"

"Well, from my distant vantage point of handyman neighbor, she seems okay, comparatively."

"You're like Schneider to Taylor's Valerie Bertinelli."

"What?"

"Never mind. I watched too many reruns in the eighties." Amanda looked at him, admiring his rough hands, clean fingernails, and flat stomach. But then she stopped herself. She definitely didn't have room for another branch on the dude tree right now. "Do you ever feel like you're just messing everything up and running out of time to fix it?" she asked.

He grunted knowingly. "Isn't that the precise definition of middle age? When you're fucking everything up and running out of time to fix it?"

"So what do people do? Aside from buy sports cars and get divorced? Give up? I can't stop trying with my kid. I can't give up on her."

"No. I think that's ultimately the only reason to have them. They make you keep trying. Keep you accountable. I'm free to throw in the towel and become an awful person," he joked.

"But you're *free*. That's the operative word."

"It's not what it's cracked up to be. Freedom."

"Isn't that what everyone wants in this country? The land of the free?" It's what Amanda wanted. To finally be free of her past. Free from these obligations.

"Freedom is incompatible with love."

"Whoa," Amanda said.

"It's true," he replied. "You can't have both love and freedom. That's a basic American misconception. If you want love . . . if you have love, you cannot also be free."

Amanda thought about it for a second, and then said, "Unless you're a shitty lover."

"Exactly."

"You don't seem like a shitty lover to me," she said. "You come across as someone who's good at loving."

Ben blushed. "Well, I've had some mixed feedback in that arena, but a lot of it is good."

"Sorry. I embarrassed you. I'm sorry. I'm just really tired."

Amanda's phone beeped and she stood up, cutting the interlude short. "I have to see if this is Taylor."

"No worries, I should be going. I have a date with a Lean Cuisine," he said, extricating himself from the balcony railing.

"You should come over sometime for Hot Pockets," Amanda said as she showed him out and looked hopefully at her phone, but it was not a text from Taylor. It was from Agent Stevens.

Tick. Tock.

11

She didn't care what Bruce had to say about her desperate parenting, she slept on Taylor's floor again because proximity was all she had to work with right now. And besides, was she really going to take parenting advice from a vicious narco? If that's what he was. She could see the true-crime memoir now: *My Stepfather Was a Vicious Narco*.

Taylor hung her head over the side of the bed at 7 AM, her hair drifting to the floor in wavy blue ombré ribbons. "You're pathetic," she said in her raspy morning voice.

"No, I'm not pathetic, because it worked and you just spoke to me, which was my goal. I'm sorry I couldn't get to you yesterday, Taylor. My boss, my creepy boss, would not let me off work."

"You're *always* sorry though, Mom. Do you know what it's like to have a sorry mom?"

"Um, do you even have to ask that? At least I apologize. Tay, I'm trying."

"I'd live with Dad if it wasn't even more of a shitshow at his house."

"Ooof. Well, kids really do know how to push buttons, don't they?" Amanda said. "I'm secretly elated that it's a shitshow over there, too, though."

"Yeah," Taylor said, sitting up. "You get to a certain age and you realize that every family is just a traveling shitshow."

"That age is supposed to be forty-five, Taylor, not sixteen. You should still have hope and optimism."

"My mother was in prison. Kind of takes the sparkle out of your lip gloss."

"Well, look at it this way, Bonnie Belle. I took the pressure off," Amanda said, getting on all fours so she could hoist herself off the floor. "Whatever you do in life will be better than my lousy performance. I set the bar low. You're welcome."

"Thanks. That's great parenting," Taylor said.

"Good talk," Amanda joked, dragging the blankets toward the door. "I love you, Taylor."

"That's something, I guess."

"It's everything, TT." Amanda opened the door then, and Joyce fell into the room still holding the rocks glass to her ear. "Ah geez. I love you, too, Mom," Amanda said, helping her up off the floor.

"I was just checking for termites," Joyce said, and she knocked a little on the doorframe.

"Whatever, Grammy," Taylor said.

—

By eight Amanda had gotten another text from Stevens. *I'm waiting*, it said.

She wondered why he was so impatient about this so she googled him using Taylor's computer on the dining room table, and there he was. A younger, beefier version of him in uniform and a military crew cut flashed onto the screen. His graduation from the police academy in 1986. He definitely was in law enforcement. But aside from that, it was difficult to get anything on him. Which was intentional, she was sure. How were you going to nab your perp if the perp could just follow you on Facebook and kidnap your whole family while you were away in Paris posting snapshots of yourself beneath the Eiffel Tower?

While she was at it, she switched to private browsing mode and typed in "Evan Nardini." She spent two years of her life anticipating his every move, siphoning tiny amounts from his bank accounts while he paraded her all over Vegas.

She gasped when she saw his bleached teeth smiling back at her from his headshot on a press release announcing the opening of his first casino, and she instantly closed the page, glad that piece of her life was over.

Before she turned off the computer, though, she couldn't help googling the anti-Evan. "Benjamin Altman Van Nuys," she typed into the search field and then filtered for images. Turns out even carpenters in LA needed headshots. And why not? His head was definitely a selling point in his case. Extremely photogenic. She reached for the mouse to probe deeper into Benjamin's Internet story, but before she could click, Joyce snuck up behind her and said, "I spy something stalker-y."

"I'm not stalking," Amanda said.

"I already told you, honey. He has no money."

"I'm not in it for the money. I have a job. At Markdown."

"Don't remind me. So you just stalking him for cheap thrills?"

"I want to get to know him."

"Uh-oh."

"What?"

"You weren't bred for that."

"For what?"

"Intimacy. Domesticity. Surrender."

"How is it surrender? Never mind." Her phone beeped again with a text from Stevens. "I gotta go."

—

Van Nuys, in the area of L'Affordable Storage, looked a lot like Baghdad after Bush (and Cheney) got through with it. Tan rubble spilled everywhere from beneath chain-link fences that surrounded sand-colored warehouses and broken-down parking lots plagued by acres of dry brush. The only splashes of color came from the scattered labels of littered soft drink bottles, the occasional red Ford Ranger pickup on its last legs, and the poorly tagged graffiti adorning every cement structure in a three-mile radius.

It was so hot here, east of the ocean, that no buildings dared to grow above a single story. It was a flattened, dried-out, impoverished plain of desperation, Amanda thought as she pulled into L'Affordable's gravel parking lot. She waited for the dust cloud around the van to settle before climbing out and heading to the "office," which was designated as such with the gold and black rhomboidal stick-on letters you get from Home Depot.

She opened the screen door and an automatic doorbell rang alerting whoever was inside to her presence. But it didn't need to because there Bruce sat, haphazardly shaven and, aside from the robe, dressed for business in slacks and a white button-down shirt. He had on his reading glasses and looked down his nose through them at an ancient boxy PC standing upright on his desk that was littered with labeled manila folders. What shady front of a business would bother with manila folders? Amanda already knew this was a waste of time. So much for her memoir; *My Stepfather Was a Vicious Narco* would have been a best seller, too.

Bruce lifted a full brown paper bag saturated with grease spots, read the receipt underneath it, and unstapled the menu from the top. He was about to throw the entire bag of food in the wastepaper basket when he looked up and noticed that it was Amanda who had walked in the door.

"Hiya, Mandy. What're you doing here?" he asked, lifting himself painfully out of his faux leather chair and hobbling to the front desk. He held the bag out to her. "Want some Mexican?"

"Oh. No, thanks." She eyed the bag. "I thought you hated Mexican."

"This neighborhood has some good authentic stuff I've been trying. Still. Can't do too much of it, you know." He rubbed his belly in a circle a little awkwardly.

"I brought you this," Amanda said, remembering her alibi and handing him a bottle of oxy prescribed to a Judith Martindale. "Thought you might need it for your leg."

"Thanks," he said. "Membership has its privileges, I guess. While you're here, why don't I give you the grand tour?" he said and then very smoothly, trying to do so without her noticing, leaned on the desk as if to support himself and then flipped over a spiral notebook that acted as the logbook for people coming in and out. Then he put his arm around her shoulder and escorted her back out the screen door and into the sun, which if it had a soundtrack, would sound like the shower scene music from *Psycho* right now. Not that she'd ever seen the shower scene from *Psycho*. She did not watch scary movies, her life being scary enough as it was. The sun screeched down on them, though, in that kind of horrific beating pulse.

Amanda shaded her eyes with her hand and Bruce walked her down the first row of sheds with their louvered tan garage doors that blended in with everything else around here. "You know, self-storage is a twenty-four billion dollar industry," he bragged. "And this is my little piece of it. Forty thousand square feet of Bruceland. It has an ancient history, too, storage. Six thousand years ago, the Chinese used to bury their extra stuff in clay pots and hire guards to monitor it."

"Wow. You're really passionate about storage. So what about security? You don't have any cameras?" she asked, squinting into the sun, scanning the eaves for any nosy lenses that might get in the way of potential surveillance.

"Cameras make people nervous. I'm the security. People do business with me, pumpkin. They trust me."

"Maybe I can work here. I can talk to my parole officer. It would be better than Markdown. I could help you, like, brand yourself or something. It's all about the branding . . . apparently. We could paint these doors, for example. Or even better, have local graffiti artists or art-center kids or someone paint a different mural on each door. This neighborhood needs a little color," Amanda said, trying to think on her feet about ways to infiltrate the business and find out what was really going on.

"You don't want to work here," he said, a little nervously. He fiddled with his keys, a little too much, popping out the Swiss Army knife on the key chain and using the corkscrew to swipe some dirt from beneath a thumbnail. *Remind me never to drink wine with him on a picnic*, Amanda joked to herself. "You're an aesthete," Bruce continued. "You would die in all this beige."

"Exactly. Which is why we could paint the doors. Maybe Taylor could help."

"This is not a wholesome environment for a teen," Bruce said, just as a conveniently timed lowrider with blacked-out windows and vibrating bass hummed by slowly and menacingly in two-four time. "Gangs," Bruce said as if it were the final word. "Why the sudden interest in the storage business?"

"Well. My mom was right. The Markdown job is no less a scam than her operation. My boss. This guy, Russ. He's using me to run his own game, skimming goods off the top and then selling them somehow. I'm afraid I'm going to get caught. So I thought I could work here maybe. Help you with the books."

"Well, they have software for that, Mandy. And Maria's been with me for five years and would not appreciate any nepotistic shit edging in on her territory. I mean I know you two are acquaintances, but I'd have to talk to her about it, capiche?"

"Got it," she said. She looked him in the eye, trying to do the mother test on him. If he were guilty of something heinous, he'd turn away or look down or turn a whiter shade of pale. But he didn't. He locked her in his gaze. A true professional—or an innocent man. "So," Amanda said, breaking the intensity and taking another tack. "Say you were moving some hot merch from the Mark. How would you do it, hypothetically?" she probed, trying to get anything that could indicate Bruce knew something about the dark side. "I think he's going to move me into the sales end and I don't know what to expect. I'm sure he'd want to avoid a cyber trail."

"Why don't you tell your parole officer?"

"I think he's in on it, too."

"Seriously?"

"Yeah."

"Well, he might be stupid enough to move it on the Web. If not, he could head to Venice and just lay it all out on a blanket. Cops there are too distracted by the fake medical marijuana operations to worry too much about what's being sold on the blankets. He might even rent out a cheap storefront. But now that I think about it, I think I would just use Craigslist for that kind of junk."

Craigslist. Could Bruce be communicating with his narcos on Craigslist?

They headed back to the office and Bruce took a call in the next room out of earshot. She leaned in and tried to hear him, but she got nothing. Maria, his assistant, sauntered in then, sipping coffee infused with cinnamon. She wore a pencil skirt and crisp white blouse. She took this job seriously. She had mouths to feed. "Aye, Amanda. Welcome home," she said awkwardly. "I mean, it's good to see you." She was a gentle soul and held out her arms for a hug.

"We should go out and catch up," Amanda said, wondering guiltily if she could use Maria to get to Bruce. "How's the old man doing, anyway?" she asked, gesturing her head in the direction of Bruce in the other room.

"Oh, him. You know. Same old, same old."

"Yeah," Amanda said, glancing down at the logbook. It was supposed to be the names of visitors to the site. Walk-ins. Mixed in with the regular old Jennifer Morrison–type names were some suspicious ones. Glen Dale. Bob Hope. Syl Mar. S. Clarita. V. Princessa.

Maria reached for it and slid it into a drawer. "Sorry for the mess," she said.

"Sorry," Bruce said when he came back into the room. "Storage needs," he said, pointing to the phone. "Her deceased father was a trophy-hunting taxidermist. Tricky one."

"Um. Yeah," Amanda said. "I'll be on my way. See you back at the ranch?"

"You know your mother. I'm in the doghouse. Maybe tomorrow."

"Tomorrow, then."

—

Amanda stopped for coffee on her way home and overheard a group of women her age having a middle-class, middle-aged, normal-person conversation.

"Yeah, we booked the ski trip for January," one of them said. Her face was dewy fresh and unblemished like Amanda's was before prison, when Evan was paying for the facials, the fillers, and the Botox. "I always *dread* skiing," she said, looking down into the foam of her latte and probably calculating its calories.

"Right," said another one. "I detest the entire skiing *project*. The packing. The schlepping. The fear of injury. Until I actually get my ass on the lift."

"Then I wonder why I don't do it more often."

"That's how I feel about sex," deadpanned the brunette of the group. A brunette in LA had to rely on her wit to gain access to cliques like this one.

"Ha! Yes. The five stages of middle-aged sex and skiing. Dread. Avoidance. Capitulation. Hard Work. Resignation. Meh, it wasn't so bad after all."

There were guffaws followed by twittering giggles.

Amanda brought her coffee over to a stool by the window and started feeling sorry for herself. She could never just hang with a bunch of women her own age and talk about life. Unless it were with a bunch of ex-cons, but she wouldn't fit in with them either. *Poor me, poor me, pour me another drink*, she remembered from AA. It meant that self-pity usually led to backsliding. She took a deep breath, exhaled, and let it go. A woman sitting in the corner said, "Bird watching?"

Amanda jumped. "Excuse me?" she asked. It was the woman who looked like Carrie Fisher.

"You can see why they call them 'birds' in England, right?" she said, shrugging toward the tittering women. "Their concerns are so flighty."

"Are you real?" Amanda asked.

"Perception is reality. If you're perceiving me, then I'm part of your reality. But that doesn't mean I'm real."

"So I'm hallucinating you? I wouldn't put it past myself right now." Of course Amanda was talking to a ghost or a hallucination or a hallucination of a ghost. She shook her head.

"That's the story you're telling yourself—that I'm hallucinating you, when really I'm just having a cup of coffee, minding my own business. Maybe I'm here, maybe I'm not; does it matter? How'd it go with the offspring?"

"Terribly. I broke a promise. Couldn't get to our appointment on time, so she left. I had one brief conversation with her, but then she went to her dad's, and she hates it at her dad's. They treat her like a bastard servant child. An in-house babysitter."

"Well, that was bitchy of her to take off, right? Sometimes they can be bitches, too, you know."

"I guess, but this was a test, and I failed it." They were both quiet then, watching the BMWs fly by on Wilshire. "No words of wisdom?"

"Nope. You failed the test. But you tried. The results are in God's hands. Give it to God," she quoted from the Big Book.

"Thanks," Amanda said, tipping her cardboard cup toward the apparition, who was still wearing the enormous sunglasses, and then she headed for home. On the way, she got another text from Stevens. It was simply a mugshot-style photo of her mother's face Photoshopped to look like it was behind bars.

Subtle, she typed at the next red light.

Time is up. I need an update, he wrote back, and ridiculously followed it with three stopwatch emojis like he was a thirteen-year-old girl.

12

Ben was in the driveway again, using a broom to sweep up some dried-up palm fronds. Amanda tried to ignore him as she pulled into her garage space, but he stuck his head in.

"Hello."

"Hi," she said, grabbing her purse and pretending to seem too busy to chat. "You carpenters keep strange hours." It was just about 4 PM.

"It's one of the few fringe benefits. Can I buy you a drink?" he asked, holding up a big bottle of Italian sparkling water and two mini-football-sized lemons from the tree that drooped into their driveway. "I have a special place I like to go after a long day."

"Um," Amanda hesitated. She really just wanted to lock herself away from the world, flop onto her rented mattress, and play *Words with Friends* until she got a headache and had to close her eyes and sleep a restless sleep. But then she remembered the yuppie woman conversation at the café. How sometimes when you do what you dread, it ends up being worth the effort. "Okay," she said. "Let me get a jacket."

His was an old pickup truck from the sixties with the big rounded fenders and a wooden truck bed. The kind they take pictures of in front of barns and put on the October pages of wall calendars next to a haystack and a pile of red leaves. She slid her finger around the dusty crank for the window and turned it a few times in disgust.

"What? You don't like my wheels?"

"Who are you, Fonzie? Who says 'wheels'? I don't know. I'll get used to it. I think it's just like calling attention to yourself, I guess. But in a strange anachronistic way."

"It's an antique."

"I know. But like why would you want to drive something that looks like it should be in a museum?"

"Because I can. They don't have cars like this on the East Coast."

"For a reason," she said. And she wasn't even being cute about it. Right before she climbed into the vehicle, she could feel all the happiness drain out of her body and her mood swing to rageful annoyance. She should have just stayed in her bedroom and stared at the walls like she wanted to. This was a mistake. "I'm sorry," she said. "I'm just preoccupied and in a really bad mood. It's not you."

"It's not not me either, though, because I'm sitting right here and my presence and my vehicle seem to be annoying you."

"I just have a lot on my mind."

"I'm a good listener," he said.

"Of course you are," she said. *They're all good listeners until they buy the cow then they won't hear a word you've uttered. Get it? Uttered*, she thought to herself and smiled.

"What?" he asked.

"This just isn't fair to you," she said. "I'm not ready for this kind of intimacy."

"Sitting in a car?"

"Sitting in a car," she agreed.

He had just pulled into the exit-only lane for Bob Hope Airport, though, and Amanda perked up a little. Maybe Joyce had him pegged wrong. Maybe he, her hunky, humble carpenter, like Jesus, was going to whisk her away to Mykonos for two days where she could bake on the black sand and have her mind blown by the fact that geometry was invented there. Or close by, anyway. Euclid probably sat on that very beach. Or Pythagoras. She would yield to the pink pelicans crossing the narrow streets on foot as she shopped in the bazaar at the top of the hill that they had just exhilaratingly climbed by moped. Then they would dine in a whitewashed restaurant built into a cliff while they watched the sun set over the Aegean.

Maybe.

"Where we going?" she asked.

"You'll see," he said mischievously, and his eye, glowing amber in the yellow LA sun, literally twinkled.

"I didn't bring my bathing suit," she said. *Not to mention apply for a travel pass like a good parolee*, she thought to herself. He just laughed, which was not a good sign. *If he shakes his head at me I'm out.* She could not take one iota more of patronizing from a man, even if it was flirty, endearment kind of patronizing. She couldn't stomach being endearing to anyone right now. He was finding her adorable, she could tell. "I'm not who you think I am," she said, trying to cut his illusions off at the pass.

"I have no idea who you are. Hence the date," he said. He had pulled the truck off the dusty access road across from the airport. The Bob Hope Airport's screen mural hanging on the stubby control tower glowed with a reverse-video image of Amelia Earhart.

"If I were flying today, I would take that as a bad omen," Amanda said. "I hate flying. Lots of superstitions around it. Wouldn't you be freaked out about boarding a plane after being reminded of Amelia Earhart? Wait. Why are we stopping here?"

"This is my spot," Ben said. He parked his ridiculous movie-set truck beneath a banyan-type tree and grabbed a couple of those fold-able canvas chairs that seniors bring to concerts in the park. "Milady," he said as he bounced hers open and dusted it off. "Even has a cup holder," he said, indicating the cylinder of canvas hanging at the end of the armrest. "I spared no expense."

"And we're sitting here, why?" Amanda asked.

"I just like to watch the planes take off into the sunset. The sunsets here are brilliant," he explained.

"Maybe because of all the jet fuel they're dumping on our heads right now. Fires the sky right up," Amanda countered. "You don't care about the jet fuel?"

"Nope," he said. He poured her some seltzer, cut a lemon on a cutting board in his truck bed, and garnished her plastic cup.

"This relaxes you?"

"Yeah. My dad was a pilot," he said, settling in. The hills in the distance were beginning to soften and blacken into the purpling sky. And then all at once they sparkled with garlands of tiny white streetlights. The more obnoxious lights from the runway blinked on and off in some kind of wacky Morse code. A windsock swung to the west.

"He left us alone a lot. Flying off to exotic places, bringing me home souvenirs, bringing my mother home . . . never mind. He slept around a lot."

"Nice," Amanda said.

"Sorry. Anyway, so I was the man of the house. Used to cheer my mother up by telling her jokes and helping with the housework and whatnot. I learned to fix things. The good son."

"So what did you do with your dark side?" she asked.

"Good question."

"Well, everyone has one, right?"

"I drank it into oblivion as soon as I tasted my first drink. What about you?"

"Ah, well, you know Joyce."

"Yes, but that doesn't answer the question."

She taught me to harness the dark side. She never let me see the light. She taught me to let other people make something of themselves. Let other people go in for the kill while I circle them menacingly and then feed off their scraps, Amanda thought. Aloud she said: "She taught me to live like a vulture. But that's not who I am." A sudden sob snuck up on her and seized her throat for a second. She felt a tear forming in the corner of her eye but there was no way she was going to let it fall in front of him on their first date. She choked it back.

"No, you are not a vulture," he said kindly.

"I'm trying to figure out what I am exactly. I have an idea of what I want my life to look like but there are so many obstacles to getting there, you know? I can't seem to escape the dark."

"One day at a time."

"Doesn't seem fast enough."

"It's the journey and not the destination, right?"

"I guess, but it doesn't feel like a journey. It seems like I'm just stuck in a net, trying to release myself from entanglements. I'm so tangled up and I just want to set myself free."

"What does the destination look like?"

She described to him the cottage, the herb garden, the canvas shopping bags, the books on the shelves, the intimacy she'd share with Taylor for a while before she set her free. She'd never verbalized it before.

"So what's in your way?"

"You don't want to know," she said. She was pretty sure *Cosmo* would advise against revealing 1. the conditions of her parole; 2. being blackmailed by the FBI; and 3. moving stolen merchandise from Markdown on the first date.

"Let's change the subject. So how's business?"

But he couldn't answer because just then the nose of a long silver jet that zoomed straight for them hissed and then squealed like a whistling teapot as it lifted into the air. They could almost see their reflections in the shiny underbelly of the phallic beast as it roared above them, buoyed itself, and climbed, drifting away behind them.

"Whoa!"

"See? Exhilarating," Ben said. "Airbus A300."

"What? You know the model of every plane?" she asked, inching her fingers to the edge of the armrest so that they could be closer to his. She could just barely feel the graze of his knuckle before he went for it and covered her hand with his.

"Just by the sound of it, actually. Stupid pet tricks."

"You're lucky I'm old enough to understand that reference. Most of the girls you date probably wouldn't get that. Just a tip," she joked, playing it cool and pretending not to be giddy and entirely aroused by the warmth of his hand over hers. It was the first time she'd been touched, aside from Bruce's hug and Joyce's three cold taps on the back, in two whole years and her body was overreacting, firing on all synapses at once.

"How do you know I date younger girls?"

"I won't stoop to answer that. You are an empirically hot forty-something man living in LA. They throw themselves at you. You partake. Just don't use old Letterman references with them or you'll lose ground. You need to stay current," Amanda said and then surprised herself by extricating her hand and tracing a line up the inside of his forearm with her index finger.

A sleek private jet hardly made a sound as it glided toward them then whirred as it got closer and lifted itself just in time to clear the access road. It was so close to them it blew Amanda's hair out of place. "Gulfstream G650," she said. "I also know my way around a runway."

"I love a girl who knows her way around a runway," he said. His eyes were dopey and lovestruck, and Amanda could smell the heavy waves of his crush pulsing toward her. He wanted to kiss her, she could tell. She would put him off, but not for too long.

"Doesn't it bother you, though?" she asked.

"What?"

"That they're up there and we're down here. Just because we were born on the wrong side of luck?"

"See, I think we're the lucky ones."

"How do you figure?" Amanda asked, leaning forward.

"When's the last time those people," he said, leaning toward her, "if they're over forty, got lucky enough to experience a new first kiss? They probably haven't meaningfully kissed someone new in decades."

"And you have?"

"I'm going to right now."

"Oh you are, are you? You're pretty confid—"

Their lips just lightly grazed at first, gently, barely touching, which drove her happily insane. She leaned in, breathing his heavy breath, and pulled him deeper into a real kiss. It felt gentle and fierce and necessary. She touched the side of his face and the senior citizen chairs bent and creaked and they almost tipped into each other, so they stood up, embracing lightly at first and then pressing together every crevice of their bodies, turning themselves into one monolithic, geologic, lovestruck piece of the planet. It was so heavy, all of it, it felt like they might sink through the sand with the weight of their desire.

He stopped and looked at her, his eyelashes thick and black, defining his brown-eyed stare. "Uh-oh," he said.

She traced his lips with her fingers before lightly kissing them again.

"Yeah. Uh-oh is right."

They moved toward the truck bed. Every cell in her body wanted to push him in there and climb on top of him. It had been so long since she'd felt the exhilaration of mutual attraction. Even with Evan she had to visualize some film scene or memory of a past boyfriend before she could get turned on in the least. This was instantaneous. Goose bumps like the olden days. She felt the thing you think you'll never feel again as long as you live, and it had to stop. She bit his lip a little as she pulled away, straightened her clothes, and said, "Date over. Take me home, please."

"Okay," he said, looking almost painfully into her eyes for a second. "I guess we should take it slow." He folded up the chairs and placed them neatly into the truck. On the way home he bought her a strawberry shake at In-N-Out.

"Thanks for the nice time," she told him as she jumped out of his truck and dreamily climbed the garage stairs that led to their apartments.

"Hi, Mom," she said to Joyce, who was sitting at the dining room table looking through her narrow reading glasses at some spreadsheet on her laptop. "Is Taylor back?"

"Hi. Yes. She's in her room."

"Oh. Thank god. She wasn't answering my texts. I'm just going to go take a bath."

"Sounds good," said Joyce, seemingly distracted by the figures on her laptop. Amanda had never seen her using a computer before.

"Okay, then," Amanda said, heading down the hall a little dreamily.

"And Amanda," Joyce called, taking off the glasses and staring at her over the computer.

"Yes?" Amanda asked, loudly slurping down the last of her strawberry shake.

"Don't shit where you eat."

13

Ever since childhood, Amanda had found it comforting, every once in a while, to lock herself in the closet. When she was younger, she would hide there if her mother brought home a gentleman caller, stuffing her ears with cotton and sandwiching her head between two pillows and her Winnie-the-Pooh. Perversely, it was actually one of the things she missed most when she was in prison, the ability to lock herself away. Everything in the correctional facility was laid out in the open. There was nowhere to hide.

Seclusion is not the craziest of human behaviors, Amanda thought. Women in Manhattan Beach spent thousands to "float," sequestering themselves for hours at a time, in creepy space-age sensory deprivation chambers. Amanda's closet worked just as well. And it was free. Well, as long as her mother was paying the rent.

That morning she sat in the dark and tried first not to think at all for a while, and then, fluttering her eyes open, began to make a plan. She zipped open the top suitcase and counted the money again: twenty stacks of one hundred hundreds. It might seem like a lot, but making a down payment somewhere in California and then paying tuition for both her and Taylor, and adding in food and expenses—it would be gone in a couple of months. Which is why she also needed to finish her parole on good terms, get a job, and sell the ring to supplement their earnings. She just had to wait. There was still too much suspicion surrounding her with Agent Stevens poking around, and

Evan still frequenting the Four Seasons, according to Roderigo. She couldn't travel until her parole was up, and she didn't want to tip Evan off by selling the ring anywhere near LA. He had probably alerted every pawn and jewelry shop in California and Nevada, and if she sold it now, it would lead him right to her.

Some wacko *Star Trek* beep tone on her phone that she had never heard before interrupted her solitude. She dug around the shoes at the bottom of the closet trying to find where she had left her phone. She swept her hands around the shoes, reading the carpet like braille until she felt the slick rectangle of technology that connected her to the rest of the universe. She flipped it over and felt the smooth, satisfying weight of it in her hand and then gasped to see the stark, scarred face of Agent Stevens staring back at her. *FaceTime request* the phone said. And Amanda instinctively threw the phone back across the closet.

Where it rang again.

She knew he would not be ignored, so she crawled to the other side of the closet, retrieved the phone, and pressed the green button. No dummy, she pretended not to know how to FaceTime and clumsily held the phone in front of her cleavage, trying to knock the wind out of him or at least knock down some of the hate and aggression. It's how you handle them. Men.

"Um," he said. "Amanda?"

"Agent Stevens?" she asked stupidly, angling the camera straight down her shirt then giggling. "I don't know how to use this thing."

"Hold it in front of your face."

"Right," she said, moving the phone up, finding her face in the square and then trying to get her best angle in the frame.

"This is taking too long," Stevens said.

"I'm sorry," she said. "I've never used FaceTime before."

"Not that," Stevens said, pounding his fist onto his kitchen counter and then breathing in and sighing, trying to compose himself.

"What, then? You seem so tense."

"Do I? Do I seem tense?" he asked, slowly raising his voice.

"Well, yeah. A little. Yes."

"Ahem," he said as he cleared his throat and started over. "If I seem tense, it's because I need this operation completed on East Coast time, not . . . ahem," he cleared his voice again, trying not to curse. "Not California time. Do you know what I mean?"

"Born and raised here, so no. What do you mean East Coast time?"

"I mean," he said, then turned away, coughed, and threw his empty beer can across the room. "Excuse me." More throat clearing. "What I mean by East Coast time is competently completing a job in a timely manner and clearly communicating your results. In a timely manner. East Coast people work with a certain, shall we say, *exigency*, that seems to be absent in my relations with people of the West Coast persuasion."

"Didn't you just abduct me four days ago?"

"Four days? Days? In New York I could have had this cleared up in three hours! And I didn't abduct you." From the thud and the ensuing squealing sound, she thought he might have just kicked his cat.

"Oh sorry. Carjack."

"I didn't . . . Just, ahem." More throat clearing.

"I think you're barking up the wrong tree, here, Agent Stevens. I've checked Craigslist. eBay. The *PennySaver*. He is not broadcasting any cryptic messages. I hate to say it, but I don't think he has the energy for that. You've seen the robe. He's a mellow guy."

"Just get me some shit on your fucking stepfather before you go back to prison, or worse."

"What's worse than prison? Did you just threaten me?"

"Whatever works," he said and then the phone went blank.

She threw her phone again as if it were suddenly poisoned or on fire. She packed away the suitcase and hid it beneath some clothes then dressed as fast as she could despite her hands still shaking. Perhaps she'd underestimated him. It was time to take him seriously and get herself a job at L'Affordable.

She knocked on Taylor's door on the way out, just to say good-bye, but there was no answer. She pushed the door open slowly and could tell that she just missed her. High school started early these days, and the kids exhausted themselves getting to school on time. Amanda had just read on the parenting blogs she was following that they (the mysterious "they") were discovering that most of what we think of as the inherent behavioral issues of adolescence could possibly be caused by how early we make them get up in the morning.

The cloying smell of Taylor's fruity hair conditioner clung to the post-shower steam hanging in her bedroom. Her bed was made, which Amanda found a little bit heartbreaking, actually. Taylor was clinging to some semblance of order, and the only way she could find it was by continuing to make her bed even if no one cared. Joyce had bought a desk for her at the flea market and it was stacked with folders, binders, and textbooks. Wedged in a stand-up file holder between a school calendar and a physics textbook was a bright-pink slim leather Moleskine notebook. A journal. A well-loved one, with a banana sticker in the corner and pages softened and dog-eared from frequent use. Amanda fingered the corner and tipped it toward her. Then she slid it out. The cover shone with the oil of its skin, tanned from being held and adored and toted everywhere. Why didn't Taylor have it with her today? Was it a sign? Did Taylor *want* her to read it? Had anything ever been so tempting?

She knew she shouldn't.

She couldn't, right?

But then she did.

November 1

Dear Diary:

Nothing good re: motherlessness. For example, if had mother around, would probably not have hooked up with football player at *Halloween party*. Would not have had to walk home at 7 AM on weekday dressed as *Wonder Woman*. Little girls, on way to school, skipping to bus stop in polka-dot tights, would not stop in tracks, point, and say, loudly, "Mommy! Wonder Woman!"

Middle-aged, slack-faced mommy of girls would not stop, stare, judge, feel. Emotions visible on wrinkly face: rage *(how dare you co-opt powerful girl heroine and turn into slut)*, jealousy *(I used to have those thighs)*, shame *(for us all)*, pity *(I remember being young and stupid. Youth wasted on young)*.

Would not have shaken head at me.

If had mother of own, mother would discourage hooking up. At least, perhaps warn about: if hook up, make sure wearing street clothes. Street clothes useful for: *walk of shame.*

When home, still rue motherlessness, because, while might not tell her whole story, mother would still hug and listen to crying.

November 2
Dear Diary:

Nothing good re: being motherless. If had mother, would own small quilted zippered pouch in which to store tampons. Would know where to buy such a thing and in which strategic pocket to place it in backpack I would also own. Would also know how to knit. Together, mother and I would knit enormous striped hat for Clownarina statue. Winter is coming.

November 3
Dear Diary:

Mr. Hunter says: must do homework. Can't pass me without some proof of work. So. Read *Great Gatsby*. Discover on page 42 that Nick Carraway = obviously gay. Has anonymous sex with man after bender in city with Tom and Daisy. Then some smutty dialogue about touching the elevator boy's "lever." Have people just ignored this fact for a hundred years? Or people just down with: Roaring Twenties = Everyone gay = One big party. Write paper about Nick Carraway. Nick Carraway not infatuated with money, old or new. Infatuated with Gatsby himself. Because Gatsby totally hot and sensitive and loyal and good-hearted. Get F. Because teacher = homophobe.

Meanwhile, enjoy sleeping in. When Lauren texts me this: photo of Clownarina sculpture . . . *My* Clownarina sculpture, in Venice. Wearing enormous knit hat! Someone beat us to it. Secret: I miss my mom.

November 4
Dear Diary:
Always knew: people = not what they seem.
Never realized: Amanda = person.

Amanda's heart had stopped after page one, and she gasped now, trying to breathe some life back into herself. She had uncovered the soul of her girl-child, and she felt simultaneously guilty (who does that? Reads their kid's journal?), relieved (her kid was so smart and emotionally intelligent. What an amazing kid!), and *devastated* (Amanda had abandoned her one true purpose in life at the moment when she needed her most). Amanda sniffed and just grabbed at the first thing she could to try to wipe away her tears. It was two pieces of folded, stapled printer paper that had slipped from between the journal pages.

She dabbed and scraped her tears away with it and then unfolded it.

The document was covered in red ink with a big F on the top. Amanda gasped. The F was even underlined with bold angry strokes of the red pen. Was this the *Gatsby* paper?

Taylor was failing? She tried to breathe deeply but the breath wouldn't come. Her entire sense of stability hinged on the assumption that at least Taylor's grades were intact. Even during her imprisonment Taylor would send her every report card to sign from prison, because she was so proud of them. If Taylor was failing, it meant that Amanda hadn't set her up for success. A parent's only job, aside from shielding them from loneliness, was to set them up for success, right? With the early exposure to books and the stocking of the art supplies and the weekend visits to the library and the museums and fresh air and exercise and monitoring screen time and feeding them fresh vegetables and teaching them "please" and "thank you." Above all, teaching them gratitude so they didn't become entitled assholes. Amanda, in the early years anyway, had done all the things. Set her living room up like a preschool with a sand table and a dramatic play corner with costumes and puppets and dolls of every race, ethnicity, and gender. In spite of her recent fuckups with Taylor, in the early years, she had done all the things. So that she wouldn't get an F on a paper in high school. How do you even get an F if you turn the thing in? In her mind, turning it in was an automatic D.

If Taylor was in academic crisis, it was even more important for her to get Stevens off her tail, protect Joyce, and get the heck out of Dodge so they could start over. She shoved the essay into her boho bag and promised to stop by the school after work and talk to this . . . Mr. Hunter it said in the corner heading. Room 307E.

As she drove back to East LA to the neighborhood of L'Affordable, she thought about what the title of her life story would be. *Roadblock*, she joked. Or *Bad Karma*. Prison and her work-order job at Markdown seemed like roadblocks enough, but this Stevens BS was sending her on another seemingly useless detour. And now Taylor's F. Why were some people just blessed with a direct route to the good life? What even the heck? Sometimes she thought she must have been a serial killer in a past life. She was paying off some huge karmic debt, she was sure. Otherwise she would have been gifted with easy ways out like all the folks who lived in Santa Monica.

"Bruce," she said, hopping down out of the van. The gravel crunched under her feet as she approached. He was stooped in front of the front office watering the succulents with a green plastic watering can.

"Need to keep up the curb appeal," Bruce said somewhat jokingly as his body creaked to standing.

"Funny you mention that," Amanda said. "I was really serious the other day when I asked if I could help you out."

"I know. And I was serious when I said we didn't need help." He glared at her over the top of his reading glasses. He was handsome once, when everything was coiffed and lubricated. Now his handsomeness had retreated deep within and he was all shrunken scruffiness and stray hairs. He did still have a bit of a gleam in his eye, though, and Amanda tried to read it. *Was he hiding something?* He usually gave her whatever she asked for.

"Please, Bruce," Amanda said, resorting to the pleading tone of her childhood that she knew he couldn't resist. "I could really use the extra cash."

"I can give you cash if this is about cash," he said, pulling his wallet out of his back pocket.

"No. It's about more than cash, Bruce. If I eventually want a job that's not in a big box, I'm going to need to prove I can handle some managerial tasks. They're going to ask me questions like 'Describe a problem you had at work and a system you created to solve it.' They're going to be asking me about *systems* and *processes.*"

"Honestly, Mandy, that's what I'm afraid of. We're all systems go around here. We don't need anyone coming in and messing with our systems. You know what they say about reinventing the wheel."

"Well, if you can give me some exposure, you know?" She followed him around the corner of the building where he hung his watering can next to the perfectly wound-up hose.

"See," Bruce said, pointing at the hook. "Everything has its place. This is the L'Affordable system for plant watering."

"But I could help you with marketing. Or sales. Make some cold calls. Do you have an Instagram?" she tried.

"Insta-what?"

"Pleeeeaaase, Bruce. I'm dying in that big box. I need to feel productive. I'm like a caged animal in there."

"Nobody puts Baby in a corner," he said, smirking, quoting another one of their favorites. Joyce had no patience for film, partly because she had such sour grapes that she hadn't made it in the industry, so going to the movies was what they did together in the eighties as a father-daughter kind of thing.

"Right. Get me out of the corner."

"Okay," he said, capitulating.

"Okay?"

"Yeah. Stop by when you can, and Maria will show you the ropes."

"Thank you!" she squealed, hugging his terry-cloth robe and inhaling the sharp drugstore cologne that used to mask his smoking but now barely disguised his old man smell. "You won't regret this," she said. *But I might*, she thought. She had to do it, though. She'd weighed all the options. It was Bruce or Joyce. And Bruce was probably clean, anyway. She couldn't imagine him dealing in anything illegal. She slunk to the van where she texted Stevens. *I'm in*, she typed, but left it there, stagnant on the phone for a full two minutes before she finally, impulsively, hit Send.

14

After her shift at the Mark, she found Mr. Hunter, a thin white man in wide cords the color of peanut butter and a tight plaid shirt, at his desk in 307E. He had a red pen in hand and sighed and moaned out loud as he scribbled and slashed it through entire paragraphs of the underdeveloped thinking of teenage children.

She knocked lightly on the door. "Mr. Hunter?" she asked politely.

When he looked up, clean-shaven and baby-faced, she was at first taken aback by his youth and then hit with an eerie feeling that they'd met somewhere before. Since turning forty she had that feeling a lot and it led to some awkward encounters on the street. She would pause for a second looking at a face, knowing she'd seen it somewhere before but unable to place it. Was she/he a barista, or someone from AA, or a shopper from Markdown who came through her line, or someone she should actually be saying hello to like a friend from high school or one of Taylor's friend's mothers? Usually she gave a little sideways grin that she hoped said "Have a nice day," but probably said, "I'm a lonely cougar on the prowl."

Forgetting faces made her think of Alzheimer's and the prospect of dying young, but very slowly while Taylor watched her drift into oblivion and forget who she was. "Mom! I'm your daughter, you have to remember me!" she would scream.

"Ahem," Mr. Hunter broke through her reverie and she gave him the friendly, slightly cougary grin. He stood up and said, "Hi. May I help you?"

"Yes, I'm Taylor Cooper's mom, Amanda."

"Oh," he said, turning a ghostly shade of grayish white. If it were a paint sample it would be called "pebble." He turned pebble and then regained his composure and came over to shake Amanda's hand.

"Sorry," he said. "We don't get a lot of parents traipsing through here. Once they hit high school, the parents kind of get busy with work or family or something."

"Midlife crisis," Amanda said. "We're just barely trying to hold it together and parenting has to go on autopilot for a while. Just have to hope for the best." At this they both kind of nervous-laughed. "Speaking of that, um, hoping for the best, not midlife crises . . ." God, she may as well start babbling about vaginal dryness and hot flashes. This wasn't going well, but she ploughed forward. "It doesn't seem like Taylor put forth her best effort on this paper." She pulled the paper from her bag and pointed to the giant F.

"Oh. That," he said.

"I mean, I read it . . ." Amanda continued. "Mind if I sit?"

"Of course," he said, motioning toward a half desk.

"Anyway," she said, sitting down, "I read it and it seems like a masterful analysis of Nick Carraway. Perhaps even a literary discovery! I'm not sure how she could have done better."

Mr. Hunter looked embarrassed. Caught off guard, his pebble complexion bloomed with hive-like splotches of pink in the shape of jigsaw puzzle pieces, so Amanda continued on her rant.

"They're just teenagers," she said. "Their frontal lobes are not yet developed enough for the kind of analytical thinking we expect from them these days. They chemically can't make the deep connections between things that make a good essay until at least nineteen years old." She had read this in the education section of the *LA Times* next to an article about how everyone expects kids to get up too early for school. "Plus, we're exhausting them by making them arrive before eight in the morning. Exhaustion does not equal Excellence." She had read the last part on a bumper sticker that was parked in the parents' parking lot.

"Ms. Cooper," he said, sitting across from her and clearing his throat. "Actually Taylor is one of my best students."

"Wait, what? She is?" Amanda glowed, her face flushing with instant uncontrollable pride. "So . . ."

"This," he said pointing to the paper, "was just a draft. I do this sometimes to push her along when she's being a little lazy with her thinking. Her final grade will reflect her true performance, which is excellent. No need to worry."

"Really?"

"Really."

"Well, that's kind of sucky, giving her a fake F."

"How so?"

"Listen. I know you." Amanda said, pointing at him and staring at him over her finger.

"You do?" He turned pebble again.

"Not personally. God, I'm speaking metaphorically. You're an English teacher; get with it. Californians are so literal. It's boring explaining things to you all the time. Metaphorically. I know you. I know people like you. You have the power here, right?" she said, pointing at the big F. "And you know you have the power. And you're—now be honest with yourself here, Mr. Hunter—you're getting off a little bit on having all the power in this situation."

"No, I . . ." he stuttered.

"Well, this is not going to happen again," Amanda said, pointing one more time at the F. "Are we clear?"

"Yes, ma'am."

"Good."

She gathered her belongings and moved toward the door, when she turned around and said, "So can you maybe . . ."

"I'll keep this meeting confidential."

"Perfect," she said and she spun to escape the encounter. In the hallway, she ran into a woman carrying a bright orange ream of still warm, freshly xeroxed paper that flew into a little tornado and then floated calmly to the floor.

"I'm so sorry," Amanda said. "I was distracted. Let me help." She squatted down and slid the papers together. They were printed in three columns, and each column listed three amazing prizes a person could win if they bought a raffle ticket. A $20 gift card to Tito's Tacos. A free facial at Yolanda's Day Spa. An iPod with an "o."

"Hi, I'm Anne," the woman said. "It's raffle season, as you can see. So nice to see another parent in the hallway. Once they get to high school it's like the parents scatter to the four winds, you know? And this is when they need us most, I think. Who's your kid?"

"Taylor," Amanda said. "Taylor Cooper."

"Hmmm. Don't know her. My daughter is McKenzie. She does cheer and track and math league."

"Sounds like a smart girl," Amanda said, trying to shut down the constant stream of crazy coming from this poor lonely woman's mouth. "I really should be going," she said, handing Anne the papers she had collected.

"We're having a meeting next week," Anne said. "To collate these and add the final touches to the Winter Festival. Trying to earn enough for the new gym. You could come, if you want. We're always looking for new meat," she joked awkwardly, then handed Amanda a home-made business card. "The info for the meeting is on the back."

"You have a business card? For your PTA office?" Amanda asked, immediately hoping it didn't sound as judgy as she thought it did. She was just shocked by this detail.

"It's important for me to take myself seriously," she said as if re-peating some psychobabble her shrink taught her.

"I see that," Amanda said. "Well, it was nice meeting you."

"Will we see you at the meeting? There's wine and cheese and good times. We'll need a head count soon, so make sure to RSVP."

"Right," Amanda said, trying to back away slowly. "I'll see what I can do." She walked briskly through the halls trying to escape any further encounters, but as she approached her car, she thought, *Maybe I should go.* She flipped Anne's card over. It was red and white and had the school's wolf mascot in the corner and read, *Anne Schiller. President, PTO. Vice President, Tricky Tray.* What the heck was a Tricky Tray? Then she wondered, *If I went to PTA meetings, Taylor would feel like a normal kid.* That was Amanda's release plan, after all. Join the PTA. Bake some shit for the bake sales. Maybe she would go. WWCFD? she asked herself, and then she heard her higher power as if she were a projected hologram from R2D2: *It's not easy to hang with people who think they're normal. Usually they're crazier than you are, because they don't recognize their crazy. But you should try it anyway. For your daughter.*

———

At home, said daughter was taking notes while watching Alex Guarnaschelli butcher a pig on the Food Network. Amanda flopped down next to her on the couch and dropped the F paper onto the coffee table.

"What the heck?" Taylor asked, grabbing the remote and pausing Alex, who had the cleaver above her head about to hack viciously into the porcine rib cage. "What are you doing, going through my things?!" Taylor asked, horrified. "I can't even."

"People are saying that a lot. What does that mean? Finish your sentence. You can't even what?"

"I can't even fucking believe that you went through my stuff," Taylor said, standing up and shaking the paper at her mother. That was the first time Amanda had ever heard Taylor use the F word and she did not like it at all. It made her face look pale and mean and ugly. "You're the one on parole, Mom, not me. *You* can be searched without a warrant. I haven't lost my right to privacy."

"I'm here now, Taylor."

"Obviously. But for how long?" she muttered.

"For the rest of my life, Tay. I'm going to be near you for as long as you want me to be. I know how hard this must have been. But I'm here now and I can help you take care of stuff like this," Amanda said, pointing at the paper. "He shouldn't be trying to intimidate you like this. Do you need me to get you switched out of his class?"

"No. I got it."

"You sure? Because I met some powerful people today." She smiled as she put her arm over Taylor's shoulders and pulled her in for a hug. "I met this lady," she said, and showed Taylor Anne Schiller's business card. "I think I might go to their meeting. Help with the Winter Festival. What do you think?"

"No. You can't play their game. They're all a bunch of phonies."

"Okay, Holden Caulfield. But maybe I will. I would do it if it meant you would feel more normal."

"Wow, *Catcher in the Rye*. You really did read a lot in prison," Taylor said.

"Well, what else was I going to . . ." Amanda started, but Taylor's face got a different kind of ugly then. Her chin went up and the sides of her mouth went down as she tried to stave off the tears. Her eyes got really big and then the first one fell and the rest streamed down after it.

"I missed you so much, Mom."

"I know, baby," Amanda said, pulling her in closer and kissing the top of her head. "I'm so, so sorry." And there was nothing else to say after that.

15

During her first shift at L'Affordable on Sunday, Amanda forgot for a second why she was actually there. She got caught up in the training Maria was providing her and actually thought for a second that she was beginning a career in storage. They even gave her a pamphlet from the trade association called *So You Want to Be in Storage*, and she read it with glee, absorbing all the graphs and pie charts, hopeful about her prospects in this new industry.

After that they showed her a video on a VHS tape that they popped into the mouth of a mini television with a built-in slot. Amanda hadn't seen one of those since high school. The video was peopled by sharp women in hard hats holding clipboards while directing the slow dance of forklifts. It was a dance. It was exciting. Cartoon arrows shot across the screen in animated graphics that pointed in the many directions a career in storage could take you.

Maria, too, made it seem so alluring. She was snappily dressed and walked in crisply in her pointed heels, showing Amanda the "Board of Storage," a giant whiteboard where she recorded the ins and outs of the daily transactions of L'Affordable. She was so gracious about sharing what she knew and so organized about how she planned her day. Amanda might never figure that out: how to organize and plan for things in a real way that required products from Staples. All she had was her wimpy dude tree.

Maria's first task today was to prepare Bruce for the annual storage convention in Kankakee, Indiana.

"There's only one passable hotel," Maria explained. "A Days Inn across the border in Momence, Illinois, so I have to book him early. I also need to get him a rental car. It's about sixty miles from O'Hare. Someday I can get him one of those cars that drives itself because it's such a straight shot on one highway through nothing but farmland and billboards for megachurches. And when I say straight shot," she said, donning her official phone headset before calling the rental car company, "I mean there isn't even a curve in the road or the tiniest of hills."

"Have you been there before?"

"Yes. He brought me there once. You couldn't get anything for breakfast that wasn't . . ." She tapped her fingers on the desk, searching for the right word. "Glazed," she said as it came to her. "Everything was glazed in sugar. All those farms and not one piece of fruit. All those cows and not one drop of real milk for your coffee."

"Nondairy creamer?" Amanda asked in disgust.

"Yes."

"Ick. They didn't even give us that in prison."

"Aye, *mami*. Don't say *prison*. This gorgeous face was not in prison. I can't think of it." She gave Amanda a little sympathy hug across the shoulders and then pointed at the spreadsheet open on the computer, whose monitor buzzed and blinked in an arrhythmic static.

"Why doesn't he get you a new one?"

"He hates all this," she said, swirling her hand around the monitor. "I had to beg him to use Excel and Quicken for the accounts. He finally gave in."

Quicken, Amanda thought in her imaginary evil villain voice and imagined herself tapping her creepy villain fingers together one at a time. *That might be where he's hiding his shady beeezness.* "Can you show me the Quicken program?" she asked.

After Bruce was confirmed on a flight and at a hotel and registered for his three-day Midwest Storage Conference, they spent a couple of hours on the accounting side. Printed and mailed some bills, collected the checks from the mail, and zipped them into a special bank deposit bag.

Amanda opened a new account and learned how to assign keys and take payment from a young couple who started their own adult coloring book business on the Internet and needed a place to store their extra inventory.

As much as he hated computers, even Bruce admitted that the Internet was a boon for the storage business. "All those ladies selling mittens on Etsy need places to keep their inventory," he had said earlier that morning. "Forty percent of my customers sell shit on the Internet." And with that, Amanda had added a new goal to her "who she wanted to be" wish list. She would live in a stand-alone house with an herb garden, shop at the farmers' market, listen to NPR, *and* sell some shit on Etsy. She wanted to be one of *those* ladies.

The young couple signed their contract and Amanda showed them to Unit 32 and rolled open the door for them.

"Coloring books, huh?" Amanda asked. "You don't think the market's already saturated after the trend boomed last Christmas?" On their most depressing visit to the women's prison last year, Joyce and Taylor had brought Amanda colored pencils and three adult coloring books filled with mandalas and seascapes and trees and intricate henna-looking elephant prints. "It's supposed to relax you," Taylor said, shifting nervously in her chair and trying not to cry. Amanda never opened them.

"We have niche market coloring books," the man said, taking off his Ray-Bans and inspecting the space. "When we say adult coloring books, we mean"—he raised four fingers to make air quotes—"'adult coloring books.'"

"Oh," said Amanda, trying not to make a face. "That's an interesting spin on it."

"This will be great," the wife said as she shook Amanda's hand.

Amanda had made her first deal. It felt good. And when she got back to the office lunch was waiting: another enormous brown bag of Mexican food bleeding so much grease that the brown paper had become almost translucent.

Bruce came out of his office and took the receipt from under the bag, looked inside, and lifted out a container of enchiladas. The thin rings of jalapeño slices were visible through the plastic cover. "Want some, Amanda?" he asked. "Help yourself."

Amanda lifted out a second container, also filled with enchiladas, which she hadn't had in years and was kind of psyched about.

Bruce ripped the stapled menu off the bag and took it with him back into his office where he sat and proceeded to pick off the green peppers and stack them in a tiny poker chip tower on a napkin next to his plate. He hated jalapeños; always had. Amanda pretended to be busy with Quicken as she eyed him through his door while he unfurled the menu, studied it for a second, and then tossed it into the trash beneath his entire plate of enchiladas which he tossed in after it. He'd only taken two bites.

Ulcer? Amanda wondered. *Why does he keep ordering Mexican?*

The next time Bruce got up to use the bathroom, Amanda snuck into his office, reached into the trash, and pulled the menu from El Triunfo out from under Bruce's discarded plate. It had seven items circled on it. And none of them were enchiladas.

16

At home that evening, Taylor had agreed to watch *Paper Moon*, starring Tatum and Ryan O'Neal. It was a family favorite because Amanda looked exactly like Tatum O'Neal, then and now. And the film was what gave Joyce the inspiration to use her kid as a shill in the first place. It's where she learned all her first con jobs like Mommy's juice and the targeting of recent widows. It soothed them as they watched, their limbs entwined like the roots of an old mangrove.

Joyce poked her head in, a little jealous of their intimacy, Amanda could tell, and tried to interrupt it with random meaningless conversation.

"Hey Mom, since when did Bruce start eating Mexican?" Amanda asked, voicing the thought that had been niggling at her.

"Since never. Can't even get him to eat guacamole, which is like just eating mush, right? It has no taste. Or no offensive taste, anyway."

"Maybe he's one of those people whose taste buds can't deal with cilantro," Taylor said.

"What?" Joyce asked.

"It's a genetic thing," Taylor continued. "I learned about it on the Food Network. To the people who have the gene, cilantro tastes like toothpaste." She snuggled a little closer to Amanda on the couch and Amanda almost visibly swooned with contentment.

"He's never mentioned that," Joyce said, grabbing a handful of popcorn from the bowl on the coffee table.

"There's butter on that," Amanda snidely warned, knowing her mother would eat butter over her dead body, but Joyce ate it anyway, which was a little jolting. "Anyway," Amanda continued. "The two times I've worked at L'Affordable, he's ordered Mexican for lunch."

"Tastes change, I guess," Joyce said, a little more contemplative than usual. She grabbed nervously for another fistful of popcorn. "Maybe he's having an affair."

"What? Mom. No," Amanda said.

"A man starts eating Mexican out of the blue after sixty years without it. Sends a red flag. Either way, he owes me a Margarita Night. Been trying to get him to Jose's Tortillas for ten years."

Joyce left and they fell asleep on the couch before the movie ended. Amanda woke to the insistent buzzing of her phone in her back pocket.

"Fuck!" Amanda sighed, disentangling herself from her girl-child and looking at her phone.

Time's up! the text read. *Sad, really. Old women don't do well in prison. Rheumatism, etc.*

Wait, Amanda texted. *Family emergency! I have good stuff for you. Promise. But I need a little more time.*

Please, she texted again, and got the three bouncing bubbles of anticipation. They kept bubbling and bubbling as Stevens presumably crafted his response, until finally she got: *Two more days. LACMA, Tuesday. 8 pm. Urban Light. Wilshire entrance. This better be good, I shit you not.*

Fine, Amanda texted, and then after some equivocating decided to include the emoji for smiling pile of poop.

You did not just poop emoji me, he texted back.

And Amanda sent him thumbs-up, fist bump, and flexing bicep.

To which Stevens replied with a photo of a real gun.

Do they teach this at Quantico? she wondered. Seemed like a violation of code. But she could tell he was serious and her heart sank a little bit at the prospect of giving him any intel on Bruce.

—

The next day, when she emerged from her bedroom, Bruce was there, clad in neatly pressed golf shorts, a checkered top, and some loafers. He sat in the recliner smoking.

"Your mother dressed me like this. Do I look like a yodeler?"

"What do you mean, yodeler?" Amanda asked. She wondered if it were a new old-homophobic-white-man euphemism for gay person.

"You know, yodeler. Like *yodel-ay-hee-hoo*. These shorts look like lederhosen. Real men don't wear short pants, right?"

"No. You look good," she said. She tried to look him in the eye to gauge whether he'd gone to the dark side like Stevens suggested. She looked at him to figure out if all his shady take-out Mexican *almuerzos* were a change of taste or something else more sinister. An affair? A way to communicate with Mexican drug dealers? But he was super cool. She couldn't read him. He lowered his newspaper for a second and locked her in the briefest of evil eyes before relaxing again into his fatherly face.

Joyce interrupted, whisking out in a midi skirt, tight top, and espadrille sandals with a posh straw handbag on her forearm.

"Let's go, babe. First race is at eleven. Did you pack what I asked you to pack in the trunk?"

"Yes dear." He winked at Amanda as he hoisted himself from the chair and then tapped Joyce on the rear with his rolled-up newspaper. "Let's go, sugar mama," he said. And they were off.

She heard the deep rumbling boat engine sound of the Acura leave the driveway and then called out sick at Markdown. Everyone else did it all the time, she figured, and then she headed straight to L'Affordable. She had a plan. If anyone knew anything about the dark underbelly of L'Affordable, it was Maria. And if she couldn't loosen up Maria's lips, she could at least steal her master key.

"Hi, Maria," Amanda said. Before working with Maria, Amanda had spent time with her at the company picnics Bruce used to throw in the olden days. It was usually just Joyce, Maria, Amanda, and Maria's kids having hamburgers at some park, but Bruce always made a go of being the generous boss. Which is why Maria believed her when Amanda said, "Bruce took the day off, so he told me to come take you for a drink."

"Drinking in the daytime, Amanda?"

"It's California, right? All this time in California and we forget to live like Californians. Yes. Drinking in the daytime. Why not?"

The worst thing about the con artist life was having to con someone you really like. Maria was caring and smart, funny and cool, and now Amanda had to do this. Get her hammered and steal her master key.

"So where to?" Maria asked.

"Well, you know the neighborhood . . ."

"Right. I know the place."

Maria directed them to a tucked-away alley cantina with a hidden patio in the back complete with a wooden pergola draped with Jacaranda vines. Sometimes East LA was freckled with tiny pieces of Carmel. You just had to know where to look.

They ordered margaritas and told the waiter to keep them coming. Amanda dumped hers in the ceramic floor vase next to her, while Maria, on her third, began slurring about how hard it was to raise kids who gave a shit about anything.

"Maria, they're only nine and eleven. It's going to get worse before it gets better. Trust me."

"How do you know? You have the perfect child."

"Nobody's perfect," Amanda said, remembering the bearded man at the Four Seasons, the F paper, and the sad, lonely journal entries she'd read. "At least she won't be perfect after I'm through with her," she lamented. "God gives them to you perfect, and then you turn them into the same messed-up piece of angriness you've become, because you don't know any better. You chisel away at them with your own neurosis until they're just as damaged as you are."

"Whoa! Amanda, stop. Too deep. Too negative. We're drinking in the daytime, right?" Maria said, swinging her drink in front of her for a toast.

"Right. You should maybe have some food," she said.

"Yes. Order me some guacamole. I need to pee."

Luckily Maria failed to take her purse with her. Amanda reached for it just as Maria turned around and said, "You are a good mozzer. Don't forget it," she said, pointing at her.

"Okay," Amanda said and when she turned the corner, grabbed Maria's keys. Three for the office door and the master key for all the units.

"So Bruce is still a good boss to you?" Amanda asked when Maria returned, probing a little to see what she could get.

"Oh, yes, yes, Amanda. He pays for private school and piano lessons and also the fancy summer camp at UCLA. He gives the kids two hundred for every report card."

"And he never . . ."

"Asks for anything in return? No. I am not a prostitute, Amanda."

"I didn't mean to imply. It's just I've been wondering about Bruce lately."

"You should stop all that wondering. It takes your mind to some shitty places. Bruce is a stand-up guy. You know. Trust your instincts."

"So there's no funny business?"

"I don't know what you mean," she said and she stared Amanda flatly in the eye. *Ooo. She's good at this*, Amanda thought. A good secretary guards secrets with her life. The word *secret* is in her job title.

"Okay. Sorry," Amanda said. "I'll drive you home."

"This was fun," Maria giggled, wobbling drunkenly in her high heels as Amanda grabbed her elbow and guided her through the parking lot.

—

After driving Maria home, she sped back to L'Affordable. It was getting dark by then. As she crept along the gravel, a motion sensor light snapped on, paralyzing her, a deer in headlights, reminding her of prison and jailbreaks and handcuffs, which thankfully were never used on her. She had these post-traumatic moments sometimes, remembering the horrors of being institutionalized, but usually she was able to push the sounds of evening sobbing, the smells of shit, piss, and collective vagina, and the taste of pasty instant mashed potatoes deep, deep into the recesses of her consciousness. There were no cameras on the premises, she remembered, and she continued tiptoeing to Unit 56, which was marked as "Occupied" on the spreadsheet Maria was training Amanda with, but happened to be blank in the OWNER column.

Unit 56, however, was filled with two crates of LPs, a stack of CDs, some cassette tapes, a rolltop desk, and a giant stuffed giraffe. Unit 43, another unit whose OWNER column was left blank, held a brown suede sectional couch, some football trophies, a big-screen TV, and a mini jukebox—obviously bachelor stuff some guy couldn't part with when he moved in with his stylish girlfriend. *People just need to let go of this crap and drop it off at Goodwill*, Amanda thought.

She continued opening a statistically significant number of storage units and found nothing but mildew, bad pastel-colored abstract art from the eighties, lots of really long skis, some musical instruments, fondue pots, bread makers, espresso machines, home microbrew kits, and those lethal jarts. *God, people are boring*, she thought.

She crept her way to the office, which reeked of cigarillo funk trapped in the upholstery, and she—first donning gloves because who even knew who Bruce was anymore and if he'd be dusting for fingerprints (God, this was worse than finding out about Bill Cosby)—leafed through all the Mexican restaurant menus scattered on the desk. They were marked up with ballpoint, like Joyce's racing papers. And each had way too many items circled for one man's lunch. She wasn't sure what they meant, but something told her they were important. Why would he save so many of them? She grabbed a couple of menus from a bottom drawer and headed out.

In the van, she checked her phone, which she'd been ignoring in an effort to concentrate. A text from Ken, her parole officer: *Watch it. Russ told me you called out sick.*

One from Russ: *No one calls out sick during holiday shopping season. You better recover quickly. Or else.* Then he attached a link to a GIF of a beheading from the opening scene of *Game of Thrones*.

A text from Lupita: *Russ is angry.*

And Joyce: *Is this thing on? I got an iPhone. Love, your mother.*

From Stevens: A photo of Joyce on a park bench in Santa Monica handing over what presumably was a buttload of pills stuffed into a cardboard cylinder marked PRUNES to a pernicious-looking muscle man entirely covered in tattoos.

"Ah, Jeezus H. Christ, Joycey," she muttered. She usually had to go through the fifty states alphabetically in order to tire her mind, but that night in bed she only got to Delaware before she was fast asleep.

17

Urban Light was a contemporary art installation at LACMA consisting of 202 different historical streetlamps from the various neighborhoods of LA. It was set up in an enormous, closely packed chessboard of lamps, and it was the perfect place to meet Stevens. Although the lamps were lit, it was impossible to really see who was moving in and out among them. Amanda felt entirely invisible in the middle of a city that was designed for maximum visibility. Most people wanted to be seen. There were few places to hide.

"So," Stevens said, biting into an arepa that he bought at the food truck across the street. Outside the installation, they could hear the muffled conversation and the clinks and clicks of the waiters setting tables in the outdoor patio restaurant, while a jazz band set up to provide ambiance for hipster date night.

"So. Here," Amanda said, handing him a few menus.

"What's this? I already ate." Stevens neatly wiped the corners of his mouth with a napkin, took his last bite, and looked her in the eye. A tiny drop of salsa still hung on the scar across the left side of his face that went from nostril to earlobe. He must have been knifed by some shady perp. Or the scar was evidence of some hot water in Afghanistan. He cracked his knuckles. "But if you haven't eaten, I'm happy to take you out." He bit his knuckle then and sighed, shaking his head. "That ass. You are one fine piece of ass, Ms. Cooper. I find it distracting, I have to admit."

Amanda leaned against the light post behind her, bent her knee, and slid her foot up the side of it. She had been sure to wear her most lacquered of lacquered pumps and she instinctively lowered her gaze. "You're not too bad yourself," she admitted. He had a swarthy East Coast edge to him, sharpened and shaded in all the right places. Stoically hiding some deep and damaging secrets. California men, in contrast, were so baldly and nakedly transparent. New, smooth, bouncing-baby souls with no distinctive suffering. Pain is what makes a person interesting. Stevens was actually very interesting.

"So can I take you for dinner?" he asked. "You can tell me what you really know. Maybe a meaty Cabernet will get it out of you."

"You're currently blackmailing me, threatening to put my mother in prison, and asking me to betray my stepfather," Amanda said, torturing him by sliding her pendant back and forth along the necklace that hung above her cleavage. "But let me think about that for a second." She tapped her forehead in faux contemplation. "Do I want you to take me to dinner?" She then looked him in the eye and said, "Absolutely not."

Stevens practically slurped as he inhaled and said under his breath, "God, what I would do to you. You have no idea what you're missing." Then he shook himself out of it and said, "Well, this is crap." He waved the menus in her face.

"The taquerias might be some kind of network. They might communicate somehow with menus and delivery boys."

"Menus and delivery boys," he said. It was not a question but a statement of incredulity. He shook his head. "I give you all this time, and you give me Taco Tuesday?" His face turned red with fury.

"Yes?" she asked.

"Is this all you have? A bunch of menus?"

"You asked me to tell you how he's communicating. This may be how. The man doesn't eat Mexican, but he's swimming in these menus. And he circled items that don't match his orders. There's something here, I know it."

"I need more," he said, exhaling.

"More?" Amanda held out her arms. "You're the agent. You figure it out. I even broke in to the storage units yesterday. No weapons. No drugs. He's not storing anything at L'Affordable."

Amanda could feel his frustration rise. Like most people, he hated not getting what he wanted when he wanted it. His anger was a tangible thing that grew between them next to the pillar cloud of lust that was already hovering there. They really should just have sex and start over, Amanda thought, just to clear the air.

He calmed himself down and then said, "Fine. I'll have my guys look into this, see if anything pops."

"Good," Amanda said, and then headed home after taking a requisite selfie inside the yellow hoses of *Penetrable* by the front entrance of the museum, managing to get Stevens in the background of the shot. She was so relieved to have one monster off her back that she could only think that she'd done the right thing. She protected Joyce, and left Bruce to his own devices. He'd understand, right? She didn't give too much away. Not enough to pin anything on him. She did what she had to do for family. "To family," she imagined herself saying to him. It was the very last line of *Moonstruck*.

—

"Amanda, watch this," Joyce bragged when Amanda got up the next morning. It was Wednesday, and Taylor was still asleep. Joyce sat at the dining room table, wearing her expensive orange and green tortoiseshell glasses attached to a gold chain and pointed to the screen of her MacBook.

Amanda wasn't used to her mother being facile with the computer. Her mother was born not only on the wrong side of luck, but on the wrong side of the digital divide, which is where Amanda thought she would stay forever. Just two weeks ago the woman even signed her own texts. *Amanda, bring home milk. Your Mother.* But look now.

Here she was adeptly hacking into some woman's Patient Account at UCLA Medical Center. She had Cedars-Sinai open in another tab. St. John's in a third.

"These ladies don't know that they can request refills online or trigger their Medicaid refunds just by logging in to this website. Silly old widows."

"Mom. These poor old ladies."

"Old, maybe. Poor, they are not, Liebchen. First I filter for the towns ending in 'Hills.' Beverly, Manhattan Beach, Hidden, and Rolling. Then filter by 'Canyon' and then add 'Malibu' and 'Palisades.' I am collating for myself one wealthy subset of widows who have done nothing to deserve their wealth aside from give blow jobs to assholes just like the rest of us. They just chose luckier assholes. I am in the business of wealth redistribution."

"Um, yeah," Amanda said. The language. It felt like being back in prison and hearing one *blow job* and two *assholes* before her first cup of coffee. "Since when have you ever used the word *subset*?" she asked. The rest, Joyce's Robin Hood spiel, she'd heard a million times before.

"I took a little computer class at the senior center."

"And they taught you how to hack into patient databases?"

"No. They taught me how to filter. The rest I taught myself, with my uncanny wisdom about human nature. These old bats are so stupid about passwords that most of them use their dead husband's name and birthdate. They're so self-abasing and devoted to their servitude, even in death, they would never even use their own names. Then voilà. I'm in. I change the address in the profile, request my refund and my refills, and I'm flush with oxy, Prozac, Paxil, Zoloft, Klonopin, even medical marijuana. These ladies are on some heavy shit; no wonder they can't drive around here. . . . And their refund checks get sent to a PO box. The money? They won't even miss it. And the drugs, they'll just ask for more. Everybody wins! I'm taking this operation into the twenty-first century. I can't believe how easy this is."

"Mom . . . Maybe you should slow down just a little. There's nothing easier to trace than a cyber trail. Did they teach you *that* at the senior center?"

"No. But they taught us Facebook and that is a gold mine of a hacking opportunity right there. Old ladies all over that thing telling everyone where they're going and when's the best time to rob their houses. Why don't you join me? You can help me cover up the cyber trail. I know you know how to do this. And I know the other things."

"What other things?"

"You have social media. I have social capital."

"What does that even mean?"

"It means I know people in high places. Jimmy at Wells Fargo. Marge at the DMV. Janice at Kaiser Permanente. And."

"And what?"

"I watch people. I have an uncanny way of figuring them out. For example," Joyce said, exhaling from her third Benson & Hedges of the day. She only allowed herself three a day. She had amazing self-control.

"Yes," Amanda said, distractedly leafing through *People* magazine on the table.

"So at bingo, I sit with the old ladies and I hear them chat. Idle chatter about their grandchildren, their deceased husbands, their boy-friends in the assisted living who've given them the clap."

"Mom!"

"You don't like the heat, get out of the kitchen. You put a bunch of single seniors in a coed dorm they're going to revert to their col-lege days. Plus. Viagra. Blew the field wide open. Anyway. Was playing with this lovey-dovey couple Frank and Marla and he kept calling her 'Pippie.' So I come home, find her Facebook, and log in as her. Pass-word: Pippie01. See a bunch of ads for Chico's. So I go there. Chico's website. Log in as Pippie. She has her credit card on file so I order myself a couple new sequined jackets. Bada bing. We'd make a great team."

"Mom . . ." Amanda started. Her mother looked small and with-ered sitting there in the chair. Her lifetime of dieting had left her vulnerable to osteoporosis, and she was literally melting before Amanda's eyes like the Wicked Witch of the West. But inside the shrunken, elven shell of herself, her spirit was still so fiery. *What is feeding that?* she wondered. *What keeps her fighting?* At forty-two Amanda was already exhausted by it all. She looked again at her mom, pleading with over-sized eyes that had taken over her shrinking face.

"You can help, Mandy. It could be our little project. Look, I have this map. We need to randomize it so it's not all happening in the same place. You could do like . . . what's the word? Some kind of algorithm."

"I have a job, Mom."

"It's not a job if you're not supporting yourself."

"It's not a job if it's a crime," Amanda countered.

"Pulllease, Mandy. Everything we do in this consumerist free market economy is a crime against humanity. The market has no morals. Dog. Eat. Dog. They set it up this way. So, we eat each other. You have to be in it to win it. And none of it is legal or moral. What I'm doing is entrepreneurial."

"It's stealing."

"Uh huh. Just like the big banks and the CEOs. Just taking my piece of the pie. Never mind. I just thought we could do something together," Joyce said, looking away.

And, cue the guilt. Her mother had no idea how much Amanda wanted, craved even, engaging in a collaborative project with her, spending time with her before it was too late, laughing with her, finding out her *story*. The way mothers and daughters do. But she wished the project could be making a family quilt, or taking a spa vacation or Mediterranean cruise, spending a week in Hawaii.

"Why don't we spend a week in Hawaii or something? When I can travel again." Amanda asked.

In one sad, wise look Joyce acknowledged the fact that that would never, in a million years, happen and that in spite of their both craving some kind of deep connection, it could never happen because they were born very different people, in different times, who wanted different things. "Sure Mandy. Hawaii would be nice," she lied. And then Amanda thought she caught the beginnings of a tear. Her mother was as lonely as the rest of us, she realized. And last night Amanda betrayed the only thing her mother really loved. But she did it for Joyce, she reminded herself.

"So what about Bruce, Mom?"

"What about him?"

"Could he maybe help with this?"

"This is women's work. He's busy with his own stuff."

"Why haven't you two gotten married?"

"There are different kinds of married, Liebchen."

"So, you love him?" Amanda ventured, getting up and pretending to put some extra milk in her coffee so she wouldn't have to see the truth on her mother's face.

"I love him awful," her mother said with a sigh. It was another quote from *Moonstruck*. Amanda hadn't realized Joyce watched the movie as closely as she and Bruce did. She always thought it was her thing with Bruce.

"That's too bad," Amanda said with a wink, staying on script. But she realized, too late, the ramifications of her action last night. She'd set the dogs after Bruce. And if they took him down, her mother would go down, too. It would finally kill her spirit. The only thing she had left.

18

An hour later, a knock sounded at the door.

Amanda opened it to find Ben. He was wearing cleaner jeans this time and his plaid shirt was somewhat pressed. The usual base layer shirt printed with a cat face wearing an astronaut helmet was replaced with a plain black tee. *Dressed to impress*, Amanda thought. "Just here to check on the faucet," he said.

"Sure you are," Joyce mumbled. "I'm sure the pipes are fine right now. She's only forty-two. Stuff gets jammed up pretty quickly after forty-six though, so you better act now."

"Mom," Amanda gasped, but she was secretly grateful to hear that after their conversation, she'd quickly snapped back to her snarky old self.

"What?" Joyce asked without looking up from her screen.

"Please. Ignore her," Amanda said. "I'm taking her to the dementia doctor this afternoon. Come in."

"Actually it's a nice day, so I thought . . ."

"Imagine that. A nice day in LA. Really, is that all you got?" Joyce said sarcastically. "I thought better of you, Ben."

"Mom. Two words. Assisted. Living." Nothing shuts up a senior person better than the words *assisted living*.

"You're just jealous, Joycey. I know," Ben said and walked over and gave her a hug that she struggled out of. "So afraid of the intimacy, Joycey, what were you raised by, bears?"

"No. Worse. WASPs," she said, turning her focus back to the computer.

"Taylor! I'm leaving," Amanda called down the hallway.

Taylor wouldn't dare grace them with her full bodily presence, but she hung her head out her bedroom door to take a look. "You are? With him?" she asked, quickly putting it all together. Amanda could see the gears of her daughter's brain slowly turn from *Ew, gross* to capitulation. *Huh. Ben. It could be worse. At least she's not hiding it from me.* "Ben, keep an eye on your wallet," she said and then ducked back into her bedroom.

Amanda threw on a jacket. "Back soon," she said to Joyce.

"Fine. Just get out of here. I have work to do," she said, waving them away.

"What's she doing on the computer?" Ben asked as they climbed into his truck. The preciousness of the antique truck bothered her a little less today for some reason. Maybe because she couldn't wait to kiss him again.

"You don't want to know. She took a class."

"That woman will rule the world."

"In her mind, she already does. So where are we going?" She'd never been on a date in the daytime before. In fact, in the business she was in, she usually slept through most of Saturday. Evan, if he woke before four, which he never did, would probably take her to a very public boozy brunch full of paparazzi. Somewhere with that new rustic industrial decor: poured cement flooring, steel barstools, communal tables, visible steel girder beams, and air ducts. "Please nowhere where you can see the inner workings of the ventilation system," she said.

"Not a problem," Ben said, and after a quick stop to grab coffee, he pulled over in two minutes.

"Wait, we're still in Van Nuys."

"Don't tell me you've never been here."

"Where?"

"The Japanese garden."

"Isn't it like a sewage plant?"

"Well. No. Snoberino. It's technically a 'water reclamation plant.'"

"The difference being . . . ?"

"I guess there is no difference. But just put that out of your mind for a second and witness the beauty of SuihoEn. The Garden of Water and Fragrance," he said as he pointed to the sign at the entrance.

"Fragrance," Amanda laughed.

"What?"

"It's just that there's no irony. No one is laughing about using the word *fragrance* to describe what's going on when you plant flowers in a sewer. They just flat out expect you to go with it."

"You'll see," Ben said. "It's cool. Not everything has to be ironic, does it?"

"Kind of. We've outlived our authenticity. Especially in this place. A sewer dressed up as a garden is kind of a metaphor for LA."

"How so?"

"Well, LA is just one big shitty high school, right? Dressed up as some glamorous hub for the making of art. Really it's one shallow, idiotic high school popularity contest. It's a sewer decorated with flowers."

"Except for Frances McDormand."

"Exactly! Except for Frances McDormand. She's the only evolved being in the entire metropolis," she said, clicking the plastic lid of her to-go coffee cup against his.

"Well, will you at least give it a chance?"

"You know what they say in AA, 'Don't quit five minutes before the miracle happens.'"

"First of all, miracle? That's a lot of pressure. I never promised you a rose garden."

"Actually, that's exactly what you promised."

"Oh yeah. Come on," he said, and he grabbed her hand and softly caressed the palm of it with his thumb, as her insides melted.

"You have the thumb of a master craftsman," she joked, to which he just raised and lowered his eyebrows.

SuihoEn was to gardens what sushi was to food. So delicately crafted and meticulously balanced that in controlling the nature of it, it somehow seemed more natural. It reminded Amanda of Central Park because while they could see LA beyond the boundaries of the garden, they also felt entirely removed from the city. Every sense was evoked, the sound of rushing water, and the chirping of birds, the smell of the tiny tea roses. The breeze here felt softer and less abrasive than the one that rushes past you on the beaches of the Pacific, and the colors and textures were perfectly in tune with one another. Nothing too rounded or sharp. It was a tiny paradise in the middle of Van Nuys.

They walked for a while along the perfectly planned circuitous paths, and Amanda thought how simple this was compared to her life with Evan and the other men she "dated." With Evan, she had to look the right way and say the right things to all the right people as he paraded her around like a dog on a leash. This was all just so natural and simple. No wonder AA counseled to *Keep It Simple, Stupid*. Alcoholics and all of us get addicted to drama and crisis and complexity.

She was a drama queen with Taylor's father, too. She was young when they met, and powerless. She created all this drama and jealous rage to prove that she had power, if not over anything else, then over their relationship.

It was before Amanda decided to get into her mother's line of work and after her failed year at college. She worked at the beach, managing a Sunglass Hut, and he came in with his movie-star looks, all dark, swarthy, and relaxed. Tan. And she wanted him. The second she slid the Ray-Bans onto the bridge of his nose. So much it blinded her to his weaknesses.

He was a typical Californian when he was young. Not narcissistic, per se, not then at least, but kindly unable to put anyone's needs before his own. It was a trait she'd found in a lot of people who grew up here. An inability to commingle, cohabitate, collaborate. A lack of consideration. Whereas people she'd met from the East Coast would drop everything and come to your aid if you went into labor, say, or got into a car accident or needed a ride, a West Coast person would kindly leave you hanging because the surf was up or they had a pedicure appointment.

Mike was like this. Amanda would call him at work and ask for some help with Taylor or ask him to pick up some milk and he'd happily and nicely (always so nice!) tell her he couldn't swing it because he had to go to the gym or get his surfboard waxed. Amanda would fly into a rage when he got home, trying to stir some kind of emotion in him. But he never took anything on. It bothered her that nothing ever bothered him. She was furious and dramatic and thought it was evidence of her passion, but really it was her immaturity and her secret disappointment that she had chosen the wrong father for her child.

And yet simplicity didn't have to be boring. There could be multitudes in simplicity, she thought as they paused to look at a waterfall.

"This really is beautiful," Amanda said as they stood on a rounded bridge and listened to the brook babble beneath them. "It's completely removed my snark. They should call it the Optimism Garden, because that is what it has temporarily restored in me."

"Temporarily?" Ben asked.

"Yes, I'm sure the negativity will come rushing back as soon as I hit the parking lot."

"The Optimism Garden versus the Parking Lot of Pessimism."

"Exactly. That's how fragile my hopes and dreams can be."

"What are you hoping for now?"

"I'm not hoping, just wondering."

"What?"

"Wondering why you haven't kissed me already. We're, like, standing here on the bridge," Amanda said, pressing herself closer to Ben and tracing her index finger along his luscious bottom lip.

The kiss was the kind that made you believe in the Force. Or the

Tao, which is really just where Lucas got the idea for the Force. In kissing, they became the Force. Melding their scattered weak energies into the one powerful, throbbing energy that infused all living things. *With an emphasis on the throbbing*, Amanda thought and then giggled.

"What's funny?" Ben asked, breaking away.

"Nothing," Amanda said and kissed him again. The air between them was dense and thick, as if the oxygen molecules had morphed into some heavy noble gas like argon, pulling them deeper and deeper into each other. "We need to go," Amanda said.

"We do?"

"Unless you want me to take you right here," Amanda said, shocking herself. She inhaled deeply, trying to take in as much of the heavy Ben-scented air that hung between them as she could, then slid her index finger down his chest, between his pecs, and traced an S shape with it so she could feel all the strong ripples of his abs before landing on the upper edge of his belt buckle.

"That would be exciting," he said.

"But perhaps a little amateurish," Amanda finished.

"I don't know if I can wait."

"Good things come to those who do," she said, and led him back to the car. They barely made it back to Ben's apartment, christening the kitchen at the top of the stairs and then the living room and ending up in the bedroom, which was, not surprisingly, cloaked in different shades of bachelor beige.

"Well, now I'm embarrassed," Amanda admitted. "If LA is high school, then I guess I'm the queen slut. I guess that's what happens after two years of . . . never mind."

"I think it had more to do with these guns," Ben said, flexing his biceps jokingly, "than your time in the pen."

"So you know about that?" Amanda asked, "And don't be flexing those unless you're ready for another showdown," she continued, stroking the smooth skin on the inside of his right bicep.

"You're insatiable."

"Again. Two years. Women's prison. And no, I did not have a prison girlfriend. I know that's what you want to ask. No. Everyone basically left me alone. And I read. A lot. And I went to AA meetings."

"Did you used to drink?"

"Never. I just really got a lot out of recovery theory. The accepting yourself, taking one day at a time, doing the next best thing kind of life path. It helped me through things. I can see how it works."

"It works if you work it," Ben said.

"Exactly," Amanda replied. "Speaking of work . . ." she said, getting up and checking the clock.

"Now?"

"Markdown keeps very convenient hours."

19

Her favorite thing to do at Markdown was to organize the infant/ toddler section. It was the only clothing that wasn't emblazoned with crass, slightly racist, fascist emblems of what people considered expressions of their warped patriotism. The infant section was the only place in the entire store where she could find some peace.

She kept the baby blankets and the little hats and booties and tiny little pants and onesies meticulously organized and let her mind drift back to when Taylor was a baby. Amanda was surprisingly good at parenting a baby. Babies, like puppies, are entirely without malice. And it was the only time you, as a parent, could keep things entirely under your control. She liked that about it. The innocence and the control. How you could create your own schedule and engineer your own peace as long as you didn't forget the diaper bag.

Mike was still in the picture during that first rocky year, so Amanda stayed home with Taylor and created a false domesticity that she knew, because neither of them were bred for such a thing, would eventually implode. It did. Mike was gone before she turned two. But that one year home alone with Tay was baby powder–scented bliss.

She tried to relive the feeling as she focused more and more on stocking the shipments of pacifiers and let boxes and boxes of the shirts printed with Yoda giving everyone the finger pile up in the stockroom.

She was hanging some new sippy cups and folding some baby

blankets when she looked up and noticed Anne Schiller, PTA president, checking out a tiny Christmas outfit for a boy baby that came complete with a bow tie and a tiny green velvet vest.

Amanda audibly gasped before scurrying to Automotive, trying to think of a department a PTA president would not frequent at Markdown. She could not be seen in this uniform by anyone from Taylor's school, or Tay would not hear the end of it.

If Russ was awake and not napping in his office, she knew he was watching her every move on the sales floor, so she snuck into Sporting Goods and crawled into an assembled green pup tent in the camping section. Her palms sweat in the stale air of the tent and her skin glowed a phosphorescent green. A tiny trickle of sweat made its way down the side of her forehead following the edge of her hairline. She took a deep breath and thought, *There are no coincidences in AA.* Anne Schiller, PTA president, was here for a reason. It was a reminder for Amanda to start her normal life. She had logged Anne's number in her cell phone in case she ever got the courage to RSVP to the Winter Festival meeting, and she called her to do just that from inside her secret, sweaty tent.

Anne picked up on the first ring, answering by stating her name. Amanda was surprised she didn't also announce her title, Anne Schiller, PTA president, but she didn't, thankfully.

"Hi, Anne. This is Amanda Cooper."

"Who?" Anne said.

"Um, Amanda Cooper. We bumped into each other at the high school and you gave me your card."

"Oh, yes. Are you okay? You sound like you're trapped somewhere. Muffled."

With that, Amanda knew Anne was not raised in California. Californians don't ask if you're okay, they just assume that you are. Which is good and bad. Good, because: optimism. Bad, because they know if they don't ask then they won't have to help.

"I'm fine." Amanda could hear the click of Anne's cowboy boots two-stepping closer to her tent. She peeked out the mesh window, making sure she wasn't too close, before saying, "I'm fine. Would you remind me when that meeting is for the Winter Festival? I'd like to attend."

"Oh great! The more the merrier. We have so much to do. It's today, actually. Four thirty. My house," and then she gave Amanda the address.

She could make it if she didn't run into Russ in the breakroom again. She'd ask Lupita to punch her time card at four. She watched from the tent as Anne hung up the phone and then she tried to gauge her reaction to the call. Was she really happy Amanda would be joining them or annoyed by the late RSVP? Amanda didn't notice an eye roll or anything, so maybe this chick was a person who meant what she said.

Amanda was going to a PTA meeting. In for four, hold for seven, out for eight.

—

Anne's home was a ranch near Culver City with close neighbors, a small yard, and a detached man-cave garage in the back. It was well landscaped and inside, the decor was an eclectic mix of art from Spain and Mexico, all of which was probably dusted once a week by a staff of immigrant housekeepers. But by California standards, it was modest. No pool. No second story. No security gate, and the groceries, Amanda noticed from glancing at the recycling waiting to be picked up at the curb, came from Vons and not Gelson's. Maybe Amanda could be herself here. Whoever that was.

In for four, hold for seven, out for eight, Amanda breathed, and then tried to decide whether to ring the doorbell with a trembling finger. *WWCFD?* she wondered. She tried to summon up the hologram of Princess Leia to ask it for advice. She imagined it flashing in front of her, crackling with static.

"Go for it," said the hologram. "You know what I always say. You must do the thing you think you cannot do."

"Eleanor Roosevelt said that," Amanda almost answered out loud.

"Really? What a coincidence. Anyway. You're showing signs of social anxiety. You might have used the booze to medicate it. But now, you're out here naked and sober and about to face a room full of trampy, vicious stranger-moms."

"How is that helpful?" Amanda asked the hologram. "I had already assessed the situation. How do I cope with this?"

"Fake it 'til you make it," she said, and then zapped away like Gazoo used to do on *The Flintstones*.

Amanda rang the bell.

Anne came to the door holding a glass of wine, and she ushered Amanda into the kitchen where the ladies sat around the island picking at olives and salted Marcona almonds.

"Ladies, this is Amanda," Anne said, but since this was the era of rudeness ushered in by the Internet and its ability to make everyone forget their face-to-face manners, no one bothered to halt their conversations, except a nice, shy Mexican woman, who held out her hand and said, "I'm Carlita."

"Nice to meet you," Amanda said. It was everything she could do to pull up a stool and not bolt for the door. Every warning light in her social consciousness was blaring out, *Emergency, emergency, evacuate now!* But Amanda stayed and politely listened to the chatter about colleges, SAT scores, who's dating whom, which teachers were pregnant, when Anne called the meeting to order by tapping on an old cowbell.

"More cowbell," someone said in a Christopher Walken impression. Amanda thought she could like this woman, but the other ladies didn't understand, and the room quieted.

"We have some new faces joining us," Anne said, handing Amanda a glass of red wine. She was going to refuse it, since she hadn't drunk since her first and only year at college, and then looked around and decided to sip it. It might be necessary. "I thought since we had some newbies," Anne continued, "that we'd do a little ice breaker to get started."

Uh-oh. Amanda gulped a larger sip of wine.

"There's an orange Post-it Note in front of you. I know most of you know one another, but try to think of something about yourself that none of us knows and write it on the Post-it. Fold it up and put it in the bowl in the center of the table. We'll read them one by one and try to figure out who wrote what. Fun?"

"Yes," said the ladies. Amanda eyed the women around the table. Each was shining and glowing and stunningly beautiful, using every California tool at their disposals to grasp and hold on to the final desperate shreds of their youth. It was working. They were still toned, with bright eyes and shiny hair in a rainbow of hues the color of hardwood floor samples. But every once in a while, a glance or a movement would betray the old lady inside them just waiting to poke through. A hunched shoulder, the crinkling of crepe-paper skin near someone's armpit, the traces of smoker lines around another's mouth.

The women giggled slyly and glanced mischievously around the room as they wrote down their secret confessions, and Amanda gulped her wine again. Her face immediately flushed with its warmth. Steeled with liquid courage, she grabbed her pen and wrote:

I had a three-month gig, once, where I danced in a cage in a nightclub in Vegas.

She folded it and winked as she dropped her confession into the bowl with the rest of the slips. One woman nervously equivocated, chewing on her pen and crossing out one secret before starting over with another three times. Finally she was satisfied and dropped her slip into the bowl.

Anne grabbed the bowl and shook it around and selected the first Post-it, folded so many times it must be something juicy like *I never told you about my first marriage* or *I was Julia Roberts's butt double in*

Mystic Pizza. But instead, Anne's eyes crinkled sweetly as she read, "I've always wanted to write poetry."

What? That was pretty tame for a truth-or-dare-type confession. People went around the room assigning a name to the secret. Most people guessed Sandy, when it was really Kelly who wanted to write the poetry. Amanda broke out in a cold sweat as Anne reached for the bowl to pull out the next slip.

"I was in the Peace Corps in Namibia."

Uh-oh, Amanda thought. *I played the wrong game . . .* Why did she think she could do this? Hang out at a PTA meeting? What was she thinking? What was her next move? She could dump her wine in the fishbowl or get up and leave.

She chose all of the above.

As the women were contemplating which of them was bold enough to spend two years in Africa without a blow-dryer, Amanda stood up, pretended to clumsily reach for an olive, and then dumped her red wine into the bowl. The purple liquid splattered on top of the orange paper, seeping into it in a psychedelic tie-dye pattern as Amanda apologized and grabbed a napkin, pretending to sop up the wine, but really pressing it into the paper to make the rest of the notes illegible.

"Oh my gosh, I am so sorry," she lied. "I am such a klutz! I guess that's my secret. Amanda the clumsy one," she said. And then, as if a higher power were actually watching over her, her phone rang. She didn't bother to answer it; she pretended it was a work thing. "I'm on call tonight," she said, "and I have to run. It was so nice meeting you all. Just shoot me an e-mail and let me know what committee I'm on."

The call was from Taylor, so she immediately rang her back when she was in the car. "What's up, Tay?" she asked.

"Nothing."

"Did you call me, hon?"

"Yeah."

"So what's up?" she asked again.

"I was just thinking about how you're trying to be normal."

"Yeah?"

"Yeah. I think it's a valiant, noble thing you're doing. You inspired me."

"I did?"

"Yeah. I stopped working for Grammy."

"What do you mean 'working for Grammy'?"

"Nothing. I just did her a few favors now and then, and I decided to stop doing those."

Amanda suppressed her fury at her mother so she wouldn't scare Taylor off the phone. "That's great, hon."

"I'm going to focus on my grades and my applications and stuff."

"Good, Taylor! I can help you. I have a plan for us. An escape plan. You and me against the world."

"Sounds good."

"But, hon?"

"Yeah?"

"Will you love me if I can't be in the PTA?" she asked.

"Mom, I told you not to go."

"But will you love me if I can't be in the PTA?" She needed to know.

"I love you, Mom."

"I love you, too. We'll do this, okay? One day at a time."

"Okay," Taylor said. "I'll see you tomorrow. I'm babysitting for Dad."

"Is he using you too much, Tay? I want you to have a relationship with him, but I don't want him taking advantage."

"I got this, Mom," Taylor said, a familiar refrain of the teen go-getters on Instagram, and Amanda believed her. They had this.

She drove the van back to the epitome of soullessness but because of her good mood even that bleak structure seemed to sparkle with the cozy hominess of the lemon tree and the scooters and the pink Dora the Explorer basketball deflated and rotting in the corner. It all made her smile for some reason.

She opened the garage door and closed it behind her, then got out of the car. She looked to see if the light was on at Ben's house and was tempted to drop in for a booty call, but then got hold of herself. Men hate being pursued. She'd have to remember to tell Taylor that at some point. You must always, always, always let them come to you. Always. No matter how long they torture you and make you wait.

She climbed the wooden stairs in the dark, fiddling for her keys in her purse, when she heard a deep male voice bellow from the top step right in front of her, "Hello, *Amanda*."

Amanda screamed and would have tumbled backward down the stairs if he hadn't stood up to grab her forearm.

"Come on in," he said calmly, guiding her gently to the top step before forcefully kicking in the cheap door. "I've missed you," he said, locking eyes with her.

Evan.

20

Amanda's soul exited her body, an old habit she'd developed while dating a psychopath for two years. People think psychopaths are rare crazies existing at the end of the bell curve of normalcy, frequently locked up away from the world—the freak, fictional subjects of thrillers and horror films. But that's not true. They actually walk among us. Blending in. Their innate charm blinding everyone to their inner viciousness.

"So glad to finally catch up with you. It's been a while," he said. "How have you been?" he asked casually, his voice rising dangerously at the end of the question. Amanda flinched. His hair product had been melting in the heat of the garage so his greasy bangs fell in front of his left eye. His tie was loose and his sleeves were rolled up, as if ready to get down to business. She looked directly into the green irises of the eyes that had so endeared him to his mother.

"I've been good, Evan," she said carefully. She tried to sense whether her mom was in the house and hoped Taylor was safe at her father's.

"That's good. I'm glad you've been good. See, I haven't been that good," he said.

"I'm sorry to hear that. Everything okay with your mother?" she asked, thinking it was a good idea to evoke his beloved mother and perhaps what remained of his conscience.

"Yeah. She's fine, thanks for asking. A little issue with her blood pressure meds last week, but we've cleared it up."

"Good to hear it," Amanda said, sitting down on the couch. "That's great."

"Yeah. What isn't great is that my fiancée skipped town two years ago and embezzled two hundred thousand of my assets, not to mention a fifty-thousand-dollar engagement ring. She wasn't even classy enough to give me the ring back," he said, pacing back and forth in front of the couch.

"Surely, that must be water under the bridge by now," Amanda tried. She scooched herself as far back as she could go on the couch, trying to put as much distance between them as possible. He would never hit her. It was his personal code: no physical violence against women. But he'd killed a few men in Vegas and was the initiator of more than one murder for hire. He was dangerous and she had crossed him. He'd make her pay somehow, now that he'd found her.

"Petty change, really. I was disappointed that you didn't aim higher. It's not the money that bothers me," he said, opening and closing his fist as if wanting to warm it up before putting it to good use. He looked at Amanda then, defeated. "I gave you everything," he said. "What else could you have possibly wanted?"

"You were very generous," she said, trying to quell the situation.

"You must hate me so much. So much that you'd go to prison to hide from me. That's a lot of hate."

"The prison thing was an accident, actually," Amanda mumbled. "Completely unrelated to the situation at hand."

"Did you think I wouldn't come for you? You're the only woman I ever proposed to. The only woman who met my mother."

"I'm flattered," Amanda said, trying to stand up, but he signaled calmly for her to sit back down.

"Don't get smart, *Amanda*," he said. Her real name sounded foreign on his tongue. He pulled her to standing, kicking the cheap coffee table out of the way, and moved closer to her. She knew not to back away. It would only infuriate him further. She could feel his breath on her face. A blend of whiskey and spearmint.

She gripped the recliner beside her, searching for an escape. "Did you think I wouldn't find you? That's what I don't understand. I professed my undying love for you, gave you everything that women like. Or maybe you found what you like in prison. Maybe I underestimated your hunger for the ladies." He stood right in front of her and reached around her neck to run his fingers through her ponytail. He leaned in, until he was centimeters from her lips. "I thought you loved me."

"I still have your money," Amanda said, leaning back. "And the ring."

"You think that's what I want?" he asked.

"I don't know what you want. I'm sure you've had many beautiful young girlfriends since me, Evan. I'm old now. Used up. An ex-con. You can't bring an ex-con home to your mother. I could never fit into your life anymore. You don't want me. Here. I'll go get your money and the ring. We can call it even. You can go home and spend it on your who . . ."

He laughed then. "You think I want you back?"

"I'm not sure what you want," she said, backing her way down the hall to get to the suitcase, so she could try to at least use it as a peace offering.

Breathing was not going to help the situation, so she didn't even try to relax as she thought about everything she had worked for, a suitcase full of money, just going down the tubes. How was she going to start over on her Markdown salary? Her palms dampened and her body shook in an uncontrollable seizure-like tremor. She hated him so much. She had wasted five years of her life that she could never get back, and now she'd have nothing to show for it.

She heard him rummaging through the kitchen cabinets probably looking for some alcohol. In the bedroom, she avoided looking at the mirrored closet door because she could not stomach the visage of herself at her lowest low. Hair limp, eyes bloodshot, complexion gray and sagging. She imagined writing this on an orange Post-it at the PTA meeting. *Often I have hid in my bedroom, praying that a man I know will not become enraged enough to kill me . . . Lol. Smiley face. Smiley face.*

She slid the door open and lifted the first suitcase off the pile. It felt very, very light.

A wave of feverish anxiety flushed through her body again as she pulled the zipper around the top of the case and noticed that the money was gone. The ring, she noticed as she fished around for it frantically, was also missing. *Fuck. Fuck. Fucking Joyce*, she thought, and then without even skipping a beat pulled her phone out of her back pocket and texted Taylor. *Do not come home tonight.* Then she deleted Taylor's contact info altogether in case he got hold of her phone.

She thought of climbing out the bedroom window and going to the police, but what good would that do? She'd been the one who'd stolen from Evan.

"And where the hell is the alcohol in this dump?" he called from the kitchen.

"Under the kitchen sink, darling," she said sarcastically as she rolled the empty bag behind her down the carpeted hallway. *Dead woman walking.*

She thought briefly about how easy it would be to just kill him. Stand behind him and wait until he crawled out from under the sink and then whack him over the back of the head with Joyce's weighted baseball bat. But she'd read *Crime and Punishment* in prison, and the new Franzen, and it was enough to convince her that no one ever got away with murder.

"What's that?" he asked her, pointing at the suitcase. "Where do you think you're going?"

"Nowhere. This used to be filled with your money."

"What do you mean, used to be?"

"I mean, it's gone and I . . ." she started.

Evan had found Bruce's best Scotch hidden behind the Drano and the dishwasher tabs and he'd poured a full four ounces into Taylor's

Elf glass. *I just like to smile, smiling's my favorite*, the glass read as Evan tipped it into his scowling mouth.

"You still don't get it," he said.

"What?"

"Why I'm here," he said, offering her the side with Will Ferrell's face on it.

"No. I guess I don't."

"I don't want money."

"I see that," she said. She had expected him to throw the glass across the room when she told him the suitcase was empty. "What do you want?"

"Let's discuss that over dinner, shall we? In a civil conversation? Although going to prison disqualifies you as a civil, sophisticated human. Boy, I'll give you one thing. You really had me fooled."

"How did you even find me?"

"Once we found that Vanessa Jones was Amanda Cooper, it was easy to find you. Facial recognition software. I had my hounds scan your face and hack into the Registry of Motor Vehicles. You're not the only one who can hack into things."

Just then, Joyce stepped around the broken-down door and said, "What the fuck is going on here?"

"Hi, Mom," Amanda mumbled. "Mom, you remember my fiancé, Evan?"

"Oh, Evan, so nice to finally meet you in person," said Joyce in her saccharine *I'm in the presence of a man* voice. She completely ignored Amanda's shaking hands and the empty suitcase toppled over on the floor. The woman was a fine actor. "What the fuck?" she whispered to Amanda as Evan excused himself to go to the bathroom and wash his hands. He had a hand-washing thing.

"Evan came for some money I was holding for him while I was in prison," Amanda said, staring at her mother accusingly as she watched the blood drain from Joyce's recently Botoxed face. It was frozen into a constant state of apathy to match her stone-cold heart.

"Oh," Joyce said. "Well, I'm sure you two will work that out. Evan, honey, can I get you a sandwich?" she asked loudly, opening the refrigerator in her Donna Reed act, pretending to rustle around for some bologna.

Now Amanda wanted to kill her mother, but matricide, she thought, would be difficult to discuss at her AA meeting and was definitely a violation of parole.

Evan came back into the room wiping his hands on a peach-colored towel. He got a text and said he had to go. "I have business," he said, looking at Amanda. "But trust me, I'll be back. For dinner, where we will civilly discuss your future."

She watched Evan leave in a black car, then ran to the front window and turned her head to see another one waiting in a parking lot across Van Nuys. She thought of all the black cars she'd seen. She'd thought they were Stevens's, but had it been Evan all along? The driver's face was visible in the glow of his iPhone as he paged through screen after screen and then turned it off and unfolded a big newspaper.

"You've. Got. To. Be. Kidding. Me," she said to her mother as she closed the shades. "You stole my money?"

"Oh, please. It's a sure thing, Amanda. Twenty-to-one. An *investment*. You'll have it back tenfold." Joyce waved her hand dismissively, and tried to crease her eyebrows in certainty, but continued staring blankly ahead in a creepy, paralyzed Botox stare.

"You put it all on a horse?" Amanda yelled.

"Not a horse. A sure thing."

"You have impeccable timing," she said, shaking her head. Just then she received a text from Anne at the PTA. *We put you on the decorations committee!!* it said with two exclamation points.

21

AA the next day was just what she needed to get her head together. Amanda sat in the back of yet another church basement as innocent, nonviolent people talked about remaining centered and grounded and present and not projecting into the future. Which was a perfect idea when your future looked like an eternity of being stalked by a madman.

She shared a little bit. Standing up and admitting that she'd been visited by a ghost from her past. They all spouted out platitudes about giving up the past to stay in the present and whatnot, and shared stories about how hard it is to give up your drunk friends when you choose sobriety.

A stay-at-home mom who'd been secretly drinking wine out of a Starbucks cup practically twenty-four hours a day spoke next about comparing "her insides to everyone else's outsides." "I finally realized that all those horrible women in the PTA were more fucked up than I was. I hated them for being able to fake it better than I could. Then I found compassion. And actually invited one to lunch."

After the applause for Pam, Amanda hoisted herself up and made her way to the refreshments table. Carrie Fisher's ghost was there, of course.

"Looks like a run-in with some white knuckle sobriety," she said, handing Amanda a day-old scone. "Ghost from the past was a man, I take it."

"What's that?" Amanda asked. "White-knuckle sobriety?"

"You know. Guys who use the difficulty of recovery as an excuse to beat the hell out of you. A dry drunk. A sober horse thief is still a horse thief. Etcetera."

"This guy isn't even trying to be sober and he would never hit me," Amanda said, throwing the scone in the trash.

"Abuse is not always physical. Threats are a form of abuse," she said, picking the raisins out of her scone and lining them up around the periphery of her paper plate. Amanda worried about her eating habits. Even if they were hallucinatory.

"I just think *abuse* is a strong word."

"Ah, the problem is with you, then. You are not recognizing the Force. Your own power to get rid of the douchebag. Arrivederci," she said and whisked away up the church stairs once again.

—

Afterward, Amanda had to endure another shift at Markdown, this time with a pulsing migraine. The Christmas music was constant now in mid-December and she let the familiar tunes and her nostalgia for them pull her into a stupor of false solitude as she stocked some red-and-green stockings filled with Milk-Bones in the pet food section. She felt entirely alone in her reminiscing head. The music and the stockings and the Milk-Bones reminding her of the one Christmas Bruce dressed as Santa and *I shit you not*, she thought to herself jokingly, actually brought a golden retriever puppy to the window outside her second-grade classroom.

Joyce wasn't the only one with a flair for drama. In his earnest attempt to win her heart, he didn't realize that he'd simultaneously made her the happiest girl in the world and the target of every other kid's resentful scorn. She ran out of the classroom and into the schoolyard, frolicking with her new puppy while the other students lined up at the window and glared at her, plotting their emotional revenge. Amanda was not a popular kid. But she did have a dog. *Which, honestly, can make everything better*, she thought as she unwrapped a huge rope of a pull toy tied into a frayed knot and hung it in its place next to the rubber chickens.

She was so deep in thought that she didn't see him coming, and suddenly Agent Stevens was hovering menacingly behind her like Trump in the second debate. She jumped back when she noticed him and fell into the half wall of the aisle, the hooks for the pull toys jabbing into her back and the squeaker of a stuffed squirrel whining in her ear until she finally got her balance and stood upright. Stevens, an inch away from her, waved some old take-out menus in her face.

"Did you think this was funny, Senorita Taqueria?" he asked. "Did you think I wouldn't find out this was a false lead?" He was large, looming above her like a volcano dressed in a suit, the scar on his face glowed a vicious pink-orange, like a splatter of lava.

Amanda grabbed a leather dog leash in case she needed to use it as a whip to defend herself. "I don't know what you're talking about. These are the menus that were in his desk."

"These restaurants are clean. They have no ties to Bruce or the cartel. You gave me fucking nothing."

"I'm really not feeling very well today," Amanda said, her head throbbing. He had been whisper-yelling at her; she could tell by the straining ligaments in his neck, but he sounded farther and farther away and then he split into seven angry men. "Can we do this tomorrow?" she said.

"What?" all seven Stevenses asked.

Amanda squeezed her eyes shut and when she opened them again they had collected themselves back into one person. A very angry person who was now pointing at her. "We have intel that a two-hundred-pound black tar heroin shipment is happening soon and that Bruce is instrumental in its distribution. Have you seen this?" Stevens asked and then waved a tiny plastic bag branded with a colorful head of a stag. The gang's apparent emblem. "Anything with this marking on it?"

"No," Amanda said honestly.

"No matter." Stevens shook his head then whispered in her ear, "If you don't get me the details, it's not only your mother who's going to prison. The two of you can make it a family affair. I know you've been helping her with her 'prescriptions,'" he said, putting the last word in air quotes. "Judge won't be easy on you second time around, soldier."

Soldier, Amanda thought. Yeah, this guy was definitely military, marines, semper fi. He was not going to go away until he had what he wanted.

"What else can I possibly do? I gave you everything I know," she cried. "I betrayed my stepfather for you."

"Find me something real. Something I can use. When and where is the exchange happening? He has to be planning for it. It's two hundred pounds," Stevens said and then grabbed a big glass bottle of lamb and rice dog treats, smashed it on the floor, and yelled, "Clean up in aisle five!" before stomping angrily away.

Amanda fixed the Pet Food aisle and then forced herself, her hands smelling like rawhide and dusty Milk-Bones, to schlep her tired self to the back desk that Russ had set up for her to pull up reports for the shrinkage scam. She tried to make sense of the spreadsheets fanned out in front of her, but it felt like someone had opened the top of her skull, stuck a whisk in there, and scrambled her brain. The thinking she was usually so good at—making connections between things and seeing the big picture—had been taken from her because of the stress and all she could do was sit and stare at the Christmas aisle with its tiny colored lights blinking on and off in random intervals.

She could create another dude tree to try to compartmentalize all the ways she'd already messed everything up in three short weeks.

Number one: She betrayed her stepfather. She didn't even know who this Stevens was. Was he really in law enforcement? Could he really put Joyce in prison? Put her in prison? Maybe she should have taken her time thinking things through. Maybe she should have told someone about Stevens, rather than working in a vacuum. That's the first step in AA: admitting you need help. Maybe she shouldn't have taken everything into her own hands. "There is a God and I am not it!" she remembered people chanting at her last meeting. I am not God. I can't control everything. I need help. But she truly had no one to turn to. She tried to breathe but could only inhale for two.

Number two: Letting Evan find her was going to ruin everything with Ben. Not to mention Taylor. She'd been good until now at keeping Taylor and Evan apart. He barely mentioned the fact that she had a daughter, and Amanda liked to keep it that way. She didn't want him anywhere near Taylor.

She'd ruined everything. She drew a picture of herself hacking away at the dude tree of her life, before closing her eyes and putting her head down on the desk.

Lupita found her this way and touched her on the shoulder. She jumped because her nerves were obviously shot and Lupita said, "Relax, Amanda. You seem so tense. So upset. What's going on?"

"Oh nothing," Amanda lied. "Just running up against some obstacles. You know. Life," she said, sadly.

"Well, we're grilling tonight. Why don't you come have dinner with my family after work? You like hot dogs?"

Amanda smiled slowly. She got so few offers of friendship. She had to catch a sob in her throat before answering, "Sure. Who doesn't like hot dogs?"

"My youngest, apparently. He's always with the chicken fingers."

"The struggle is real," Amanda said, alluding to the "beige food" nugget rut she'd heard other parents always complaining about. She had been lucky, though. Taylor had always been a fabulous eater. You eat what you're given when you have a faint sense that you may not eat again for a while. Not that they ever went hungry, but she thought Taylor sensed that they someday might. So she ate everything and eventually developed an interest in cooking.

"Can I bring Taylor?"

"Of course! We'd love to meet her."

—

When they got to Lupita's, a tiny one-bedroom that she shared with her sister, carpeted wall-to-wall in beige with some toys piled neatly in a corner next to a sofa bed, Lupita set the groceries down, put on some music, and put Amanda to work.

"Can you please slice these tomatoes, Mandy? And then dice some carrots and onions for the macaroni salad." It was as if Lupita knew exactly what Amanda needed—to feel like a part of something normal.

"This one should do it," Amanda said, nudging Taylor, who, less reluctantly than Amanda expected, agreed to meet Amanda's new friend from work. "She's the one with the knife skills."

"You like to cook, Taylor?"

"A little," Taylor said modestly.

"She made our whole Thanksgiving dinner," Amanda bragged.

Lupita's seven-year-old girl came skipping into the kitchen from the bedroom. "Magda, set the table outside. Get your brother to help."

Without question the little girl grabbed all the paper products and skipped out the door. After five minutes she came back in and said, "Who's that?" pointing at Amanda and Taylor.

"Oh, I'm so sorry. I forgot my manners," Lupita said, turning away from the burgers she was pressing on the kitchen counter. "Magda, these are my friends, Amanda and Taylor. Guys, Magda."

Magda wore perfectly twisted ponytails that looked like thick strands of licorice and she blinked at Amanda for a second with beautiful doll-like brown eyes. "Pleased to meet you," she said.

"Go get your brother, Magda," her mother said, and she went into the bedroom, snapped off the TV, and returned with a five-year-old boy dressed head-to-toe in fluorescent soccer-type gear from Markdown.

"Hiiiiyah," he said, as he threw a karate chop toward Amanda.

"What's your name?" Taylor asked, looking away from the cutting board where she had diced an onion into congruent, translucent squares the size of baby teeth.

"Angel," he said.

"Hi, Angel. I'm Taylor."

"Hiiiiyah," he said again, and karate-chopped with the other hand.

It was all so normal. The family, the patio, the hot dogs. It ignited a glow in Amanda's chest. Almost like ET. She glowed inside and reminded herself, *I can have this. I don't have to give up. I can fix everything.* Or God could, or something. Her higher-power Carrie Fisher might fix it. Somehow it was going to get fixed, and she and Taylor were going to be knitting some effing kick-ass mittens and selling them on Etsy, just as a side business, to help pay for tuition and the stand-alone house with the patio and herb garden.

On the way home in the car, the setting sun sliced through the passenger-side window and threw a stripe of light across Taylor's chest. Amanda took a deep breath.

"Hon," she started. But Taylor was on her phone Snapchatting like it was her job. Amanda would delete the app but Taylor seemed to be doing okay in school and getting home on time and basically doing the right things, so she let her snap away.

"Taylor." Still no answer.

"Tay!" she finally shouted.

"What?"

"Thanks for coming with me tonight. It was fun to, like, socialize for once. Like normal people."

"Yeah," Taylor said without looking up from her phone.

"I need to ask you a favor."

"Okay."

"I need you to stay at your dad's for a week or so while I straighten out some things," Amanda said tentatively.

"Mom," Taylor said, then looked up, blank-faced and wide-eyed with disappointment.

"What, babe?"

"Nothing." She turned her attention back to her phone but Amanda noticed a single tear splash onto the screen before almost slamming into the Ford truck in front of her on the 405.

"Tay?"

"It's just . . ."

"What?"

"This is not how it was supposed to be, Mom. You promised it would be different and here I am and you're sending me away and I don't know when I'll see you again. I don't know why I'm surprised."

"Hon. It's just a week, okay? I need to straighten some things out. By Christmas this will all be a bad memory. We're going to have a normal Christmas and then we're going to start over in the new year. I promise." Amanda really wanted to believe this was true, but her whole body felt empty and shaky. She scanned it and tried to find some solid, tangible weight to anchor her belief in herself, but she couldn't find it, so she lied. "I got this, Taylor."

"I just want my mom," Taylor said, and Amanda could hear her sniffle a little.

"I know, babe. I'm working on it. Here. I got you some things," she said and reached around to the backseat, grabbed a plastic Markdown bag, and slung it on Taylor's lap.

Taylor rooted through the bag, and looked at her mom. "I can't believe you read my journal."

Inside were a pair of knitting needles and a book about how to knit, another book about yarn bombing, and a quilted calico pouch, perfect for storing tampons in a cross-body purse.

"You are not motherless," Amanda said.

"Prove it," said Taylor as they glided into the garage. She grabbed her stuff, pounded up the stairs, threw some stuff into a bag, and left.

22

With Taylor safely ensconced at her father's house, Amanda took out some more of the Mexican food menus she'd stolen from Bruce's desk. *It has to have something to do with these menus*, she thought. She didn't know if it was intuition or something more, but she felt it in her gut. If Stevens's guys couldn't figure it out, she would.

She laid the menus out on her bedroom floor. Each menu item had a number. Some of them were circled. She was sure that that had to correlate with the numbers of the storage units, but the units she checked were all clean.

Maybe they were amounts. Like #87 Chicken Tacos was an order for eighty-seven kilos of cocaine delivered to Pollo Paco's or something, and #56 Barbacoa Burrito could be fifty-six AK-47s delivered to Rancho Riviera. No two items were circled twice, so she couldn't compare one menu to another or notice any trends. She couldn't decipher it without more data.

The next day, Amanda initiated Operation Taco Takedown. Whatever Bruce was doing (if he was doing anything at all!) had something to do with Mexican takeout. She was going on a take-out stake out. If she could give Stevens a credible story, she could perhaps steer him in a slightly skewed direction, prolonging his investigation and getting him off her back.

First she waited in the van, which had become her safe space. Her trusty rusted capsule of isolation. She'd grown to love this rotting jalopy. Its cushy couch upholstery, the faint sweet-and-sour smell of baked-on spilled coffee. It was the only place she could be alone.

She pulled it into an inconspicuous spot in the corner of the bodega parking lot across the street from L'Affordable and let herself enjoy some homemade churros with her coffee, because that's what TV detectives would do, and she waited.

At 11:42 on the dot, a delivery boy on a BMX bike skidded into L'Affordable's gravel parking lot with a greasy brown paper bag strapped to the front of his handlebars. She started the engine. And when he came back out without sticking any money in his pocket and climbed onto his bike, Amanda hit the gas, crashing into a plastic shopping cart, dragging it for a while before hurtling over a speed bump to get to the exit just as the boy turned left on Woodlawn. She followed him, cruising slowly now so as not to pass his pedal pace. She got a little too close at one point and he looked into the car. A young boy, maybe fourteen, who still hadn't begun to shave the soft furry emergence of his first mustache.

Amanda turned to face the road so he wouldn't notice her, and *bam!* he banged a hard, sneaky right onto Desmond. Amanda followed, cranking the van to an instant ninety-degree angle and gunning it as horns blared behind her. They were in a less industrial, residential neighborhood now. Little boxes with big sun-shading roofs lined the street, scooters and Big Wheels scattered around their driveways. She found the kid right before he turned off the road into a cement gully overgrown with vines and dipped out of sight. The gullies in LA were the secret juvenile transit system. Growing up in Van Nuys, she and her friends used to follow them all the way to the pool without ever hitting a main road. They had to watch out for rattlesnakes and coyotes, but sometimes they would take them all the way to the ocean. They were concave, and at their base only wide enough for bikes traveling single file.

Amanda, acting on instinct, parked the van, hopped out, and nabbed a pink two-wheeler with streamers flapping out of the handlebars that was toppled on its side in a driveway. It had training wheels, which would be tricky and might tip her over in the gully, but it was her only option.

She balanced the tires in the groove, gave it a huge kick start, and glided through the luge-like crevice, taking a few hairpin turns, scraping the top of her foot and squashing an innocent toad before the gully spit her out on Borden. She saw the boy on foot, ditched the bike, and ran to keep him in view.

He crossed a busy street and looked around before ducking behind a fence into the yard of a ranch house. The gated yard was strewn with palm fronds and a carpet of crispy gray leaves coughed up from a eucalyptus tree's last dying breath. The boy's feet pulverized them to dust as he slipped between the rails of the fence. Amanda creeped closer.

Euphoric scents emanated from the house. Sharp garlic, fresh cilantro, clean lime, and a diverse and multitudinous smoked-chile musk drifted from cracks in the spray-painted particle board that covered the windows.

Amanda hid behind a palm tree and tried to catch her breath. Then she crawled into the backyard where a splintered, rotten wooden play structure circa 1985 lay collapsed with the weight of its faded plastic swings. Three cases of beer swam around aimlessly in the sun-faded plastic kiddie pool filled with melted ice. Amanda crept up the back stoop and peeked into the kitchen, where a heavy woman in an apron stirred a two-foot-tall aluminum pot and danced a little, swinging her hips to a Latin beat. She cupped her hand beneath her wooden spoon and blew on it, then carried it to the young man sitting at the Formica kitchen table. She held the spoon out to him for a taste. He declined, shaking his head, and she slapped him playfully, demanding his respect for her and her delicious food.

He obliged and then gave her the thumbs-up before returning to his work, weighing out tiny piles of white powder on an old-fashioned scale and then pouring the piles into tiny Ziplocs emblazoned with the head of a stag. The same image Stevens had shown her at Markdown.

There was still a chance that this was just a hole-in-the-wall joint that served up down-home Mexican as a front for its shady drug operation and Bruce had no idea what went on behind the scenes. He was just enamored by the home cooking and ordered lunch here to buy local and keep mom-and-pop joints in business. There was still a chance this was the case.

But it wasn't likely. This scenario was many, many standard deviations from the mean. The boy came out in two minutes, looked to see if he was being followed, and continued on his way, carrying with him another greasy bag of food stapled with a marked-up take-out menu.

At least, she consoled herself, maybe now was the right time for Bruce to step into the cartels. She'd read that after the narco men basically destroyed one another with their viciousness, misogyny, and infighting, a woman had risen to the top of the Tijuana Cartel. La Jefa, they called her, and she was cracking the whip and bringing some organization to organized crime. Maybe Bruce was at least dealing with her. He liked supporting strong women.

She walked to her stolen bike and pushed it back up through the gullies, dropped it in its rightful driveway and got in her car, wondering what to do next.

If she didn't turn in Bruce, the FBI would nab her mother. She imagined her mother in prison and wondered if it would kill her spirit. Would she crumble into depression or would she start her own racket on the inside and have the warden eating out of the palm of her hand? She did not want to find out. She pulled away and eased herself back onto Desmond and made her way to work, ignoring the quick gleam of a black Integra she thought she saw in her rearview before it ducked into a Vons's parking lot.

23

Working the Markdown loading dock had a certain soothing poetry to it, especially in the morning. The spiked weeds around the parking lot were gray with crystalline dew and the few precious LA clouds had not yet burned off to mix with the pollution. They were white and soft and heavy with the smell of water as they hung in the open-door frame of Loading Dock 3, which was empty. It had not yet been crammed with the back of the tractor trailer full of schlock that was due at 9 AM.

Amanda got ready to unload it, laying out her pallets in preparation, and printing out the day's skim sheet listed with the products Russ would set aside. Since it had become such a habit, it had grown to feel more and more like a job and less like a crime. And that worried her. When you began to let your guard down, you almost always got caught.

She worried more about Lupita, actually, than she did herself. Russ had moved her to the "sales" side of the operation—an old shipping container he set up on Venice, which everyone just assumed was a legit hipster pop-up. The plus side of this for Lupita was that Russ framed it as a "promotion" and agreed to pay her a little extra under the table for running the store. It also meant she was getting closer to the end of her parole and could soon leave the Mark altogether and stop having to report to Ken.

The obvious downside was that Lupita was extremely vulnerable out on the street and if she got caught, there was no way Ken or Russ would have her back. They were basically throwing her to the wolves she was named after. Amanda drove out there yesterday to check it out. Lupita had built some stainless steel shelving and stacked the TVs, stereos, blenders, and Keurigs neatly, priced them to move, and decorated the container in dangly luau-like palm fronds and Polynesian flowers. She called it "Island Appliance." Russ had let her do her own merchandising.

"Do they have a permit for this thing?" Amanda asked her. Lupita wore a bright orange muumuu and busied herself by dusting the merch with a feather duster. The container itself was also bright orange and parked in a fire lane. "It's so conspicuous," Amanda said. "They're throwing you to the wolves."

"I'm not afraid of wolves, Mandy," Lupita told her. "I'm just happy to be working out here by the water and not in that horrible box."

"If you haven't noticed, this is also a box. If they're throwing you to the wolves, then they're throwing you under the bus. You should definitely be afraid of the bus."

"*Mami*, relax," Lupita said. "It's only one more month and then I can quit. I need the extra money." She continued dusting a set of crystal wineglasses that were originally stocked for the Pulaski-Jones wedding registry.

Amanda couldn't relax. She was so outraged at how they were using Lupita. And Amanda thought of Lupita's "babies" whom she'd just met. Magda, who had memorized and recited for her all the US presidents and Angel, who grabbed Amanda's hand so trustingly with his small pudgy one and pulled her into the bedroom to show her their betta fish named Lucy, who was really a boy.

Unbeknownst to them, this was really the kids' fourth "Lucy." Lupita had replaced him about three times, Amanda knew, because Markdown wasn't known for its quality pets department.

Anyway, Amanda knew Lupita's kids now. She knew how well she was raising them and how devastated and desperate they'd be if Lupita were deported or sent back to prison. This was all getting too risky.

"You should definitely be afraid of the bus," Amanda repeated. "They won't hesitate to throw you under it."

Lupita was reporting to Russ at the store today and after she finished unloading, Amanda popped her head in on their meeting. Russ was in a congratulatory mood, and when he noticed her, he said, "The blenders are a hit."

"You should come with me next time," Lupita said to her. "White ladies are always asking me crazy questions like, 'Does this come with a one-year warranty?'"

"Naturally." Figures the old white ladies walking their dogs would expect a warranty for something they buy out of a makeshift shipping container. Life had given them so much, they'd come to expect everything they wanted everywhere they went.

"I sold a ton of blenders near Muscle Beach. Those meatheads really like the green juice," Lupita said.

"If you're staying in Venice, you should definitely grab some touristy schlock, like Lakers T-shirts or visors that say CALIFORNIA in sunset letters," Amanda couldn't stop herself from saying.

Venice Beach had become a tourist destination where midwesterners went to verify their preconceived notions about California weirdos. It was only a micro population of Californians, but it did have its share of white people with dreadlocks, grown women roller-skating in bikini tops at 10 AM on a weekday, people who slept on the beach in tents and made jewelry out of bottle caps to pay for food for the dog they kept tied to a rope, ex-starlets dressed in big sunglasses and flowing robes who had that particular mental illness where they couldn't stop applying layers and layers of makeup to their faces. All of that was at Venice Beach. It was a veritable people zoo. And it wasn't a place that was policed very often for vendors' permits. But still Amanda worried for Lupita, so she called Ken on her break.

"So I hear you've been an asset to the Mark," he said. "I've been getting good reports."

"Why don't I have to meet with you and pee in a bottle or whatnot, like most parolees?" Amanda asked. "Is it because you don't want to be associated with me in case this whole thing comes crashing down?"

"I'm certain I don't understand what you're talking about. We get to each parolee when we can. There is a hefty backlog of ne'er-do-wells, as you can rightly imagine, so we do the best we can." Amanda had called him on his cell so he could speak freely and not worry about being recorded for quality assurance.

"Ken, why did you send me here?"

"Where?"

"Markdown."

"I thought you'd be great at sales."

"What's your cut?" Amanda asked. "You send Russ some down-on-their-luck work-order hooligans on whom you can pin the blame when everything comes crashing down."

"I don't know what you're talking about."

"And then you get a cut of the action."

"I have not had any 'action' in over a month, if you know what I mean."

"Gross. Listen, Lupita's going to get caught out there, and if you don't defend her, I swear I will send someone after you. I know some bad people."

"Are you threatening your parole officer?"

And that suddenly gave Amanda a brilliant idea. She did know bad people, and she could use them to take Russ and Ken down. Why hadn't she thought of it before? Maybe Stevens came into her life for a reason. There are no coincidences in AA. It was just a matter of dangling the right bait . . .

"I gotta go," she said. She was getting a call from Taylor.

"It was nice to hear your voice."

"Ach. God! Good-bye," she said.

—

She was probably dehydrated from spending the day under the Mark's fluorescent lights like a pot plant in a dorm-room closet, but after her shift, she had to practically drag herself up the stairs to get to her apartment. All she wanted to do was fall on the bed and pray that the gravity of sleep would pull her into its fullest darkness and not tease her with the light, intermittent, moth-fluttering-in-front-of-a-flame kind of sleep that it usually did. She opened the front door which Ben, without asking questions, had MacGyvered with a crude crisscross of duct tape, but when she went to free fall onto her bed, it was covered with a limited edition blush Herve Leger dress adorned with prism beads that caught the light and covered her walls with tiny rainbows. A note next to it read *Be ready at seven!* in Evan's scratchy man hand. The clock read 6:45.

She was too tired to cry. She just splashed her face with ice-cold water, smeared on a face mask that would hopefully pull her baggy face a little more taut, and slipped into the dress. Then she rinsed off the mask and did what she could with what was left of her pre-prison makeup. She packed a few things in an overnight bag, figuring Evan would be kidnapping her for an indefinite amount of time, and then rustled under the kitchen sink until she found where Bruce stashed the bourbon. She filled Taylor's bunny mug to the halfway mark and chugged it down, reveling in the masochistic burn that slid slowly down her body.

This was so unlike her. She usually liked to remain in control and not anesthetize herself against the world like everyone else did, but she was too tired to face reality. HALT. Hungry. Angry. Lonely. Tired. These were the times when addicts had difficulty with resistance and often gave in.

Joyce's paperwork was scattered all over the kitchen table next to her laptop. Amanda grabbed an envelope addressed to Rita Jenkins that probably held a refund check, and she flipped it over and, just in case, wrote: *Away on business. Consulting. Hopefully back early tomorrow. Be good.* Taylor was supposed to be at her father's, but she often came home early.

"Ding-dong," she heard someone say behind her. Evan stood in the doorway with a single red long-stemmed rose that made Amanda want to hurl. *What, are we going to the prom?* Evan could also be so utterly infantile. "You ready?"

"Let's go," she replied. She led him down the stairs and he guided her out of the garage with a hand placed gently, for now, on the small of her back. She didn't know what prompted her to do it, but before climbing into the shiny black limo, she looked up at Ben's apartment window and found him holding a cup of coffee and gazing sadly down at her. He held up the mug, as if to say "cheers" then walked away, letting the beige curtain swing back into place.

This is why I can't have nice things, she said to herself with a sigh. Why did she ever think she could have a normal Ben-style relationship?

24

"Isn't this romantic?" she said. "Let me go powder my nose." Evan had stolen her away to Vegas on his jet and smuggled her into the back room of TAO because any negotiating he wanted to do with her would be done on his own turf. He swept her directly to the VIP entrance beneath TAO, the city's giant gourmet Asian fusion place that turned into a club after midnight, and ushered her into a private red velvet elevator that only celebrities knew about. Stepping out of it, she saw that he had rented the entire VIP room just for them. It was empty save for one candlelit table for two in the center. Seven waiters stood in a line with dishtowels draped over their forearms, waiting to serve their every whim.

The decor was lush and dramatic. The walls were draped in red velvet. Giant stone Buddhas the size of elephants looked out at them with tentatively optimistic stares as if they were thinking: *Please don't destroy the human race. I don't like the direction things are headed, but maybe you can turn things around?*

I don't think so, Buddhas, Amanda thought. *Things are too far gone. Have you been to the Strip lately? Barbaric. End-times kind of scumbaggery lines the streets. And people come here for* vacation. *Things are too far gone.*

It's true, she thought, recalling the half-naked drunken men catcalling the half-naked drunken women as buskers tried to lure you into strip clubs with bucket-sized cocktails for three dollars each. And so crowded. More evidence of how overpopulated we've become. You couldn't avoid touching another person on the Strip as you wound around the casinos and ogled, for some reason, at the eruption of an enormous fake volcano that looked like a giant fifth-grade science experiment. It was trashy beyond trashy. Worse, she supposed, than the Jersey Shore and triple in size. Everyone who bothered to wear a shirt wore one that said something like *I'll keep my guns and Bible, you keep your change*. Amanda hated it here.

Inside TAO, the red and the dark and the closeness and the plush and the steady beat from the club music downstairs made Amanda feel like they were inside a uterus. But she didn't say so. It was too weird, and Evan did not think in metaphor. Instead, she said, "This is so beautiful. How thoughtful, Evan," and he escorted her to her seat. "But what is this about?" she finally got herself to ask.

"Great question. I'm glad you asked," he said, a wide close-mouthed smile stretched across his face. "How do you like the uni? I ordered it especially for you."

"It's sumptuous," she said tentatively. "Smooth."

"Great. That's just great," he said. And then he chewed. Baiting her. Waiting. Making her sweat through her stockings.

"So, about the money," Amanda said. "I think I can pay you back in, like, installments. We can make it legal. With a contract if you want."

"Amanda, Amanda, Amanda."

She hated when he repeated things three times. It usually signified the calm before the storm.

"Evan, Evan, Evan," she tried, smiling at him in the way he used to find endearing.

"See, now don't try that, Amanda. That's not going to work anymore, sweetheart." He wiped his mouth with a napkin and one of the waiters replaced it immediately.

"Why am I here, if you don't want my money or my body? I have nothing else to offer you."

"Well, you do have a daughter," he said. "She's almost more beautiful than you are. And at such a ripe, juicy age."

Amanda felt the sushi climb back up her throat and tried not to vomit.

"I think that would be an even trade, right? In some countries people settle debts with their children all the time. Yours is worth at least two hundred grand—well, two fifty if you count the ring. But, like I said. Who's counting? Not me. I'm not counting." Amanda's eyes filled with tears of rage. He got up and walked slowly around her chair and leaned down, about to whisper in her ear. "Just kidding," he whispered eerily. "I'm actually not that cruel."

Amanda clenched her napkin on the table and tried to surreptitiously feel around for a knife.

"Ha. Do you think I'd have them set this table with knives, Amanda? With your backstabbing tendencies? How stupid do you think I am? Chopsticks only tonight. And a couple of spoons."

"What do you want?" she finally spit out.

"I hear you did a lot of reading in prison."

"I did. You want me to write your book report?"

"Ha, so adorable. No. I read a lot myself. Have you read a little thing called Dante's *Inferno*?"

"I know that this is a circle of hell."

"I can see that you haven't. You're squirming. So I'm just going to spell it out for you," he said, sitting across from her again and staring into her eyes.

"Great," Amanda said, tired of the torture. "Please do."

"I believe in an eye for an eye."

"Fair enough. I said I'd pay you back."

"But it's not the money that hurts, Amanda. You took away my dignity. You took away my chance at true love."

"But there are other chances . . ."

"No. You took away my one shot at love. So, I will take away yours."

"What does that even mean? You can't control whom I love. Love is love."

"But I can control whether he lives. And he will not. Live. If you so much as glance sideways at a man or graze his hand with yours, he dies," Evan said, another self-satisfied grin crossing his dumpling-filled mouth. "You took my love," he said, chewing. "I'll take yours. For eternity. I'll be watching you. Forever. Just when you think it's safe again to suck another man's cock, I'll be there to cut it off. Sake?" he said, holding up a clear bottle.

Amanda swallowed. Again, *Moonstruck* entered the theater of her brain and she heard Nicolas Cage screaming, "I lost my hand! I lost my bride! Johnny has his hand! Johnny has his bride!" while standing, glistening beautifully in sweat, in front of the brick bread oven in that Brooklyn basement. But she knew that Evan was not at all like Nicolas Cage. Evan was steadfast, resolute, and even more maniacal. She couldn't tame him with a steak and a trip to the opera. He would keep this promise.

25

Evan dumped her in his private jet at 4 AM and she Ubered home from the airport. The car dropped her off at seven in the pitiful driveway where Ben was sitting on the stairs peeling an orange.

"Hi," she said, admiring the way his plaid sleeve tightened around his bicep as he bent his arm to take a sip of coffee.

"Hi," he said without looking up. She was still wearing the dress she had on all night. She took off her Jimmy Choos and held them by the strap.

"So, good news and bad news," she said.

"Bad news first," he answered.

"Well. That guy I was with? The one who took me away in the limo? If he sees you anywhere near me, he will kill you." If she hadn't been so practiced in numbing herself, she would actually be heartbroken about this. In spite of herself, she had begun to insert Ben into her stand-alone-house, herb-garden, farmers'-market, NPR-loving fantasy-world future.

"Great. And the good news?"

"You can get back to chasing all that hot, tight, well-intentioned millennial tail with the thigh gap and the skinny jeans and the Zipcars and the selfie sticks. I know you've been missing that."

"Yeah," he said faux wistfully.

"But don't worry. You won't have to miss me for long. I just got back from Vegas, and from the looks of it, civilization is crumbling. The end-times are near."

"That place is a pit," Ben said.

"Yeah," Amanda said, making her way into the garage. "Good-bye, Ben."

She hoped he would be smart enough to wait for her driver to pull far enough away before he followed her in. She hoped he would follow her and not give up too easily.

She forced herself not to look back. There was something in the Bible about losing faith, looking back, and turning everything into salt. She forced herself to continue to the garage stairs without looking back, and easily found the camera Evan had planted there. She turned it off and covered it with her scarf, when she suddenly felt Ben close in on her. She felt his thick, muscular arm around her waist. He kissed her neck. She turned and kissed him, the gruffness of his beard scratching her face, reminding her that she was, maybe for the first time in her life, with a real man. "What're we going to do?" she asked him. "I can't stay away from you and he's watching us twenty-four-seven. He'll kill you."

"I can take him," Ben said. "I have power tools."

"You definitely have some kind of tools," she said, and she slowly unbuckled his belt. Why was forbidden, dangerous sex always the best kind? God really was such a jokester.

Ben thrust her against the cheap sheetrock wall as she bit down on his forearm to conceal her final gasping scream.

—

Ben snuck out the back, and Amanda went upstairs and found Taylor in her room unpacking the old canvas paperboy bag she used for overnights. She was so responsible in spite of everything, carefully folding things before putting them back in her cheap, unpainted wooden drawers. She took three heavy binders out of her backpack and stacked them neatly on her desk, then opened one and carefully looked over her homework. Amanda had a wave of that fear/pain/existential rage feeling that is parental love. She watched as Taylor's sloppy, loopy mess of a ponytail swung back and forth and was so happy to have a kid whose priorities were straight. School first. Vanity second. Taylor finally looked up to notice Amanda in the doorway.

"Mom," she said.

"Hi, Tay. You're home early. Everything go okay with your dad?"

"Yeah, same old, same old," and then, "Gram hacked into Social Security."

"Oh no!"

"She's getting good," Taylor said, leafing through a binder and making sure her homework was inside.

"She's going to get herself arrested."

"Maybe. Hey, Mom?" Taylor asked. But all this talk of Joyce getting arrested made Amanda realize her phone had been off for twelve hours and she'd been out of touch with Stevens. Evan made sure when he took her that she was completely cut off from the world. She turned her phone back on worriedly now, wondering where she'd left things with Agent Stevens and his promise to take Joyce down.

"Yes?" she said distractedly as the texts bleeped and scrolled in from Stevens. Each insane text gained more and more exclamation points as the hours wore on. The last text was just a string of eighteen of them with no words at all. "Oh god," she sighed out loud.

"Never mind," said Taylor.

"No, honey. What is it?"

"It's about a guy," Taylor said quietly.

Taylor had never spoken to her seriously about a guy before.

"A boyfriend?" Amanda asked.

"Sort of. I'm just having trouble . . ."

Amanda's phone beeped again. This time Stevens had included a photo of Amanda escorting her shuffling mother into the doctor's office. *Accomplice to fraud: 5–10 years without parole . . . with intention to distribute, add ten. Get. Me. Bruce!*

Amanda exhaled. "Shit," and Taylor said, "Never mind, Mom. I'm late," and she finished packing up and headed sulkily toward the door.

"Wait! Well, what I think about guys," she said vaguely, "for what it's worth . . . is that you can't let them get the upper hand. I mean, you need to let them *think* they have the upper hand, without actually letting them have it, you know?" Amanda looked straight at Taylor. "You know how to do that? Make them think everything is their idea. Make them think everything is their decision, not yours, even though you were really the one who decided, you know?"

A light seemed to go on in Taylor's head. "I got it," she said. "I have an idea."

"Well, let him think it's his."

"Yup," Taylor said. "Thanks!"

It felt like a tiny win. When Taylor was gone, she grabbed her phone and texted furiously to Bruce and Stevens. She had it all figured out now. Screw the universe. Screw namby-pamby AA and their ridiculous *Let go, let God.* "Screw my higher power. I am my own higher fucking power." The last part she said aloud under her breath, and then hallucinated Carrie Fisher on the other side of the kitchen table, taking off her sunglasses and saying, "Uh-oh. Man overboard."

Come to think of it, Amanda thought after she'd left, *Taylor doesn't usually look so disheveled on her way to school.* And the dark circles under her eyes were a new development. Maybe she should have been more attentive. Next time, Amanda would handle it. It was time for everything to be *handled,* so she could get Taylor out of this godforsaken apartment.

She drove to L'Affordable, where she sat at the makeshift desk Maria had made for her out of a card table and a zebra-striped chair they pilfered from an abandoned storage unit. Her computer was pilfered, too, from a unit whose owner had already gotten the seven required notices to pay his bill or pick up his shit. It was an ancient bright orange Mac laptop that weighed seventeen pounds. She had no idea how Maria got it to work or how she was able to load it with the proper software. Amanda pretended to look busy for a while, and then at 11:42, the time Bruce usually got his "lunch" delivery, she got up and said she was going to water the plants.

Right on schedule, Marcelo, the delivery boy in loose cargo pants held up by his adorable tight, muscular biker's butt, skidded into the parking lot.

"Hey," Amanda said, intercepting him.

"Hey," he said back.

"Why aren't you in school?"

"Homeschool."

"Really?"

"Really," he said. "It's a religious thing. My six brothers and sisters and I all sit around a table while my mother teaches us algebra and the Scriptures. Plus, it's Saturday."

"Right," Amanda said. She'd completely lost track of the days.

"Gotta go," he said, trying to brush her off and moving insistently toward the door.

"I'll take that," she said. "Bruce asked me to grab his lunch and take it to Unit 74. He's over there this afternoon, cleaning it out."

"I'm only supposed to give this to Mr. Bruce," he said.

"Well, he wants me to grab it. I'm his daughter. It's okay. Really, Marcelo." She looked him in the eye. "It's just lunch, right?"

"Okay," he said tentatively. He handed her the bag and picked his bike up out of the dirt and began pedaling away.

"Stay in school," Amanda yelled after him, and he turned back for second and gave her the middle finger.

When he was far enough down the road, Amanda inspected the menu. It was from a different taqueria with new item numbers circled in black ink. Stapled to it was a receipt with a calculator printout and *Thanks from Paco Wash $8.04* written in the same black ink.

Strange name, Paco Wash, she thought. And what a coincidence that it was also the name of the concrete river—the Pacoima Wash—that ran through these parts.

Come to think of it, the Pacoima Wash would be perfect for drug dealing. It was slated for an upgrade, designed by the likes of the architects of the fancy High Line in New York City—gardens, bike paths, food trucks, picnic tables, beekeepers, public art, microbrews, a hipster paradise—but the bureaucratic red tape would hold that project up for years. Especially in California, where people were not exactly known for their exigency. Amanda imagined everyone assigned to that project—the bureaucrats and state senators, the lawyers, developers, and carpenters—probably started their days with bong hits for breakfast. No one was really in a rush around here.

So in the meantime, the Pacoima Wash persisted and languished, deteriorating every day into a veritable landfill of discarded plastic toys and bicycle parts. Homeless shantytowns popped up every once in a while beneath the overpasses. It was the land of the forgotten. A nada, *nunca*, nothing of a wasted space. A breeding ground for mosquitoes, and therefore West Nile and now Zika.

Hmmm. The Paco Wash, thought Amanda, and something caught in the back of her brain. Wasn't there a Metrolink stop near the Paco Wash? No one used the train in LA. Even in spite of the supposed "Subway to the Sea." No one took the train, so it would be easy to move around unnoticed on the Metrolink. She took out her phone and pulled up the schedule, and wouldn't you know, there was an 8:04 arrival scheduled for Van Nuys on weekdays.

—

On Monday, Amanda parked in the Target parking lot and walked around to the back where the Pacoima Wash intersected the train tracks. She had no idea if she was following a real trail or her imagination. Despite what she'd seen through Marcelo's window, she still couldn't wrap her head around the idea that her stepdad would be waiting behind Target to make a drug deal.

The sun burned through her hair and scorched her scalp, making her think of melanoma, which made her think of dying, which made her think of Taylor left alone on the planet with no one but Joyce to guide her, which made her think of the prospect of Taylor's father as her guardian, which made her sad. Mike could never really embrace her reality and show her that he loved her, while, at the same time, he seemed so adept at doing so with his other, newer kids. Taylor had to watch him give his love to everyone but her.

This hurt her heart a little, which made her think of heartburn, which made her want a Coke, which made her look at her watch and realize she still had enough time to stop in Target and pick up a sun hat, sunscreen, and a fizzy beverage to make her burp.

She donned the floppy hat, smeared some white sunscreen on her face, twisted open the Coke, and walked back to the parking lot.

And that was when she saw Bruce. *Fuck*, Amanda thought.

He sat in his shiny, low to the ground Acura Integra that he said hugged the road, but really drove like a race car, shaking passengers' heads around with every curve and bump. It made the driver feel more masculine—as if he were actually on a NASCAR track—while practically giving his passengers concussions. He had his favorite Sinatra blaring out the window and he was chewing on a Slim Jim. *Breakfast of champions*, Amanda thought. *He's going to get the big canc—*

Her thought was interrupted by Bruce suddenly turning his head and staring right in her direction. Amanda froze. Like the geckos that skittered all over the state, she paralyzed herself, held her breath, and tried to blend into the tan walls of the Target. She was wearing her khakis for work, but the floppy hat might be enough camouflage for him not to notice her.

He had his Ray-Bans on, so she couldn't be sure he was looking right at her. She didn't even blink. Finally, he turned away and then flipped open his *LA Times*, continuing to wait. Amanda exhaled.

At 8:04 on the dot (who knew California transit would be so punctual?) the Van Nuys train barreled past behind the chain-link fence, and at 8:07, Marcelo, dressed all in black, approached on the BMX bike. Without leaving the car or looking away from his paper, Bruce popped the trunk and Marcelo dropped something into it. Then, before he left, he slid a menu beneath Bruce's windshield wiper. Bruce pretended not to notice and the boy kept cycling, hunched and oversized on the tiny trick bike, and then, impressively, stood on the front tire while he swung the back tire around himself in a 360.

She expected Bruce to tell him to stop hot-dogging, but he kept his cool, ignoring the boy and turning the key in the ignition, then pulled slowly away, reaching smoothly out the window to grab the menu off the windshield.

Fuck. So it was true. Even Bruce was on the take. Everyone but her, it seemed, was in control and taking what they wanted. Why was it that she was the only one in her family getting blackmailed and manipulated? How had she let this happen? She was the con artist here. How had she lost control? She needed to stop accepting the things she couldn't change and instead change the things she couldn't accept. She could no longer accept the fact that Stevens was blackmailing her to get to Bruce. She was awakened. She should have done this the moment Stevens had the audacity to carjack her. She was going to Bruce.

26

She sped toward L'Affordable, now busting moves and changing lanes like a madwoman to get around the LA traffic. But Stevens was right. No one here moved with any sense of exigency. Didn't these people have someplace to be? Why were they meandering around her route, joyriding?

She gunned it around a pickup truck and then slammed on her brakes at the next red light. As the light turned green and she pulled away a siren wailed and a blue police light flashed behind her. Amanda flushed with anxiety. Her entire body flushed with fear as she pulled over. Her hands shook as she reached across to get her registration out of the glove box. Parolees cannot get speeding tickets.

But the man striding toward her in the side-view mirror was not a traffic cop. It was Stevens. Same black jeans, slightly bowlegged like a cowboy, but in a white shirt this time.

"Where you going in such a rush, sunshine?" he asked.

"You're going to give me a heart attack. If you kill me, you don't get my intel. That's poor management skills right there. Scaring your informant to death."

"Wow, your eyes turn a smoking shade of green when you're flushed. Damn, are you sure we can't get a drink?"

"I think you're the one who said, 'Life's about choices,'" Amanda said. "It's me or my stepdad."

"Well, I choose all of the above," he said, nonchalantly letting his leather jacket swing open enough for her to see his holster. "So, I hear from my people that that shipment is dropping tomorrow. And I know Bruce is in on it. What do you have for me?" An eighteen-wheeler sped by, almost sideswiping them. The backdraft knocked him off balance a little.

"Shouldn't we do this somewhere else?"

"Your place is bugged."

"How do you know?"

"Because I tried to bug it myself and found the wires already in place."

"That's my ex."

"Wow, you really know how to pick 'em," he said. "So what do you have for me, Amanda?" he asked as three more cars passed in three whooshing swishes. It was like trying to have a deep discussion during NASCAR.

"Nothing."

"Amanda."

"I do have an address that I staked out. But I think it's a false lead." To get him off her tail she wrote down the address of the house she'd seen Marcelo bike to. The one with his mama cooking in the kitchen. He took it and thanked her. She watched as he drove off, then pulled the minivan back onto the 405.

—

"Hey," Amanda said as she burst through the screen door of L'Affordable and found Bruce with his feet up, smoking a cigar.

"Mandy," he said sitting straight up. "What's the matter?"

"Nothing," she answered, frustrated, fed up, and on the brink of tears. "Want to get some Mexican for lunch?" she asked, staring straight into his aviator-style reading glasses and waiting for his response. A flake of dandruff fell to his shoulder.

Bruce stood up, and without looking away from Amanda's gaze, stubbed out his cigar in the coiled clay ashtray with a giraffe head that Taylor had made him in summer camp. He said nothing, then grabbed Amanda by the elbow and led her to storage unit 53. Inside was an old CD boom box from the nineties and when he turned it on En Vogue blasted from the speakers and bounced off the walls. "Free your mind . . . !" it squalled. It must have been the last CD playing when this person packed up to leave.

"What's going on?" he asked in a baritone that hopefully only she could hear beneath the music.

"This guy," she said, showing Bruce the photo she'd taken of Stevens at LACMA. "He threatened me. Said he'd arrest Joyce if I didn't turn you in for your involvement with the cartels and I was like 'That's funny, Agent Whoever-you-are, because Bruce is actually the only normal person I know.' Then I go hunting around in your office a little and find out that it's either true, what he said, or you're writing a book about Mexican takeout in East LA. So?"

"So what?" Bruce asked.

"So are you writing a book about tacos?"

"It's more like the first thing you said," he said, looking down at the ground and guiltily tapping a half-deflated purple Lakers basketball with his socked and sandaled kicking foot.

"Et tu, Brute?" Amanda said, feeling defeated and hopeless, yet no longer surprised.

"Yeah. Me, too, I guess," he said without removing his hands from his pockets. "But why would you turn me in?"

"He blackmailed me. Threatened to nab Joyce. What was I supposed to do?"

"Come to me," he said.

"I'm here now."

"It's late. Especially with this guy," Bruce said, sighing and shaking his head.

"Stevens? You know him?"

"It's a tight-knit community."

"Don't call it that. *Community*. And he's not part of your community. He's trying to take it down."

"That's what he told you?"

"Yeah. He said he's FBI."

"Ha! He's bad news, Mandy. A cold-blooded killer trained by America's finest. He's FBI, but in a heap of bad debt. In trouble with the Italians in New York, so I think he's trying to make some money off the Mexicans. He's in cahoots with a rival cartel and wants to take this one down. And he'll do that any way he can. He's pretty vicious. Tenacious. Won't stop until he gets what he wants. I can't believe he's using you. What a dirtbag," he said.

"I've been thinking about it. I may have a plan."

"That's my girl," said Bruce. "What have you told Stevens?"

"Not much until this afternoon. I gave him Marcelo's address. The place where they cook up your takeout."

"Fuck, really?"

"I had to give him something."

"God, I wish you had come to me earlier. Come on!" he said, and they rushed out and into the Acura as he screeched around some back roads and almost hit a stray cat or two. They pulled up quietly a block away from the drug den and peered around the corner.

Stevens was already there. His gun was drawn and he approached the house on foot. Marcelo, clueless, peeled out of the gate on his bike with another delivery. "Stop!" Stevens shouted, but Marcelo sped up, furiously pedaling, and Stevens, without hesitating, shot the kid in the leg.

Marcelo dropped to the ground, his bike tires still spinning in slow circles, the blood pooling beneath him in a dark, slick lake. Amanda shrieked.

Marcelo called out and writhed in pain as Stevens stoically walked up to him, kicked him like a dog, and grabbed the brown paper bag, then threw the kid a rag for the blood and sauntered back to his car with the takeout.

"We have to help him!" Amanda cried, but Bruce put a hand on her arm.

"He'll be fine. They have people who take care of things like this. We show ourselves now, they'll know we're responsible."

"Why are you doing this, Bruce?" Amanda cried. "It's too dangerous. That poor kid."

Bruce sighed. "You get to a certain age, Mandy, and you feel like you may as well be dead. Everything gets so boring, and you feel like you're just waiting around to die."

"So you go and join a cartel? Immerse yourself in drug trafficking? Why couldn't you take up golf? Waiting around to die," she said, shaking her head. "Well, you're going to get your wish. This is a death wish. Call nine-one-one!"

"Marcelo will be okay. He's a tough kid," he said, ignoring Amanda's plea. His cell phone buzzed, and he looked at it. "Hold on. I need to take this," he said, then started the car and drove away in the other direction while speaking into the phone in perfect Spanish she never knew he had.

You can never really know a person, Amanda thought.

They drove back to L'Affordable, and locked themselves in Unit 53. The boom box played Nirvana this time and Amanda, still shaking from the violence she'd seen and disturbed by her stepfather's cool complacency about the whole thing, tentatively laid out the plan she'd come up with. Bruce was pretty slow on the uptake, so they hovered over an old Ping-Pong table folded in half while she drew him some flow charts. Eventually he was brought up to speed. The basics:

She'd agree to get in a car with Stevens and lead him to Bruce. They'd follow Bruce under the assumption that he'd lead them to his cartel contacts and the next delivery. Bruce would take them on a wild goose chase, giving Amanda time to seduce Agent Stevens. They'd lose Bruce, but Amanda would ask Stevens to help her take down Russ, for which she will promise him just compensation, wink, wink.

"Wait, who is Russ?" Bruce couldn't keep that piece of the puzzle in place. There were a lot of moving pieces.

"That doesn't matter," Amanda finally said. "Don't worry about that part. You take us on a wild goose chase and then make sure you're in the lobby of the Four Seasons at this exact time," and then she wrote it down for him on a Post-it.

27

Marcelo was fine, a surface wound; Stevens didn't kill him. But that little incident made her loath to do what she had to do next. She couldn't believe Stevens would actually shoot at a kid on a BMX bike. But she had to do what she had to do. For family.

She arranged to meet Agent Stevens across the street from the McDonald's on Lincoln because, she said, that's the new place Bruce went for his Tuesday Filet-O-Fish. "I think he has some big plans today," she told Stevens. "We'll follow him. I heard something about the airport, too. Might be a big shipment."

He was already there when she arrived and she abandoned the minivan and climbed into his SUV. "Couldn't you have rented something a little less 'Secret Service'?" she asked him. "We're conspicuous."

In ten minutes Bruce arrived in his Acura and climbed out of it, not without difficulty because it was so low to the ground. They watched as he scooted into the Golden Arches and stood in line behind the other unkempt seniors in their crumpled Dockers and sturdy white Reeboks (*Where do they even buy those?* Amanda wondered) and ordered his Filet-O-Fish. He then sat near the window and leisurely read the paper, wiping his mouth between bites with his paper napkin, torturing her. *Damn him*, Amanda thought. This wasn't funny. She didn't want to spend any more time than she had to with Agent Stevens.

During their meeting in Unit 53, Bruce had showed her his manila file folder on Stevens. It was filled with facsimiles, of all things. Grainy, shadowy black-and-white photos and reports from the DEA printed on the shiny, filmy fax paper of yesteryear.

The reports showed that the DEA and the FBI were onto Stevens. They knew something had snapped inside him after he witnessed the beheading of his partner in Algeria. They knew his PTSD had taken an odd criminal turn and that he was seeking out danger. Almost in a suicidal way. Mixing with the darkest of criminals in order to get himself out of debt with some other criminals.

"One thing led to another, I guess," Bruce had told her. "He was injured in Afghanistan, too, and got hopped up on morphine. Same old story."

"And what's your excuse?" Amanda had asked him, again, as she flattened down the ears of a stuffed Easter bunny left in the storage unit to make it look like a pink gopher. She couldn't look Bruce in the eye.

Bruce hesitated for a second. "I don't know, Mandy. Boredom, like I said. Fear of death. Gambling addiction. The thrill of the deal. Maybe part of me wanted to be more of a man than your mother."

"Real men don't sell drugs," she told him. "Or use fax machines. God, where do you even find this technology?" she asked, holding up a fax by its corner and wobbling it as it made a plasticky crackle.

"It's below the radar. No one tracks this stuff anymore," Bruce said, grabbing it out of her hand.

"You may as well use Morse code."

"I'm out after this. I promise. Retirement. I hate golf, though."

"Maybe you can join Fight Club. That's dangerous. Or Taylor and I are going to start yarn bombing. There's some danger in that."

"The first rule about yarn bombing . . ." he joked.

"That's also the second rule," said Amanda.

But Amanda was worried about him trying to live without the thrill of the deal. Maybe he could start day trading, she thought.

Now in the parking lot, she looked over at Stevens in the driver's seat. He was playing some Yahtzee game on his phone and sucking the remnants of his lunch out of his teeth. Quinoa and chickpea salad. That body didn't just happen.

"So." She decided to get this over with. "Are you married?"

"Why do you ask?"

"Just making conversation. I figure you've got a few kids at home. Two point five of them. And a dog and maybe a goldfish. Pretty wife who has a steady manicure appointment and dyes her hair medium gold blond at the Vidal Sassoon in Bethesda." She made sure to mindlessly finger the gearshift as she spoke.

"I have some of that," Stevens said, gaze lingering on her hand.

"Which part?"

"The goldfish," he said, finally looking up into Amanda's eyes and revealing his deep inner loneliness. This was going to be too pathetically easy, albeit in a creepy, scary, sad way. She looked him up and down. She could tell he was damaged, even without Bruce's reports. His PTSD would perhaps be an obstacle, but because of it, he hadn't been with a woman in a long time, which might make things easy. He did have a really handsome face in spite of the scar.

Bruce stood up then and took a last sip of his coffee.

"What is it with senior citizens and McDonald's coffee?" Stevens asked as he sat up and threw the truck into gear.

"I don't know," Amanda replied. "I guess they just like the price point."

The engine idled as Bruce waited outside next to a plastic patio umbrella and jangled some change in his pocket until he found what he was looking for, a mint-flavored toothpick, which he stuck between his cheek and gum. Then he finally climbed back into his Acura.

They followed the car out of the parking lot as it drove slowly down Lincoln for five minutes. He kept going until he got to a pawnshop. Bruce got out and stood again, lighting a cigarillo this time, and smoking it on the sidewalk.

"He won't smoke in his car," Amanda explained. "Or he's going to sell some old storage-unit stuff to the pawnshop."

But Bruce did not go into the pawnshop. He finished smoking, got back in the car, and made a U-turn just as the left-arrow light turned red and drove down Lincoln in the other direction.

Stevens waited a few seconds before banging the same illegal U-turn in the middle of the busy street, almost taking out a woman pushing a stroller in the crosswalk.

"Easy does it," Amanda said, exhaling. It was another slogan from AA.

At a 76 gas station, Bruce got out and talked to a mechanic in coveralls as they watched from the other side of the road. Stevens leaned forward to get a closer look, clearly expecting Bruce to duck into the mechanic's shop to make some kind of deal. But Bruce simply handed the mechanic his keys, then climbed into a big black Uber that was rolling up to him past the gas pumps.

"This is getting ridiculous," Stevens said, but he took a breath and followed Bruce's Uber toward the airport.

"See. I told you I heard something about the airport," Amanda lied. "He might be picking up a shipment."

As they drove, the landscape to the right became bleaker and bleaker as its toxic-waste dunes stretched toward the ocean. To the left, a massive tumor of newly constructed condos, dividing and multiplying like cancer cells gone wild, rose up beside them and Bruce's Uber turned left, beneath the WELCOME TO PALM VALLEY sign.

"Huh, I guess he's not going to the airport," Stevens said.

"Maybe he's just making a stop first. Follow him."

They wound around the loopy drives of the enormous complex that were named after different cacti, and drove beneath some magenta-and-purple Disney-like archways getting turned around until, finally, they lost him.

"Fuck!" Stevens yelled. He instinctively reached into the glove compartment and pulled out his revolver.

"Whoa," Amanda said. "That's not going to fix anything."

"Where is he? I'm done with the cutesy bullshit."

This wasn't Amanda's first time on the other end of a pistol. She breathed. Remained calm and focused on the job at hand.

"We'll get him, Agent Stevens. What's your first name, again?" she asked. "I feel like we should be on a first-name basis." She calmly pushed the gun to the side with her finger and then moved her other hand from the gearshift to Stevens's rock-hard thigh and looped her finger along the cotton blend fabric of his pants in an infinity shape. He lowered the gun.

"Antoine," he said. "My mother was French."

"Looks like we lost him. It's okay, Antoine. It just means we'll have to do this again sometime," Amanda said, squeezing his thigh. "We'll get him," she said, letting her finger slide just a tiny bit toward his in-seam. Stevens reluctantly stuck the gun into his boot and started the car. "Actually, I have a favor to ask," Amanda continued.

"I'm not in the mood to do you any favors."

"I don't expect you to do anything without compensation."

She leaned in and let him kiss her. It was the sloppy kiss of some-one who hadn't kissed in a while, but then it grew in intensity for the same reason. She had to break away first before it got too serious.

"So," she said before he could gain equilibrium. She dragged her finger down his chest and let it rest on his belt buckle. "You know my job at Markdown. The special condition of my parole?" she asked, leaning toward him and using her biceps to squeeze her tits together.

"Of course," he said, letting his fingers drift to her leg. Amanda adeptly shimmied away from them.

"Well. It's all a scam. They're forcing the ex-cons, like me, to run their own skim operation. Stealing goods from inventory and selling them on the street. If they get caught, they're gonna pin it all on us," Amanda said, looking up at him with sad, wet puppy eyes.

"Who's they?" he asked brutishly.

"The bad guys."

"Rustling up bad guys usually comes with a reward," he said.

"Of course. To the victor go the spoils. Rustle me up some bad guys at Markdown," she said, reapplying her lipstick, "and you'll be justly rewarded."

"I can't do anything without probable cause," he said, shifting in his seat. "Give me a reason to get them."

"Not a problem," Amanda answered. "Ten-fucking-four."

28

Everything was in place. All she had to do was send Stevens some proof of the scam, which she and Lupita could easily steal from Russ's office, and then she'd be finished with her parole. Once Russ was in jail, she could use it to threaten Ken, who could forge some documents and put an end to all this ridiculous Markdown work-order business. She could go to school, get a real job, head out of town with Taylor. Start over. She would finally be free.

She felt a sense of calm, and actually felt hungry for the first time maybe ever in her life. She was starving, and she rummaged through the cabinets, looking for something to eat.

She pulled out a can of tuna fish and some white bread and said a little prayer that there might possibly be some mayonnaise in Joyce's fridge. Which was a long shot, she knew, because: fat grams. Effing Joyce.

She moved things around in the fridge when she was startled by a knock on the door. It was not the gentle knock of a friendly neighbor.

"Police," someone said. "Open up."

Fuck, Amanda thought. *They really say that?* She was living inside a *Law & Order* episode. Her appetite disappeared.

They'd figured it out; the Markdown scam, her mother's business, Bruce's bullshit. Stevens turned them in, she thought. Why was she stupid enough to trust Stevens? At least prison wouldn't be such a shock the second time around. Numb, she opened the door.

"Amanda Cooper?" There were two of them. A blond female with a neatly looped ponytail tucked under the back of her cap, and an enormous weightlifter kind of guy who could break the woman in two. They looked more like a circus act than partners in a squad car.

"Yes," Amanda said.

"Are you the mother of a Taylor Cooper?"

"Oh. Um. Yes. What's this about?"

"We'd like to ask her some questions about a Mr. Jake Hunter. She wasn't at school, so we thought we'd find her here."

"Jake Hunter? Isn't that her English teacher?" Amanda felt panic burn through her body.

"We can't say anything else until we talk to Taylor."

Amanda remembered Jake Hunter's red pen, hipster cords, his pebble-colored complexion, and then the flush of bashful humiliation pooling across his face during their meeting. Shit. Why hadn't she put two and two together? That F paper was not just a power play, it was a seduction. She flashed to Taylor's face asking her for help with a boy problem and remembered how quickly she had brushed her off. "Oh my god. What did he do to her?"

Amanda could almost feel the blood draining from her body, leaving her standing there, a gray and ashen shell of dust. A gentle breeze could scatter her to the winds. As horrible as this feeling was, it was more familiar than her recent contentment.

"I don't want to say any more until we see Taylor. Is she here?"

"What do you mean, you're not going to say any more? This is my daughter, and you are going to tell me, right now, what that scumbag did to her."

"Can you check and see if Taylor is home? We'd like to ask her some questions," they repeated like robocops.

Amanda knocked on T's door. "Honey," she said. "Are you in there?" No answer. Amanda pushed the door a tad, and it was sucked open by the draft from the open window. The cheap translucent dollar-store curtains fluttered in the breeze. Could she have possibly jumped from here to the driveway? It was twenty feet up. Amanda turned her head and noticed that the drainpipe—painted the same peachy tan as the rest of the stucco structure—was bowed and bent and broken. She must have shimmied down the drainpipe. As one does.

Amanda frantically walked around the room looking for clues. Taylor's backpack was gone. Her sleeping bag and Maurice, her stuffed lamb. If she took Maurice, she was planning to be gone overnight.

"She's gone!" Amanda told the police.

"We're putting out an APB," the male cop said to the other and then pressed the screechy talk button on his walkie-talkie.

"Don't put out an APB," Amanda said. "I can find her. I'm her mother. I just need to know what this is about."

Frick and Frack looked at each other, which wasn't easy, considering their height difference and the circumference of the big guy's neck. Finally the big one said, "She's been accused of blackmail, Mrs. Cooper."

"She's been getting Jake Hunter to pay her large sums in order to keep their affair quiet," said the little Donna Reed police officer, who they probably sent to all domestic disputes because she looked so, well, domestic.

"Allegedly," Amanda said. "She *allegedly* did the thing with the large sums and *allegedly* had an affair. You people are supposed to use the word *allegedly*."

"Allegedly," said the big one. "It's incriminating, though, that she fled. Tell her it's important for her to come tell her story."

"She didn't 'flee,'" Amanda said.

"We saw the drainpipe," the big one answered.

"Oh."

"When you find her," said the smaller cop, handing Amanda a business card, "give us a call. Here's my direct line. We'll be looking for her as well." And then they left, pulling the squad car out of the driveway, the light bar still swirling around silently without the siren. At least seven neighbors stood in their windows in different states of undress and pulled their blinds aside to get a peek at the scandal.

"There but for the grace of God go all you losers," Amanda yelled at them, but since they couldn't hear her they stood gaping for a minute longer before letting their curtains drop and starting their days.

Amanda pounded quickly on Joyce's door and then stormed into her bedroom. She found Joyce sitting cross-legged on the floor with her sleeping blindfold on, doing her vocal exercises and facial yoga. "Me, me, me. Mahhhhh," she breathed.

"Ma," Amanda said.

"Mahhhh," Joyce exhaled blissfully.

"Ma!"

"Yes, Mahhhhh."

"No, Mother! Look up. We have a problem."

Joyce, obviously annoyed, lifted one eye of the blindfold. "What?" she barked.

"Taylor. She's wanted by the police and she fled! We need to find her!"

"Shit!" Joyce said, her flushed meditative complexion turning instantly gray.

"Get up now!" Amanda paced back and forth in her mother's bedroom.

Joyce untangled herself and got up, pulling on a long sweater over her yoga pants. "Fuck," she said, nervous and angry. "I hate to say I told you so."

"What the hell is that supposed to mean?"

"You come in here all pious and self-righteous," Joyce said, "ranting about wanting her to have a better life, and think you can just break the cycle with one hug and a gallon of ice cream? It takes more work than that to break the cycle of things, especially when you can't see which way's up because you're caught in the cycle yourself. I told you so."

"Just come on. This is an emergency."

Joyce threw off the blindfold and poured herself a cup of coffee. Amanda flipped open her laptop.

"What are you going to do with that?" Joyce asked.

"Hack into Taylor's computer."

"Oh. Can I watch?" Joyce asked. "I'm learning that this is the source of all power, and my teacher says it's so important for seniors to cross the digital divide. Seniors are isolated enough without becoming disenfranchised by computer illiteracy."

"Right. She wants you to figure out online checking, not hack into the mainframe of Wall Street banks."

"Potato, patata," said Joyce, donning her reading glasses and peering through them at the screen while Amanda typed furiously.

"Did your teacher have a computerized voice and wear a scary clown mask?"

"What? No. What are you talking about?"

"Never mind."

"Did you find anything?"

"Not yet." Amanda completed some toggles and clicks and eventually pulled up Taylor's e-mail account. "You've got to hand it to her. She's very organized. Look at all these folders."

"What's that one?" Joyce asked, pointing to a folder labeled COLLEGE FUND.

Amanda clicked, and inside were dated subfolders filled with receipts from a PayPal account. Was she siphoning money from Jake Hunter using PayPal? Amanda opened the most recent one. This month she had received seventeen payments of eighty dollars each remitted to a company called Lakers Girl Inc. "What the heck is Lakers Girl Incorporated?" Amanda asked, feeling all of her flesh turn rubbery with dread.

A link to the Lakers Girl company led them to a private, blacked-out web page that required a password. "Subscribers Only," it said. Amanda hacked into the page from the back door and they were in. The site was filled with pictures of headless Taylor dressed in skimpier and skimpier Lakers attire, her body contorted into different flexible cheerleader poses, so "subscribers" could see her torso, her flank, her underwear, her cleavage, her bent-over ass.

"Turn it off!" Amanda shouted, gasping for breath. She couldn't seem to catch it right away, though, so she stuck her head in the freezer like they tell you to do with a baby who has croup.

"Is that what you were looking for?" Joyce asked.

"No. God. That was bonus material." Amanda looked at the in-box files again. "There," she said, pointing to a file named IN MY HEART OF HEARTS.

Just as she had feared. All thirty-five of the e-mails in that file were from: Hunter, Jake.

"You would think the idiot would use a fake name or encrypted e-mail for his pedophilia," Joyce said. "Tsk, Tsk. He knows he's a dead man if he laid a hand on her, right?"

"There will be no dead people," Amanda moaned. Her dry toast was stuck in her craw, as she sized up the situation. She was so close to bagging each of the dickheads in her way. She was so distracted by her dickhead-bagging plan she'd taken her eye off the prize. Taylor. "You read them. I can't," she said, swirling her hand in a circle in front of the computer screen.

"Hmmm," Joyce said. "Oh!" And then "Wow!"

"No editorializing! Just absorb the info," said Amanda, grabbing the Pepto-Bismol from the remedy section of the kitchen cabinet and taking a long swig.

"Okay. Done," said Joyce, slamming down the lid of the laptop. The glowing apple beamed up at Amanda, accusing her. As if she were the particular Eve who took the innocent bite out of it and fucked everything up. Wait. Did Steve Jobs name the whole shebang Apple because he knew the digital shit would be so tempting, distracting, and mesmerizing that it would take down the entire human race? Was Steve Jobs the serpent? "Earth to Amanda!" Joyce yelled, bringing her attention back into the room.

"That was fast," she told her mother.

"They have speed-reading at the senior center, too."

"Well?"

"Well, what?"

"Did she ever ask him for money?! They want to question Taylor about blackmail."

"Oh. Well, you never said. Let's see," she said, scanning back over the file. "Nope. And nope. Never. Per se."

"What do you mean, per se?"

"Well, he bought her a yogurt one day when she forgot her lunch money."

"That's it?"

"Yes."

"And did he?"

"What?"

"Mom! Stay with me here. Did he touch her?"

"Well, he certainly wanted to. But there's no direct evidence that he actually did."

"Come on," Amanda said, grabbing her jacket and putting it on over her PJs. "We have to find her."

"Don't you think we should do something about this mess," Joyce said, swirling her finger around the Lakers Girl Inc. web page.

"Purge!" Amanda said, pushing her mother out of her seat at the dining room table and clicking furiously. "We can't leave a trace of that anywhere on the Web."

"Good job," said Joyce, taking in every keystroke, a quick study. Just as Amanda was about to leave the apartment, the phone rang.

"Amanda Cooper."

"Ms. Cooper. I'm Whitney. Whitney Hunter."

Amanda's eyes widened and she gasped and silently mouthed the words "the wife" to her mother as she pointed at the receiver. "What can I do for you, Mrs. Hunter?"

"I don't know if you're aware by now, but your daughter is in big trouble."

"Allegedly. We don't have the whole story," Amanda said, "but I've heard a version of it."

"Well, here's my version. Five thousand a month has mysteriously gone missing from our bank account, and I think your little tramp has been blackmailing my husband." Her voice was East Coast private-school calm with a bit of Valley Girl vocal fry drawing out some of the final syllables. Whatever this woman was, she was not a distraught victim. "Give me the money back and we won't press charges."

"Press charges? Taylor is sixteen. Whatever your husband did with my little tramp is considered statutory rape, so how dare you threaten me?"

"According to him, he has never touched her."

"Well, thank god for that," Amanda said and hung up the phone. She needed to find Taylor.

Evan's men were still parked in a black car, watching from across the boulevard. She stormed out the door and crossed the busy street without even looking and almost got hit by a pickup truck. She pounded on the black-tinted window and it lowered only a quarter of the way down, exhaling a white cloud of smoke. The two tattooed men vaping inside coughed a little and lowered their sunglasses.

"Which way did she go?" Amanda asked them.

"Who?"

"My daughter. The one who shimmied down the drainpipe while you watched her escape."

"She's none of our business, ma'am. Boss told us to focus only on the target. Target's you."

"And any man that looks at you," said the one in the backseat.

"Which way did she go?" Amanda said again.

"We really didn't pay attention. I'm sorry," he said and closed the window.

"Assholes," Amanda yelled. "What good are you?" and she kicked their tire before crossing back across the street, looking up at Ben's apartment. She wished she could enlist his help but she couldn't risk his life by being seen with him. She'd have to figure this out on her own.

29

Her first stop was Venice. In fifth grade Taylor had to create a diorama of her special sacred place. Most kids made papier-mâché mountains surrounding their second homes in Lake Tahoe or rings of palm trees encircling sandy beaches of Kauai, where they spent their Christmas vacations every year. Taylor, bless her heart, made a diorama of Venice Beach, a gray winding sidewalk lined with rows of T-shirt shops and psychics and miniature homeless people she made out of clothespins and stood next to little tents she made out of pieces of her old windbreaker. It was Taylor who had dubbed it the "people zoo," and she used to love coming here in the olden days just to watch the people and witness, with a certain dread, the confusing world of adults play out in front of her.

Amanda was sure Taylor would be here. She walked down the gray sidewalk trying not to get hit by tourists on rental bikes. She was accosted twice by medical marijuana pushers and prayed that she wouldn't see Lupita here still selling Russ's crap.

She wound her way past the undulating gray cement of the new skate park that was camouflaged against the gray sand dunes. She checked to see if Taylor was among the skaters popping into the air in a random sequence, like rolling, skate-rat popcorn. She wasn't there. She wasn't at Muscle Beach, either, watching the body builders kicking it old school pulling themselves up onto crude metal and stone equipment from the dark ages, celebrating the purity of their exercise.

She strolled the beach a little, screaming "Taylor" into the wind. Joyce had rented an old cruiser bicycle and rode along the paths scanning the horizon for Taylor's blue hair. But it was useless. Taylor wasn't here. She could feel it. Mother's intuition, Amanda supposed, but then she laughed cruelly at herself. It was her lack of intuition that got them into this mess. Taylor had practically pulled a fire alarm right in front of Amanda's face, attempting to alert her to the problem, and Amanda blew her off. She was too caught up in her own ego. Living in the future. Promising she'd pay more attention to Taylor after she just fixed one more thing. If this one thing could be fixed, then she could finally start living. She should have been living one day at a time. Meeting one challenge at a time. Not blowing off Taylor until she was ready to face her. People are never ready. She was an idiot.

Bruce had been cruising Hollywood, which was another people zoo, where a kid could easily and purposefully get lost. A wacky blue-haired teen child dragging a sleeping bag and a Maurice around would be par for the course up there, too.

"Anything?" Amanda asked him.

"No, babe. I'm going to go head up to the sign."

"Why would she go all the way up there?"

"I dunno. Seems poetic."

"Okay. Stay in touch."

Amanda went out to the street and stood under Clownerina. The ballet dancer sculpture with the giant clown face that Taylor photographed and made into an Andy Warhol–like lithograph project in seventh grade, demonstrating her understanding of Hi-Lo. The one she'd wanted to yarn-bomb.

Joyce pulled up on the bike and Amanda took a moment to notice her spryness. Not bad for a sixty-eight-year-old. "You look good on that thing," she said.

"Any ideas?" Joyce asked.

"I don't know."

She got to thinking. Hi-Lo. Ramshackle chic. Topanga Canyon.

A tiny piece of the Berkeley Hills in the middle of Los Angeles. They had lived there when Taylor was ten or so and they had to hide from the fallout of one of Joyce's schemes gone sour. Joyce's actress friend let them live in the house while she was on location in Croatia. Taylor used to call it the "Fairy House" because it was tucked in the woods and looked like it was made of sticks and rocks and flower petals, but was actually a whimsical design by one of the area's most expensive architects.

"Topanga?" Amanda asked Joyce.

"Hmmm. Maybe," she said. "But also maybe the observatory. I'll have Bruce pick me up and take me up there. You hit Topanga."

Joyce returned the bike and called Bruce. Amanda hopped in the van.

After taking the curves at breakneck pace and spiraling into this other world—the smell of sage and oregano wafting in from the side of the road, the ramshackle cabins very studied and deliberate in the way they arranged their precious wacko junk on the front lawn—Amanda parked in the lot of the vintage clothing store, hoping no one would mind, and followed the creek bed up toward the Fairy House.

She found the dirt road and knew she was close when out of the corner of her eye she spotted a flash of neon green. Taylor's running jacket. "Taylor!" she cried. But the neon stayed put, so Amanda climbed into the woods and down the embankment where Tay sat on a tan rounded boulder that used to stand in the middle of the creek, damming it for a moment and letting the water collect in a still pool. Taylor used to stand in it with her plastic bucket and try to collect pollywogs.

"Why did we ever move from this place?" Taylor asked now, gazing up at her mom with her tear-streaked face.

"It wasn't ours, honey."

"I wish we never had to leave it," she said, mourning the loss of her innocence and her childhood.

"I know, babe. But everyone has to grow up."

"There's no water," Taylor said as if in a kind of shock. "There used to be water."

Amanda kicked at the dirt, trying to find any evidence of moisture, trying to give her daughter a tiny bit of hope, but dry cinnamon dirt just formed a dust cloud around her boots. "So what happened, Tay? They need to hear your side of the story."

"Nothing," Taylor said, rubbing Maurice against her nose like she used to do as a toddler.

"Tay. Did he touch you?" Amanda asked as she climbed onto the boulder and put her arm around Taylor's shoulders.

"No. We kissed once. And then I freaked out. I was just sort of seeing how far I could get him to go. I felt kind of powerful. He said he would leave his wife for me. But she was apparently not much of a prize. He went a little crazy when I tried to put an end to the flirting."

"As they do. Tay, did you ever ask him for money?" Amanda had her fingers crossed behind her back and was praying to the hippie god of Topanga that Taylor was innocent.

"Money?"

"Yes."

"No. I had my own money."

"That's another thing we need to talk about," Amanda said, cringing.

"What?"

"The . . . Oh god." Amanda had a hard time spitting it out because her heart was where her voice was supposed to be. She watched a dragonfly hover above a dying fern. Iridescent. Translucent. Magical. *We really should have tried to stay here in this magical wood*, she thought. *Maybe our lives would have been different.* Then she brought herself back to the present. "The Lakers Girl fiasco. We found it."

"Shit." Taylor wiped her nose with the back of her forearm. She had completely regressed back to the ten-year-old that used to live here in an attempt to shield herself from the present.

"Yeah," Amanda said. "Taylor. The Lakers Girl. Explain."

"It was an idea I got from my business administration class. Subscriptions. The future of business is all about subscriptions. So people would subscribe, and I would send them tasteful photos that did not include my face. Sometimes I'd write them encouraging letters," she said without looking up. She peeled the tops off some acorns as she spoke and then arranged them into a peace sign on the big rock.

"What do you mean, encouraging . . . ? God, do I even want to know?"

"Well, I figured if they were lonely and desperate enough to send for pictures of girls, then they were probably really hurting inside. So I would tell them things like 'Hang in there' or whatever."

"And that made you feel good about yourself? Tay . . ."

"No," Taylor said, her tears beginning anew. "But it made a lot of money. Like first-year tuition money."

"TT. What if someone had found out? What if a classmate had seen it? Honey." Amanda's entire body felt heavy. A deep sadness coiled around her throat and squeezed until a tear came to her eye.

"I didn't know what else to do. I want to get out of here, Mom."

"Porn has never been a stepping-stone to anything I can think of. Except more porn."

"It wasn't p—" She couldn't say the word. "They were just like the pictures that girls send to their boyfriends all the time."

"Tay, it was like practice porn."

"I learned a lot about Internet security."

"And you were hacked by your mother. So . . ."

"So . . . what?"

"So why is Jake Hunter's wife claiming you blackmailed him?" Amanda asked, switching to the issue at hand.

"I honestly do not know. Revenge? She must have found out he was into me," Taylor said.

"Did you send any of those Lakers Girl pics to Mr. Hunter?"

"Not directly."

"What is that supposed to mean?"

Taylor shrugged. "He may have been a subscriber. I don't know everyone's real name."

"Taylor . . ."

"Okay, yes, he was one of them. Mom . . ." Taylor began. "I'm sorry this got so out of control. I was trying to grow up. Do everything by myself. You said to take matters into my own hands. So I tried, Mom, but I don't know how," Taylor said, then started sobbing. She had her mother's eyes. They got greener and greener the sadder they got.

"You did fine, Taylor. I can't believe how well you've survived the hell of the past two years. Look at you. You're doing great. You're not a cutter or a binger or a drinker or a drug addict or pregnant or suicidal or starving or depressed or OCD or ADHD or allergic to peanuts or a narcoleptic. You're not having panic attacks; you don't own a gun or a Porsche and you're probably still a virgin, yes?" Taylor nodded. "That puts you in the top ten percent of your class, mental health–wise. Look at you. You're fabulous. Okay. This is my fault. And we're going to clean this up," Amanda said, thinking to herself that she just had to clean up a few other things first. Russ, Ken, Stevens, Evan, and *then* Whitney Hunter and then . . . "and then we're starting over, okay? You and me." But she did not say the last part, "against the world," because this time they were going to work with it, the world. This time they were not going to fight.

30

All Amanda wanted to do was hang with Taylor for days, side-by-side, escorting her through life and helping her fix her problems so they could start over without this teacher thing hanging over their heads. That's all that really mattered to her, but she knew she had to put that aside for now. She had time for a quick meeting before work, so she went to see if she would run into you-know-who. She could use some advice or encouragement, but her higher power wasn't at the refreshments table this time.

Amanda hit the ladies' room before leaving, though, and someone in the stall next to her knocked on the wall and said, "You know what they say on an airplane."

"What's that?" Amanda asked.

"When your life is crashing and burning: Put on your own oxygen mask before assisting others," the voice said and then stuck her hand under the stall and asked for some toilet paper.

"Ah, yes. Thanks," Amanda said, handing her a wad. The voice was right. Taylor could hang in there for a couple more days while Amanda saved herself and initiated the plan.

First step: Operation Probable Cause. She had to send Stevens some incriminating evidence on Russ, so he'd take Russ down, and free her from her work order.

After her shift, she waited until after close. Russ was so satisfied with the whole damaged-goods skim operation that over the last few weeks he had entrusted Amanda and Lupita with more and more responsibility. Tonight Amanda arranged it so that she'd be closing the store alone. It was *Lord of the Rings* trivia night at the Bloody Sheep, so Russ left at six.

She waited for the last of the cashiers to cash out, locked the cash and checks in the safe, reconciled the credit card transactions, and shut off all the lights. As per her habit, Amanda also unlocked all the condoms and pregnancy tests so they'd at least be accessible the next day until someone noticed. Then she locked up all the guns.

She met Lupita at the side door of the building that led to the Garden Center. "Why couldn't Joyce come?" Lupita asked.

"Bingo," Amanda said.

"Bingo at ten PM?"

"Late-night bingo. With glow-in-the-dark cards and stamps or something."

"They should call it Binglow," Lupita joked.

"Hilarious," Amanda deadpanned.

The Garden Center was damp and soily and loamy and rich with the smell of peat. It was also the only place in the store without a camera. Amanda had propped the door open, a gecko skittered up the concrete wall, and then gave Lupita a basket of supplies from different departments: rubber gloves from Surgical Supply, face masks from Men's Outerwear, night vision goggles from the hunting department, pointy tools for lock picking from Hardware, and black Lycra unitards from Amanda didn't know where, and three red Santa hats from Seasonal. It was overkill, but fun nonetheless. They may as well be prepared and dress the part.

"No way I'm getting in that catsuit," Lupita said.

Once dressed, they snuck around the perimeter of the store and picked the lock to Russ's office. It took Amanda only five minutes to hack into the computer and change the surveillance feed to a continuous loop of that video of a pet porcupine eating a miniature pumpkin that everyone loves on YouTube.

"Clear," Amanda said when she was finished, and then Lupita snuck in, dressed head to toe in black and peeking through night vision goggles that were blinking with tiny green LED lights.

"Maybe the night vision goggles were overkill," Amanda admitted.

Amanda and Lupita stared at the glowing rectangle on Russ's desktop that was prompting them for a password. Russ's profile picture in the circle above it was a shirtless photo of Jon Snow wearing only the matted black furry cloak of the Night's Watch.

"Try JonSnow," Lupita said. "Or, wait—JonSnow1."

Amanda tried to type with the purple medical gloves, but they didn't fit properly, and the rubber tips flopped all over the keyboard. She thought she had typed JonSnow1, but she actually typed KinDriaq2, and the computer gave them the message "Password incorrect. You have four tries left."

"Amanda! Fix your gloves!"

She stretched them tighter and tried again, but the password was incorrect.

"Sansa?" Amanda asked Lupita. "Or Hodor? Or Frodo?"

"Too short, right? Go for a longer geek word."

They had two tries left. She decided to try the hot incestuous brother of the nasty *Game of Thrones* queen Cersei, because whether he knew it or not, Russ was in this for the homoeroticism of it all. And "the Kingslayer" was possibly as hot as Jon Snow, with the added bonus of having indecipherable morals. *It must be TheKingslayer*, Amanda thought, and she typed it carefully with one finger, and then for the hell of it added the number one at the end.

"Bingo!" Amanda said and the screen opened up right into Russ's Quicken accounts.

Lupita photographed everything as Amanda opened and closed different screens. When she clicked on his in-box she noticed he kept everything in organized folders: the skim spreadsheets. The damage claims Russ sent to Corporate. The deposit receipts for the cash he deposited into his own account. The piles of merchandise Amanda was forced to set aside on the loading dock. And the pièce de résistance: on the desk they found a register of checks he had written to Ken. They could take Ken down along with Russ.

And then they e-mailed it all to Antoine Stevens. Now all they had to do was wait.

—

In the ensuing hours Amanda sent Stevens four naked pics of her torso before she could get him to fully commit to taking down Russ and letting her know precisely when. She wanted to be there when it happened. And she needed to get back to fixing Taylor's situation. The girl was moping around at home, afraid to go back to school until Whitney Hunter was off her back.

Pleeasse? Amanda begged Stevens. *I need to do this on East Coast time. Let me know what's happening.* Naked pic. Winky face. Finally, at 7 AM the next day he texted back. *It's a go. Tomorrow. Noon.*

Working the next day was like trying to sleep on Christmas Eve when you were six years old. The suspense was killing her. She had told Lupita to call out sick just in case there was any residual fallout and the blame spilled over irresponsibly. But Amanda had to face it. She couldn't wait and couldn't wipe the smile off her face as she punched her time card for the last time in the clunky old clock.

She folded and refolded the onesies in Infant and Toddler. She took the hangers from the cashiers' bins to recycling. She vacuumed the floor mats at the entrance. She hung up all the unwanted clothing from the fitting rooms. Finally, at two, "Silver Bells" playing on the Muzak, it happened.

An entire SWAT team of men and women dressed in black surrounded the building and filed into every available door like ants into an ant trap. They had rifles, which was a bit of a scary reality check for Amanda. Talk about overkill. This was Russ they were taking down— a blender burglar—not Saddam Hussein. They shouted gruffly at everyone, even the customers, to hit the deck and stay lying on the floor as they filed quickly to the back and broke down the door to Russ's office. One woman screamed. A baby cried.

Amanda watched the surveillance cameras as the SWAT team broke down the door and filed into Russ's office.

"Freeze!" she heard them yell. And then she heard gunfire. *Gunfire?* This whole thing was much more dramatic than she'd expected. Did they shoot Russ? Why would anyone shoot Russ? Did Russ shoot himself? What was going on? She'd expected an undercover cop, perhaps dressed in an Under Armour mock turtleneck like the guy who took her down, to knock on Russ's door, read him his rights, and then strap his hands behind his back with the As Seen on TV Handy Bundler machine that makes plastic loop handcuffs or, alternatively, bundles your electrical wires together in a neat little log behind your entertainment center. Not gunfire. Not SWAT teams. Thin plastic "bundler" handcuffs. That's all that was required.

Apparently Russ had seen them coming, because: surveillance, so they found him standing on his desk wrapped in straps of ammo and shooting his Markdown rifle into the ceiling. "Why is it always the innocents who suffer most, when you high lords play your game of thrones?" he screamed, quoting George R. R. Martin. But after a short tussle in which his toupee fell off, they escorted him, hands behind his back, his big belly preceding him, his shirt buttons stretched to popping, out the main entrance.

Amanda felt a little sad about not being able to say good-bye. But aside from that she was elated. Step one of their plan was complete.

Agent Stevens came up behind her and helped her up off the floor in the produce department, where she had been restocking pints of strawberries before the SWAT team burst in. No one had turned off the music and Bing Crosby still crooned about dreaming of a white Christmas.

"Good work," Amanda said to Stevens.

"You're the one who took the initiative. Have you ever thought of a career in law enforcement?"

"Never," she said, and looking up at him, she noticed a glimmer of familiarity in his eye. A collegial "we're friends because we shared this" kind of twinkle. Amanda remembered how easily he was able to shoot a kid on a bike and her stomach turned. *We share nothing in common*, she thought to herself. And she couldn't wait to get him out of her life. If all went well, she'd have only one more step to endure in the master plan concocted by her and Bruce.

Just then, Jane from Corporate, dressed in a sensibly cut red-skirted business suit ushered what customers were left toward the front door and pushed Amanda and Stevens out, too, before getting her muscly bodyguard to padlock all the doors with heavy chains so the store could begin its investigation.

Amanda and Agent Stevens stood in the parking lot while police lights still swung around in red and blue and the black SWAT team truck pulled away. They heard Russ being read his rights as they ducked his head into a squad car. Amanda felt like she could finally take a deep breath.

She had one more thing to do to officially get herself released from her work order.

She called Ken's home number, and his wife answered.

"Officer Ken Johnson please," Amanda said. She could hear kids fighting in the background about who gets to put the red icing on the Santa cookie. And then she heard Ken's wife shushing the kids and handing Ken the phone.

"This is Ken," he said.

Amanda launched into it. "Listen, you sorry asshole, I have it all."

"I've always said you had it all," Ken answered. "The most potential of all my scumbags."

Amanda ignored him and carried on. "Phone records, your texts to Russ, photos of his check register, and as we speak I'm standing right next to an esteemed senior agent of the FBI in the Markdown parking lot where everything just went down."

"I see," Ken said calmly, clearly not wanting to scare the children whom she could still hear bickering, now about sprinkles.

"I can send the FBI to your house to interrupt your cookie-decorating party, or you could mark my work order as 'complete' and never speak to me again. Amanda Cooper will heretofore have no further responsibility to the State of California. Got it?"

"That might be possible," he said.

"Make it possible."

"I'll see what I can do."

"Lupita, too, obviously."

"Obviously," Ken said and then hung up quietly.

The special conditions of her parole were over. She could find a "job job" and get herself enrolled in college.

She sent a text to Lupita and told her the good news.

"When can I see you again?" Stevens asked, as he leaned against a squad car.

Amanda had just hung up the phone and was basking in the after-glow of her takedown of Ken, and in her reverie, she kind of forgot he was still there. "Well, this definitely calls for a celebration," she said, "and I did promise you a reward. I'm learning from AA to keep my promises." She tried not to gag a little as she said the words, breathing deeply through her nose to calm the back of her throat. She spread her legs into a power-pose position and put her hands on her hips for strength. "Tomorrow," Amanda said. "I have something special planned."

31

She was too amped to sleep that night in the hot cubicle of her bedroom. The special rubbery fitted sheet that was supposed to prevent bedbugs from penetrating the rental mattress kept crinkling every time she moved and she was just hot and agitated. She knew what she needed to do, but when she snuck out of bed and pulled the curtain aside, she noticed Evan's men outside. There were two of them again, playing poker in the black SUV parked across the street.

She had called Evan earlier that day, just to put the operation in motion.

"I have your money," she told him.

"Do I look like a loan officer to you? Or a bail bondsman or something? I know those are the types you surround yourself with these days, but this will not be resolved with money. How vulgar do you think I am?" he asked her.

"I was just hoping . . ."

"Abandon all hope, ye who enter here."

"What?"

"You, by spurning me, have entered the gates of hell, Amanda. There is no hope in hell, sweetheart. I thought we'd been over that."

"Can we just meet, please? At four thirty tomorrow. Our regular suite at the Four Seasons. I have your money. I know it won't absolve me, but I just don't want it. I need to pay you back."

Finally, he agreed.

Thinking about the conversation now just made her toss and turn even more. "Shit," she mumbled to herself. It was 2:22, and there was no way she was going to fall asleep. She got out of bed, snuck into the garage, and went out the back door that led to the enclosure with the garbage cans. The walls of the enclosure were just high enough, if she could climb on top of them like an alley cat, for her to reach Ben's bedroom balcony. If her core was strong enough, which was doubtful these days, she could perhaps swing her body up onto the balcony and sneak into Ben's bedroom without Evan's people noticing.

She grabbed the top of the wall, used the garbage can as a stepladder, and then stepped her long leg up so that her foot was wedged between planks at the top of the fence. Then with all her energy, she stepped her other foot up until she was squatting like a frog on top of the garbage can enclosure. It hadn't even occurred to her until that very moment, how desperate her actions had become. What would Ben think of her if she tried to sneak into his bedroom? What if he found her like this? What if there was another woman in there right now? She hadn't been thinking straight, and she froze for a second, but then she began to wobble and her only choice was to reach for the rails of Ben's balcony and then leap from the fence to the balcony.

It was not a graceful landing.

Ben's cat started howling and Amanda could hear his covers rustling, and then before she could even sit up and check for blood (something was definitely bleeding), Ben shined his flashlight out the sliding glass door and into her face. She shielded her eyes and whispered, "Don't turn on the light. They're watching us. Shhhh," and then held her finger up to her lips like a librarian.

"What do you mean, shhh?" Ben whispered. "What are you doing?"

"Booty call?" Amanda tried.

"Most people use a telephone."

"Let me in before they see me."

Ben slid open the door and invited her under the covers. They sat under there with the flashlight like a couple of kids in a couch-fort on a playdate. Amanda checked for wounds, found some, and Ben reached for a tissue on the nightstand.

"This is so romantic," Ben joked.

"I just couldn't relax until I saw you. You have a soothing effect on me." It was true. Seeing him just made her feel safe somehow. Something she'd actually never felt in her entire life. Safe.

"So, if you don't mind me asking, why can't you go to the police about this Evan guy? Get a restraining order or whatever? I don't know if you realize, but this seems like an abusive situation . . ."

"He is a very, very bad man. But I stole a lot of money from the very bad man. And in this country the law prioritizes money over the safety of its womenfolk."

"Can't you give the money back? It's not like you've been spending it from prison."

"I could, except . . ."

"Except what?"

"Except Joyce bet it all on a horse."

"All of it?"

"A whole suitcase full."

"Fucking Joyce," he said. It was the first time she'd heard him say anything negative about her mother and she loved and hated it at the same time. "How much do you need?" he asked.

"Too much. And he won't even take my money. He just wants to torture me like I apparently tortured him."

"Then what are you going to do?"

"I have a plan, I think. I've been accepting too many things and I need to get the courage to change the things I can."

"Sounds dangerous."

"Yup. Which is why I need you to help me relax," she said. He wore a thin worn-to-translucent Virginia Tech T-shirt and she slid her hand underneath it letting it slide lightly over the contours of his torso. Which were hard, smooth, and sharply defined like the fossilized rippled sand of an ancient riverbed. "Swinging a hammer does a body good," she said, ducking her head beneath the T-shirt.

"That's part of why I do it."

"What's the other part?" she asked.

"I like being able to see what I've accomplished in a day. Step back and admire what I've made."

"That must feel good. I don't think I've ever really made anything."

"Taylor."

"Yeah, Taylor. That's a little messed up, too, at the moment," she admitted.

"What's wrong? Trouble at school? Did Joyce have her running numbers again?"

"She did that?" Amanda asked.

"Only for a short time."

"God. Joyce. Anyway. Taylor got herself in trouble this time. She was trying to be entrepreneurial, I guess. Going about it in the only way she knew how. Flirting with her teacher. She even, gulp, sold pictures of herself on the Internet."

"No. Taylor?" Ben was genuinely surprised. He'd been helping her with her geometry while Amanda was away. He'd known how smart she was. Thought she was pretty straitlaced and focused.

"She was trying to raise money for college. God," Amanda said, shaking her head. "I can't believe I dropped the ball on this. There were some signs I missed but I was so distracted. Parents are always blind to the most vital issue at hand. It's embarrassing.

"Like a speech pathologist who doesn't realize her kid has a speech impediment. Or a shrink who doesn't realize her kid is depressed. I was a criminal who didn't believe my kid capable of committing crimes. Stupid."

"At least she has goals," Ben said. "Even if her means to an end were questionable."

"Yeah. I'm proud of her for just surviving the past two years. Sometimes I do step back and admire her and think, 'Look what I made.' Well, if I didn't make her, at least I fed her the right things. Look at her, right?"

"I'm looking at you," he said, glancing down her body lasciviously. "Someone fed you the right things, too."

"Really?" Amanda said, sliding farther down under the covers and letting herself disappear beneath the luscious weight of him.

32

It was so nice to sleep in and not have to worry about her Markdown schedule ever again. Taylor was gone when she woke at eleven. The note she left on the table said she was "studying." Amanda had told her to keep a low profile. She was still staying home from school, but Amanda had asked her to keep up on her work. "I don't want you falling behind," she'd told her. Taylor seemed to be living up to her word.

Now came the hard part. Russ and Markdown were just a tiny appetizer. An *amuse-bouche*. A tiny bite of criminal vengeance to excite the palate for the big feast. But she was not going to enjoy this feast one bit. Just the thought of it made her wretch and she went to the kitchen and swigged a whole shot of Pepto-Bismol straight from the bottle. Breakfast of champions.

A quick glance across the street let Amanda know that Evan's private-eye buddies were still watching her every move. They sat in the car with the windows wide open to air out the oniony smell of their breakfast burritos from Astro Burger on Melrose. *Might as well get this over with*, she thought.

She called Bruce, because he still didn't have a texting function on his phone, and said: "Commence Operation Two Birds."

"With one stone," he said gruffly, and then quickly hung up.

Then she got on the horn with Agent Stevens and told him how grateful she was. He had rescued her from a certain trip back to prison or a future in box-store retail. He had helped her finally take charge of her life. She wanted to thank him with a special celebration in Suite 413 of the Four Seasons. "Champagne," she said. "Etcetera."

"I like the sound of etcetera," he said.

"Four o'clock," she confirmed and then shuddered a little as she hung up.

She checked with Roderigo, the concierge, to verify that Suite 413, the one she practically lived in with Evan two years ago, was available and booked in her false name. She also confirmed that Roderigo had spoken to Evan and made dinner reservations for him, and she had asked him what time he planned to arrive at the hotel.

"Definitely four thirty, Miss Vanessa. He's always on time."

"Excellent news. Thanks, Roderigo."

At three when Amanda pulled up to valet parking in the carport, she disembarked from the van and noticed her higher-power Carrie Fisher, sitting outside, smoking on a bench. Same poncho. Same big sunglasses.

"What are you doing here?" Amanda asked.

"I had a life outside AA. I used to lunch here with my agent."

"I don't like how I'm always running into you."

"I wonder why that is?"

"You are not real."

"Like I told you before: perception is reality. If you're perceiving me, then I'm part of your reality. Maybe I'm part of your conscience. It seems like you're maybe up to no good."

"How do you figure?"

"Aside from the fact that nothing good ever happens at the Four Seasons? Um. You just look guilty. Sort of rushed and impulsive. That's when the worst mistakes happen. That's when you do things that will haunt you forever. Maybe you should sleep on it."

"This is the only way out."

"It's not *out* if it pulls you deeper *in*," she said with some complicated arm movements that were slightly vulgar and not necessarily helpful in illustrating her point.

"I gotta go."

"You read the new Franzen, right?"

"In prison."

"And *Macbeth*?"

"A person reads a lot in prison."

"Perfect. Then you know what I'm talking about."

Amanda held her hand up to the woman and grabbed her overnight bag from the backseat.

"Did you just do 'talk to the hand'? That's so nineties."

"Good-bye," Amanda said, and she stormed to the front desk to get her key before she lost her resolve.

Upstairs in Suite 413, she laid out the chocolate-covered strawberries, popped the champagne, and let it sit in the ice bucket to breathe. She put on her raciest black negligee and put on Jimi Hendrix's *Blues*. Not typical seduction music, but she liked it.

At three forty-five, she began to meditate, sitting in lotus, staring straight at a candle until her vision blurred and then clearing her mind by sending all thoughts away. *In for four, hold for seven, out for eight.* She put the precious glowing ball of light that was her self outside the physical thing that was her body so that she could continue on with this dirty business.

At four, Antoine Stevens knocked on the door. His hard-body outlaw look still intact, he dressed impeccably all in black, his jeans hugging his slightly bowed, muscular thighs, his leather jacket expensive, well tanned, and soft to the touch. "Come in," she said and she pulled the drawstring of her robe so that it would fall open as she whisked the flowers he'd thought to bring away and put them in a vase.

"Can I get you a drink?" Amanda asked. Her phone was stationed next to the vase, and she pressed Call and then quickly hung up, which was her signal to Bruce to get in position.

If he received the call, which Amanda hoped he did, he would plant himself in the lobby, loitering there in case Amanda needed to be extracted.

"Cheers." Amanda smiled as she sauntered over and sat next to Stevens on the white French Colonial couch with the golden lion's feet. The whole room was decorated in colonial style with a swooping damask valance over the window gathered together in half-circles like a bunting on the Fourth of July. It felt like they were in Lincoln's bedroom or something but all in white, which would be problematic if things got messy.

"You look beautiful," Stevens said, taking his glass. "And this room is perfect. Luxurious."

"You think? To me it kind of feels like we're here to sign the Declaration of Independence." She walked over to the thin bowlegged desk and flipped the hinged colonial drawer pull so that it flopped down with an annoying clink.

"That's romantic in my neck of the woods."

"Which is?" Amanda asked.

"Around DC."

"Right," she said. "You're not drinking," she noticed.

"Yeah. I have a bad relationship with the sauce. Used it to self-medicate as a kid," he said, looking to the floor. "And I didn't have a lot of luck with the ladies. Anger management."

Scary town, Amanda thought.

"Still dealing with some of the lawsuits," Stevens continued. "Bitches got lawyered up," he said somewhat jokingly.

"I hate that," Amanda said. "Lawyered up. God. What bitches."

"You wouldn't do that."

"No. I take care of my own business. I don't need the suits."

"That's what I like about you. Come here," he said.

"One sec, I'm just going to use the ladies'." It wasn't close enough to four thirty for her to begin Operation Two Birds. She was stalling and stood in front of the mirror trying to tap the bags around her eyes, hoping they would shrink a bit. And then she jumped when behind her she saw you-know-who, her higher-power Carrie Fisher, trying to scrub her hands in the bathtub faucet.

"Out, damned spot!" she said.

And Amanda countered, "You are not real. You are not real." This whole thing was making her lose her mind.

She hesitated but then mustered up the nerve, opened the bathroom door, and walked over to Agent Stevens. If she was going to do this, she needed to get it over with. She stood powerfully in front of him, let him grab her behind her right hip, and pull her closer to him. Then he buried his face into her torso, working his way downward.

"Um," she said. Her palms were sweating and her legs trembled. Not because of what Stevens was doing, but because she suddenly realized she might never live this down. She was second-guessing the plan. Could she really go live some innocent life in a stand-alone house with a patio and an herb garden knowing she'd set this man up? Would she really be able to live with herself and create some new identity, selling mittens on Etsy? After masterminding this whole criminal plot? Karma would catch up to her, right? No one would buy her damn murderer mittens. *Murderer.* That was the first time that word slipped into her consciousness.

"I know I made some promises here, but I think I need to urgently call the whole thing off." She stuck her fingers into his thick black curls and tilted his neck backward to get his face out of her parts.

"Did you get your period or something? What?"

"Ew, no. Gross. It's just that this could get dangerous for you in a minute, and I need you to leave. Quickly," she said, trying to get him to stand up.

Amanda looked down into his face and saw a glimmer of boyish disappointment grow quickly into abusive rage. "Do you think this is some kind of game?" he asked.

"No. It's very serious, actually. I need you to go." She tried to lift him up from where he knelt shirtless on the rug, but he was dense and unmovable, like a stone monument to the cockblock.

"I don't get it. You owe me." He was trying to stay calm but she watched his face flush with uncontrollable rage. The telltale artery on the right side of his neck bulged and began to throb. He opened and closed his fists and counted to ten beneath his breath.

"Whoa, now. It's okay, Antoine. I changed my mind. I need you to get up and go. I don't have time to explain but it's a matter of life and death."

He stood up, finally, and she tried to pull him toward the bathroom in order to hide him in the tub, but he cranked his arm back and then whacked her with the full force of the back of his hand. She found out from the gash on her cheek that he wore an enormous ring signifying his membership in the fraternal order of Freemasons. She was woozy for a second and then said, "Is it true that you guys are in possession of the Holy Grail?"

"What?" he asked.

She cleared her head and looked at the clock: 4:28. "Seriously, Antoine. You need to go."

"Not until I get what I came for," he said, pushing her onto the bed. He was so powerful; she was helpless. He climbed onto the bed, stood over her, and kicked her in the stomach. She curled into a fetal position and reached to the nightstand for her phone. She wanted to give Bruce the "abort mission" signal, but then another blow came crashing into her ribs.

"Listen," she tried to tell him once more. She could feel a giant gumball of a bruise growing inside her cheek where he'd hit her with the ring. "Someone is due to arrive any minute, and he's not going to take kindly to you being here."

"Well, he'll just have to wait his turn then, won't he?" Stevens was in full-on rage at this point. Out of his body, separate from his soul, whirring and whirling a mile a minute. A soldier bent on raping and pillaging. She couldn't break through his rage.

He pinned her to the bed, and Amanda struggled to free herself but he was too strong. And then he was unbuckling his belt. He slid it from around his waist, and it made a sibilant whoosh before it threatened to crack down across her face.

When the clock struck 4:32, he was on top of her, and she heard Evan's key slide in. The automated lock responded with three purring clicks. She heard the clunk of the door handle as he pushed it down and then she heard her name. "Amanda?"

Amanda kicked at Stevens's rock-hard torso and gave him another urgent look. "Leave!" she whispered but he kissed her, hard, and bit her on the lip, drawing blood.

The next thing she knew, Evan was in the bedroom. Without a second's hesitation, he grabbed Stevens's belt and then wrapped it around his neck. Stevens gasped and coughed and gagged, kicking as Evan lifted him a foot off the ground and continued to pull the belt tighter.

"Stop!" Amanda yelled. She understood now what she'd done, and the guilty outside layer of her skin burned with shame. She checked the clock: 4:35. If Bruce had done his job, he would have called 911 at 4:20, giving the Beverly Hills cops sufficient time to mosey on over and get to the fourth floor just after the worst had happened. But she needed them here now, so they could end what she had put into motion.

"Stop!" she yelled again, but after another minute of struggle, Stevens's face turned the white-blue of slate. His tongue swelled and hung to one side, and his body fell to the floor in a heap, like someone had cut down a punching bag. His breathing had stopped. Amanda noticed streams of tears had been making their way down her temples and pooling in her ears. She ran to Stevens and tilted his head back as if to give him CPR. She even pinched his nose and breathed into his mouth and then pumped on his chest, four quick pumps with the heel of her hand.

She kept it up, hoping to breathe some life back into him, waiting for the rise and fall of his chest to resume. "Come on, Antoine," she yelled at him. "Breathe!"

"See," Evan said, ignoring her efforts and whipping out a pansy-ass handkerchief and swabbing his brow with it, as if this were his normal post-murder ritual. "I told you this would happen the moment you looked at another man. Did you have to test me, Amanda? Did you not think I was a man of my word? Now help me wrap him in this blanket." He pulled the white comforter off the bed with a flourish, like a bad magician doing the tablecloth trick, and just as he let it drift over Stevens's dead carcass, the police kicked in the door.

"Don't move," they barked, pistols out and pointing at the two of them. A policewoman ran to Stevens's body. "No pulse," she said.

"What happened here?" the bald cop asked.

But they were both still gasping for breath from the struggle and in too much shock to answer.

"You." The female cop nudged Amanda with her boot. "What happened?" She kept her gun pointed at Evan.

"He killed my boyfriend in a jealous rage," Amanda droned, completely devoid of emotion. She was in shock, but she knew enough to finish the job she set out to do since she couldn't put a halt to it.

"What?!" Evan looked at her incredulously and stood up, about to hit her. The bald policeman restrained him and twisted his arm behind his back. "She was about to be raped," he lied. "I was rescuing her."

"Why would I be resuscitating my rapist?" Amanda asked.

"I've seen stranger things," the policewoman said and then looked at Amanda woman-to-woman, and Amanda shook her head, slowly, like, "No. He's lying." Then the woman, an Officer Gutierrez, said "Let's go" to Evan. And then she read him his rights as the other officer pushed Evan out the door.

"I'll get you for this," Evan screamed, shaking his fist in the air on his way out. "She set me up," he yelled.

Amanda wished he'd said something that wasn't straight out of a comic book. She sat at the foot of the bed unable to move.

A coroner came up and took Agent Stevens out in a body bag. She'd never forget the sound of that durable zipper. A social worker was sent to sit with Amanda. She wrapped her in one of those silver Mylar après marathon blankets to help her recover from the shock.

"Do you need to get checked out?" she asked Amanda. "We can take you to the ER."

"No. Thanks," Amanda said, but she probably should have taken them up on it because she was in so much shock that she didn't remember anything that happened after she found Bruce waiting in the parking lot across the street. Somehow she'd ended up in her own bed, wearing Joyce's flannel pajamas, and had slept for seventeen hours.

33

The yellow LA light, usually so aggravating to Amanda, softened into a liquid warmth and flooded her curtainless bedroom the next day, filling her with a sense of calm she had never felt before. Forty-two years old and she'd never, ever, as far back as she could remember, felt safe and relaxed. This morning the sun had injected her with a liquid equanimity. *A good name for a blog,* she thought. *Or a really bad new-age slow jam.*

Normal people probably felt this every day. She couldn't imagine how different her life would have been if she had made all of her big decisions from this grounded, centered, soft place and not from the frazzled, sharp, and harried one that usually took control of her frontal lobe or cerebral cortex or whatever it was that made all the stupid mistakes. Maybe this was what it was like to be a man.

She tried to make it last, in for four, hold for seven, out for eight, before she let the dark thoughts seep in and trickle down the walls of her happiness like in a horror movie. Stevens was dead, and it was because of her. Sort of. In for four, hold for seven, out for eight. But even that thought didn't completely destroy her calm. She'd tried to warn him. And he'd have destroyed Bruce and Joyce in one fell swoop. She did what she had to do. For family.

She took down Russ, Ken, Stevens, and Evan, and left herself with a clean slate. She couldn't let guilt get in the way of her fresh start. She did what she had to do, she repeated to herself. To survive. She'd have to compartmentalize. Like a dude would. Compartmentalize. Compartmentalize. Compartmentalize. The secret to dude success. Don't let the horror of your past bleed into the present.

The calm stayed with her as she put on a robe. It stayed with her as she opened the fridge and poured some orange juice. It was luscious, this calm. She let herself enjoy it for five more minutes. It stayed with her as she toasted her toast and as she scooped in the six scoops of coffee grinds into the filter. Then she knocked on Taylor's door.

"Mom!" Taylor said.

That's when liquid equanimity left the building.

Taylor sat on her bed, held up her laptop, and tilted it toward her mother. "Look. Look what she's doing now," Taylor said.

On the screen was a collage of Taylor's body parts presumably ripped from Lakers Girl Inc. before they were able to purge them. In an e-mail, Whitney was threatening to show them to the principal and get Taylor expelled if she didn't pay back the money she extorted.

"We ignored her for too long, Mom. You said you would fix this," Taylor whined. "I didn't extort anything!"

"Now what?" Joyce asked as she sauntered in with Bruce in tow. It was lunchtime and the two of them got to work making sandwiches, which was uncharacteristic. Their family wasn't really motivated or comforted by food the way others were. Maybe that's why Taylor had gained such an interest in it. It filled a gap.

"She didn't do it," Amanda said.

"Thatta girl. That's what you tell them. First three rules of interrogation: deny, deny, deny," Joyce said. She'd already poured herself a drink. She swirled the ice around, took a drag of her Benson & Hedges, and pointed at the cold cut platter on the ugly table. "Have a sandwich."

"Mom. She really did not do it. The wife is up to something. Whitney Hunter, I think her name was. But we need to prove it."

"Let me just finish my drink, and we'll come up with a plan." Taylor went into her bedroom and shut the door. "Man down," Joyce said. "She should help."

"Just give her some space, okay," said Amanda.

"This her?" Joyce asked after only two minutes of clicking around.

Amanda looked at the photo Joyce had pulled up. It was a professional headshot in black and white: a posh young woman in a business suit. Her LinkedIn profile picture. "Could be," she said. "That's what she sounded like, anyway. Tay, come here for just one second."

Taylor emerged from her bedroom, dazed and groggy from her drama hangover. "Is this her?" Amanda asked her. "The wife?"

"Yes. That's her."

"What does she do?"

"Some, like, consulting thing. Does anyone even know what that means?"

"No," Amanda said. "No one does."

"I can't look at her," Taylor said, and she walked away from the computer, flopped on the couch, and flipped through the cooking channels.

Amanda viewed the LinkedIn profile and used it to find Whitney Hunter's Facebook profile. Around thirty-three years old, Whitney Hunter was like the anti-Amanda. She posted often to social media. Pictures of herself in a huddle of old sorority sisters at some fancy fund-raising event—cleaned up now, impeccable and well-shod. Or in the middle of a group of T-shirted women at the end of some charity races, glowing and blushing and healthy. Or at weddings, bar mitzvahs, reunions. She was constantly surrounded by people who pretended to like her and then probably talked about her behind her back. But at least Whitney Hunter got to believe that she was well liked. And got to project that image out into the world.

If Amanda had a Facebook feed, it would be filled with pics of the green felt black jack table she took while she sat there and waited for Evan, or the ice cubes melting in someone's drink at the strip club she was forced to attend with him, or a close-up of an abusive man's pinky ring before it smashed into her cheek, or God forbid, a shot of her orange prison jumpsuit pocket stamped with the number 3922492.

But the snapshots of her life were changing bit by bit. She could imagine posting a close-up of the shiny underbelly of the airplane as she sat beneath it at takeoff with Ben. Or a picture of the two of them on the bridge at SuihoEn. Or a selfie of her and Lupita on the loading dock of Markdown, flashing their similar Madonna-like, gap-toothed grins. Or a picture of Taylor sitting on a sun-dappled boulder at the Fairy House, while behind her a dragonfly hovered and silently wished them luck.

Joyce brought out Taylor's computer and tried to figure out where the Hunters banked. Amanda looked over her shoulder and asked what she was doing.

"Well, if she was trying to frame Taylor, then she was probably withdrawing the money herself and making it look like it was the dumbass. We just have to prove she was the one deducting the money."

"I know where they bank," Taylor said.

"How do you know that, if you weren't involved in the blackmail?" Joyce asked.

"He was a client in one of my other concerns," Taylor said without looking away from the television. She had microwaved some popcorn and ate it in a daze one kernel at a time while Alex Guarnaschelli told some schmo what was wrong with the concoction he prepared on *Chopped*.

"That microwave popcorn gives people Parkinson's," Joyce said. "I just read it on the Internet. Poison."

Taylor ate one last piece and then put the rest of the bag on the coffee table and brushed her hands off, her eyes still focused entirely on the screen. "Wells Fargo," she said.

"Oh, Wells Fargo." She slammed the computer lid down. "We can just go talk to Jimmy. Come on. It's a little chilly out. Grab your jackets," she said as if she were taking them out to the ballgame.

Joyce drove them to a very inconspicuous Wells Fargo branch in La Brea near the tar pits. No fancy marble or posh bank-y decor. Only worn industrial-gray carpet and some rubber welcome mats and heavily used rental office furniture from circa 1967. It didn't even have a revolving door. Amanda slammed into it for a second as they approached. "It says 'pull,' dummy. God, play it cool," Joyce whispered and then, as she entered, turned on the sugar. "Jimmeeee," she sang as she sauntered in like Joan Crawford and took Jimmy's hand.

"Joyce," he said. "It's always a pleasure."

Joyce, though seemingly a one-woman show, was actually supported by an entire network of losers around the city who were easily persuaded to do her criminal bidding with a wink and a nod and a couple hundred-dollar bills. She had Marge at the DMV, Yung Li at the CVS, Janice at Kaiser Permanente, and this man, Jimmy, from Wells Fargo. Jimmy dressed in the archetypal uniform of a banker. Greased-back hair. Dress pants. Suspenders. The only thing missing was his money-counting visor.

"Thanks for taking us on such short notice, Jimmy," Joyce said, reaching for his hand again with both of hers, while she expertly slipped a couple of Benjamins into his palm.

"Anything for you. You know that. Step into my office," he said and gestured for them to follow him into the one space in the bank that actually had a door and walls that reached high enough to intersect the ceiling. He had a couple of pictures of his kids in a hinged frame that stood on his desk.

Joyce sat down and unraveled her notes, passing them over the desk to Jimmy. "So we're interested in tracking some withdrawals," she said and then explained the whole situation.

Jimmy made some small talk while he clicked away and then waited. After a minute of tapping his fingers on the desk, he looked up from the screen. "Okay. I have it up," he said, squinting. "If what you say is true, she was at least smart enough to make the withdrawals with his debit card."

"Crap," Amanda said, sighing.

"What about the cameras," Joyce asked. "Did you get the special access that we talked about, yet?"

"I have access to our branch's security feed, but I'm not sure if I can tap into other branches. Let me try. This particular withdrawal on his card was from a Santa Monica Third Street Promenade branch, a week ago at noon."

"That's when we have English," Taylor said. "It couldn't have been him."

Jimmy concentrated, put on his reading glasses, and got down to business. He entered a bunch of complicated passwords and they let him run a program to sift through the digital camera feed files until he found the one he wanted. He opened up the link, and there she was. Yoga bag slung over her back like a bazooka, nervously tapping her foot like she had to pee. Whitney Hunter.

He continued the process with each large ATM withdrawal made on Jake's card, and every time she was there.

"We got her," said Joyce.

Jimmy printed up the stills, handed them to Joyce, and said, "Pleasure doing business with you."

"Here you go. Do with these what you will," Joyce said, handing the documents to Amanda. "That was almost too easy. I still have time for church circle. Want to donate five dollars? We're sending water and porta-potties to Syrian refugees in Turkey," she said and then pushed open the door to the bank ushering all three generations out into the intrusive LA sunlight.

—

On a tip from their favorite, tortured, and caught-between-a-rock-and-a-hard-place idiot of an English teacher, Amanda found Whitney in the Barneys shoe department, which is where she herself would go, actually, if she was stealing $5,000 a month from her own self. (She wasn't stealing it from Jake, obviously. Teachers didn't even make $5,000 a month.)

Amanda pretended to peruse the Blahniks, while keeping the

lovely Whitney in her peripheral vision. She was a beautiful, if a bit plain, slim, and put-together five foot nine, with a long neck and shiny chestnut hair that fell past her shoulders. She delivered a sample sling-back to the attendant and asked for a size seven.

"Bullshit . . ." Amanda disguised beneath a dry cough. There was no way she was a size seven. Was she so insecure that she had to lie about her shoe size? Well, she was insecure enough to try to take down a sixteen-year-old, so, yes.

Amanda inched closer to the center of the department, where Whitney sat neatly in a leather chair as if awaiting her prince charming and his glass slipper. She waited patiently at first and then finally, bored, stood up.

No time like the present, Amanda thought. "Whitney?" Amanda chirped like a socialite as she approached the chair. "Whitney Hunter?"

"I'm sorry. Do I know you?" Whitney said. "I pride myself on never forgetting a face. It's a business thing . . . But I don't seem to recall . . ."

"Hi. I'm Amanda," Amanda said, offering Whitney her hand. "I'm on the decorations committee for the Winter Festival at the school—Jake's school—and I heard you sometimes like to help out with those things, so I thought I'd introduce myself. You are Jake Hunter's partner, aren't you? He's such a dear."

"Oh. Yes," Whitney answered, looking down at her phone, not deigning to give a lowly PTA mom the time of day. *I went to Princeton, for God's sake*, Amanda could hear her thinking.

Little did Whitney know that she would try to transfer her Ivy League skills to the mundane work of the PTA herself one day, so desperate would she be to gain back the imagined power she lost as an executive. She would make the PTA her queendom and use it to define her entire existence. Sad, really.

"He seems to really love my daughter," Amanda added.

It was then that a glimmer of recognition started to take hold, as she must have begun to recognize Amanda's voice from the phone call they shared. She slowly looked up.

"Do you have my money?" she asked.

"Actually, Whit—can I call you Whit?" Amanda said. "We've done some research, and you've been a little sloppy in your criminal masterminding."

"Impossible," Whitney claimed. "I mean, what criminal masterminding?"

"We can prove beyond a shadow of a doubt that you were withdrawing the money. Not Jake. We even have surveillance-camera footage from the Wells Fargo," Amanda said. "So I think you better change your story. Here. See for yourself." Amanda handed her the photos.

"How did you get these?"

Amanda ignored the question. "How could you possibly try to scapegoat an innocent sixteen-year-old girl and wreck her life?"

"Innocent? What a joke. And with a mother like you, her life was already ruined. I wasn't about to let some trash destroy my marriage. Delta Gammas do not get divorced. At least never in the first five years of their marriage. My life would be ruined. It was her life or mine, and after a simple cost-benefit analysis, it was easy to choose mine. My life is worth much more to society."

"Wow. You're more disgusting than I thought," Amanda said. "Stay away from us." The shoe attendant arrived then, carrying a few boxes of size sevens. "Those are never going to fit you, by the way. Don't even bother," she continued and then stormed off, forgetting that she was still carrying the patent blush Blahnik floor model until the alarm went off when she tried to exit the store.

34

Amanda decided to go to one last AA meeting before she headed out of Dodge. It was a juicy one, too, with lots of stories about celebrity hot-tub hookups and waking up sand-burned on the beach. Amanda was going to miss this crowd. She imagined the folks in Northern California would be a little dopier and crunchier and less in tune with their own narcissism.

They had decided on the East Bay because Amanda found a program in substance abuse counseling at a local college, and because half the people there were therapists. The other half, mostly lost and lonely transplants from the East Coast, were in therapy. There would be a constant flow of business in the East Bay. And they found a great high school for Taylor where she could slow down, get her act together, and apply to some really good colleges.

Amanda listened to the final story, about a man who knew he was an alcoholic after he unwittingly sideswiped a palm tree and drove the rest of the way home from the club with the entire thing lodged in the hood of his car. He didn't even notice it until morning. "An entire tree," he said, shaking his head, "just growing out of the hood." Other folks tried to one-up him for a spell, explaining what weird things they'd unwittingly dragged home, including people, dead animals, road signs, and someone else's car altogether, and when it was over, Amanda got up and headed out without even hitting the refreshments table.

"Pssst," she heard before she got to the door.

She turned around. "Hey, I'm glad I bumped into you," Amanda said. "I'm headed out of town."

"You know, geography never solved anybody's problems," imaginary Carrie Fisher said.

"I know . . ."

"Where you go, there you are," CF continued.

"It seems like where I go, there *you* are," Amanda joked.

"That's the power of the Force."

"I guess so," Amanda said.

"So if you must go, may the Force be with you. Best of luck," Carrie Fisher said shyly, attempting to look Amanda in the eye.

"Thanks! I'm sure I'll run into you again sometime. There are no accidents, right? Thanks so much for taking me under your wing."

"My pleasure. You remind me of myself at your age."

"Well, that's a compliment. Until we meet again," Amanda said, shaking the woman's hand, which felt so real for a hallucination, and then she headed home.

———

Bruce, bless his heart, bought them a used Prius for Christmas, so they would fit in in the East Bay. He even bought some magnetic daisies to affix to the bumper so that they could make a friendly first impression. It was parked in the driveway and Taylor was packing it when Amanda arrived home. They didn't have many possessions left, and there was more room in those things than people imagine, so they didn't even end up needing a U-Haul, but the car was packed to the hilt. Maurice was squashed against the rear window, staring out at the road in anxious anticipation.

Bruce had also given them three months' rent (first/last/security) for a rental in Oakland off College, plus a little pocket money. They were so grateful. It was their own little fairy house, but rather than tucked into the magical wood of Topanga, it was surrounded by hundreds of tiny tract homes exactly like it. A tiny whimsical 1940s bungalow steeped in the history of hippies past, the woodwork painted over with an entire inch of previous tenant color choices, whose built-in dresser drawers were so gummed up with paint, they were almost impossible to open.

But it was theirs and it had a tiny patio for an herb garden, was walking distance to five farmers' markets, not to mention Berkeley Bowl, and it had an elliptical stained glass window with a dragonfly in the bathroom, which Amanda took as a sign. There are no accidents. They called it Dragonfly Ranch.

She parked the minivan in the garage and thanked it for its final voyage, slapping it on its trusty flank, then climbed the garage stairs to the apartment to make sure they hadn't forgotten anything. Amanda's two remaining black Rolie Bags, filled with clothes, had already been packed, as well as two boxes of books and photo albums. She had one box of kitchen things she had purchased with her Markdown employee discount and a few towels and sheets. What else does a person need?

Taylor smiled at Amanda as she carried out what Amanda hoped was the last of the boxes. It was overflowing a bit with nail polish, hair products, a straightening iron, a blow-dryer, and some makeup.

Taylor seemed better since "the incident." Energized by the idea of a fresh start and slowly trying to reconcile the innocent, trusting child inside her with the skeptical, scowling teen who had seen too much of the dark side. It was a process. But Amanda hoped she'd see more and more of Taylor's smile and perhaps catch a few notes of the vestigial belly giggle from her toddler days that used to buoy her through Taylor's childhood. She could only hope. It was one of the things she lived for.

Amanda checked her purse and made sure she had her wallet, keys, phone, charger, and her lease, and she was ready to go. She checked Taylor's room one more time. It was empty. The curtains were gone and she could see the drainpipe still jutting out awkwardly like a broken arm. *In for four, hold for seven, out for eight*, she breathed, and then she stepped out into the nosy glare of the LA sun. She was happy that it would no longer be all up in her business. It was cloudy up north and there were more places to think in shrouded solitude.

Bruce had showed up to say good-bye. He stood next to the Prius and asked dad questions about whether she'd changed the oil and had the brakes checked and whether there was enough air in the tires. "It looks so low to the ground," he said, kicking the tires.

"You've checked it seven times," Amanda said, but she let him do it once more, squatting with his bad leg and using his old-school slide-rule-type pressure gauge, and then she helped him up.

She hugged him and he said, "I'm going to miss you, Mandy. It's been nice having you around."

"Likewise. I need you to stay out of trouble," she warned.

"I'm out," he said, holding his hands up. "Started with the day trading, like you said. Risky, but all above board and legal-like. Promise."

"Okay," Amanda said cautiously. "And take good care of the Mrs. . . . Speaking of whom, where the heck is she? She said she'd be here to see us off."

"Give her a minute. She said she had some errands."

Amanda had run out of dadlike small talk and so stood there awkwardly for a second, and then she slowly turned to see Ben in the window. He held up a finger, asking her to wait a minute, and then came running downstairs.

"I'm so glad I caught you before you left," he said.

"Me, too," she said, stopping herself from touching him in one of the many hundreds of intimate ways she wanted to. She wasn't sure where things stood with him.

"I wanted to give you this," he said, and he pulled something out from behind his back.

"That's so nice of you. What is it?" she asked awkwardly.

He handed her a big plain canvas reusable grocery bag, which was filled with other canvas grocery bags, herb garden scissors, two library cards to the Oakland and Berkeley public libraries, and a boxed set of *Fresh Air with Terry Gross* CDs. With his other hand, he gave her a tiny potted oregano plant. "For the new you," he said.

She had forgotten that she'd shared her vision of her ultimate future with him. *Space, shmace*, she thought and she put all the things on the front seat and pulled him into a hug, which led to a kiss, which led to a longer kiss, and to Taylor's expressing her disgust and an "Ah, Jesus H. Christ!" hollered from the edge of the driveway.

Joyce was there, hobbling in from the street, dragging Amanda's third Rolie Bag behind her. There was something different about it, but Amanda couldn't tell until Joyce got closer that the entire thing was wrapped in a red ribbon.

"You almost left without your suitcase," Joyce said, and handed it off to Amanda. It was no longer empty. It weighed at least thirty pounds.

"Mom?" Amanda asked incredulously.

"Mandy, I told you it would pay out. With interest. And it paid out. With interest. Bon voyage."

"Did you walk all the way here from the OTB?" Amanda asked.

"OTB? I don't go to the OTB. That's for amateurs, Amanda. Don't insult me."

"Well, thank you, Mom. I'm so . . ." What was she? Touched, relieved, excited. All of those. With this suitcase, they could actually have a life.

"Won't you come with us, Mom? We can take care of you. Taylor wants you to live with us. Please?" Amanda begged.

Joyce opened her mouth to speak, but couldn't. She was clearly too emotional, and her voice caught in her throat. Amanda had never seen her mother's emotions get the best of her. She must be mellowing in her old age. Bruce hugged Joyce around the shoulders, rescuing her, and pulled her close. Then he spoke for her. "You know your mother, Amanda. She takes care of herself."

Her mother nodded and Bruce released her so she could embrace Amanda and say good-bye. "I love you, Mom."

Amanda felt her mother's hot teardrop on her shoulder and then her mother whisper, "Ah, Jesus H. Christ," and then she got three impatient taps on the back. And she knew her mother loved her, too.

35

"Yahtzee!" Amanda yelled. They sat around an old salvaged table from the flea market in the dining room of Dragonfly Ranch, playing board games. Board games. She never would have recognized herself a year ago. At least it was a competitive board game and not one of those cooperative ones where everyone works together for a common goal. She hadn't softened that much. Everything around here was cooperative. The food stores, the preschools, the yoga studios, the artist colonies, the jewelry stores. Amanda was at least going to keep their family fun a little bit competitive. She didn't want to completely lose her edge.

Recording her "yahtzee" on her scorecard, Amanda realized her mother was wrong about luck. Your luck can change without aligning yourself with powerful people. Luck is about doing the next best thing. It's about having faith in the good. It's about knowing the good will win out. Luck is about having patience. And she finally felt lucky.

Sitting around the table were her favorite people: Taylor, who had blossomed here and made the most of her opportunity to start over. She was rocking the school thing, working at a farmers' market, reading books, finding herself, thriving; Lucas, her sweet skate-rat boyfriend who was one of those kids who looked dirty, but wasn't, looked dopey, but wasn't, looked poor, but definitely wasn't. His parents lived in one of those huge houses in the hills with a view of all three bridges at once: Golden Gate, Oakland Bay, and San Rafael.

And Ben. They had tried the long-distance relationship thing. Meeting each other at airports like pretend yuppies, but who were they trying to kid? People built stuff in the East Bay, Amanda had told him. It wasn't like he couldn't find work here. He'd moved in six months ago, had completely refurbished Taylor's bedroom, and helped her every night with her homework.

Taylor shook her dice and let out a rare giggle as they skittered across the wooden table. She collected and sorted them into pairs, as Lucas needlessly yet adorably consulted her on a strategy, pointing at her roll with his knuckly adolescent man hands, and then Amanda's phone lit up with Joyce's name.

She got up and took the call in the kitchen where she leaned against the cool tile of the island Ben had built for them.

"I'm coming to visit," Joyce barked.

"It's polite to wait for an invitation," Amanda told her.

"I've waited a whole year. It's polite not to let a year go by before you invite your mother to your new home."

"I've been getting situated." Even though she'd invited her mother to live with them, once she'd moved, she'd realized she needed some time before inviting Joyce back into their lives. She had to get her feet underneath her and get on a roll before subjecting herself to the sheer force of Joyce and her tendency to pull her back into a life of crime. She realized she was addicted to trying to get her mother's approval and she needed some space to beat it.

"A whole year? Mandy. What are you afraid of?"

That was a loaded question. She had finally heard that Evan was sentenced to twenty-five years in prison for murdering Agent Stevens. He'd be locked away for a long while, so she was less afraid of that these days. The fallout from setting him up seemed to have fizzled out and faded away. For now, anyway. She was no longer afraid of failure or success or parenting. She had even made some friends. She wasn't afraid of creating a path to normal for herself and Taylor. And she knew her mother could not derail them.

What was she afraid of? She channeled her higher-power Carrie Fisher and thought that question at her. The dark side came to mind. Her mother practically embodied the entire dark side of her existence that she was trying to run away from. She was definitely afraid of that. "The dark side," she said to her mom.

"Mandy, don't you know by now?" Joyce said. Amanda could hear her exhale and then stamp out a cigarette.

"Know what?"

"Fear is the path to the dark side, dumb-dumb."

"Thank you, Yoda."

"Whatever. It's true. You only make bad decisions when you're afraid. You can't be magnanimous if you're afraid. And I'm not even asking for magnanimous. I'm asking for you to just let me inside."

"What do you mean, inside?" Come to think of it, the phone reception was entirely clear. Her mother sounded very close indeed.

"I'm in the driveway."

Amanda rushed to the front door and peered outside into the luscious East Bay fog that now eased her into her days, buoyed her and healed her scorched, sunburned wounds from LA. She bent over to look through the window, and Joyce suddenly appeared out of the mist and stood on the stoop expectantly, like a zombie mom waiting to feed on her brains.

"Ah, Jesus H. Christ," Amanda gasped, then opened the door and gave her mother a short hug that ended in three quick pats on the back. "Come on in."

ACKNOWLEDGMENTS

Thanks to Les and Gina at Alloy in Los Angeles for getting this ball rolling; the entire editorial team at Alloy in New York: Josh, Lanie, Joelle, and Hayley; and very special thanks to Susanna Rosenblum—I could not have asked for a better partner to breathe life into this story.